About the

Born in Cork City, Betty Cody moved to Dublin after her marriage. As a mature student, she did a PhD in Psychology at University College Dublin.

Apart from her family, sport has been her main passion in life. Having reached a number three ranking in the country at table tennis in her youth, she followed it by both coaching and playing squash and representing Ireland on many occasions at Masters level. Golf and pitch and putt followed and during that time she wrote a golf psychology column for the *Irish Independent* and features, plus celebrity interviews for *Irish Lady Golfer* magazine. Her self-published book *The Road to Perfect Golf*, sold out its print run.

Playing bridge became a passion in retirement and in September 2024 she again qualified for international bridge trials, this time for the Lady Milne trials. This year she returned to her first sporting love – table tennis. In July she competed in Rome at the World Masters Table Tennis Championship for her age category. Although losing in the first round-robin stage, she went on to win a silver medal in the lady's doubles B event with a Japanese partner. Betty was the only Irish player to reach a final in Rome.

Her motto still continues to be "*Don't ever give up on your dreams*", even when life brings sadness and sorrow, as it did to Betty this year with the passing of her beloved husband Michael. She is grateful for having had a marriage that lasted for fifty-nine years and now looks back at the good memories they shared with their children and grandchildren, during their time together.

Acknowledgments

My sincere and grateful thanks to my exceptional editor Gaye Shortland for sharing her immense knowledge of books and history with me. She has been there for me throughout this journey.

Also, to the ever-cheerful Paula Campbell at Poolbeg, who is always available to metaphorically hold my hand!

To Poolbeg Press, whose belief in books written by women has made them legends in Ireland and around the world. I give you all my heartfelt thanks.

To my friend, Rodney Davitt, from the Bohemians Musical Society, my sincere thanks for your permission to include family historical facts in my novel.

Also, my thanks to my friend Karin Kamphuijs and my granddaughter Lia for their help in proofreading early drafts of this book.

Last, but not least, to my family, Gillian and Alan, their spouses Ken and Laura, and my grandchildren Lia, Jack, Chloe, Louis and Joe, who all gave me encouragement to finish this book during a difficult time in my life, after the death of my beloved husband Michael.

Dedication

To the memory of my beloved husband Michael Cody who sadly passed away on the 7th of February, 2024

Chapter One

Hertfordshire 1866

It was early March and spring was in the air as Lady Rosita Beconsford sat by the window of her home, situated on the periphery of the extensive grounds of Hatfield House in Hertfordshire. Her home was a warm, cosy detached residence, close to the entrance to the estate. Its large garden was on two levels, sloping towards the extensive gardens and grounds of the estate below. At the side of the house, an oak tree with its massive trunk allowed Rosita to move under its wide canopy when looking for shade in the height of summer. She loved the house and gardens and, although it was only leased from the Hatfield estate, she was always welcome to visit the main house if she so wished. Many of Rosita's extended family were great friends with its owner, the Marquess of Salisbury, yet she rarely visited as she had chosen a life where her work as a nurse took precedence over society balls.

Today, the early spring sun gave a hint that the cold winter would shortly be just a memory. The flower beds in front of her home were filled with early spring daffodils, late snowdrops and cyclamen.

The moment of peaceful contemplation was interrupted as she heard her good friend Doreen Trent coming down the stairway, before entering the room like a force of nature, her bright chestnut hair loose and tussled.

"Anything in the post for me today, Rosita? I thought I heard something come through the letterbox," she said, eyebrows raised as she waited for an answer.

"Nothing for you," Rosita said. "The only letter is from Eliza, my step-grandmother back in Midleton, probably with the usual news and wondering when I'm next returning to Ireland."

"No doubt!" Doreen rolled her eyes. "But, Rosita, please say that you'll still be attending the dance near St Albans with me?"

"Of course I'm going to support a good cause," Rosita replied.

"Great! But I hope you're not going to refuse to dance with the men, for fear you're ensnared into marriage?"

"I might not be looking for a man but I will dance if I am asked!" Rosita said, smiling.

"Of course you'll be asked! The men love your elegance and good looks. You always seem to have an air of mystery about you – though I wouldn't envy the man who tries to tame you!" Doreen was now elated that Rosita would be joining her on Saturday night. "Plus, your blonde head of curly hair makes all the women jealous and all the men want to run their fingers through it! I love when I'm out with you as there's never a dull moment, especially when we're with those who know that you are Lady Beconsford. Yet, with all that attention, you still won't let any man get too close to you."

"That's funny coming from you, Doreen. I certainly don't hate men, like you seem to. I'm just wary of why men are interested in me," Rosita retorted.

"Rosita, you now know me long enough to realise that I am never going to marry. I want to control my own destiny in life and not end up like my poor mother – forced to leave County Cavan and go to Galway, where I was born and where she wasn't known. She worked herself to the bone to educate me so that I didn't have to depend on anyone. Wasn't she right? Lord rest her poor soul. She had no life after some rogue had his way with her and left her to face the consequences alone." Doreen shuddered.

Rosita knew that Doreen's mother was almost a saint in the way she had worked herself to exhaustion to ensure that her daughter had what she called a "proper" education. It had paid off, because Doreen was admitted to hospital training in England and passed her examinations without any trouble. Sadly, her mother died before Doreen could give her a better life. It almost seemed as if Edel Trent had felt her job had been done when her daughter got a good job as a nurse.

At that time, Rosita and Doreen were training together and had become very good friends. It was after Edel's death that Rosita had asked her friend if she would like to live with her and do some small household chores in lieu of rent. Doreen was grateful for the offer but it was much later that Rosita understood how truly bitter Doreen was towards the father she never knew and who seemed to have vanished before she was born.

Then Doreen's smiling personality reappeared. "I'll leave you to read your letter – I'll go and clear up your bedroom for you, Your Ladyship!" she said, laughing, only to be hit by a cushion thrown by Rosita as she walked towards the door.

Doreen grinned impishly, peeping back around the closing door.

Rosita grinned back before she opened the letter to read the latest news from Cork. Although she loved her life in Hertfordshire, Rosita always longed for those letters from home. She wanted those connections in her life.

On the day Rosita was born, her mother Fleur passed away, within an hour of her birth. Margarita Ryan, a rising singing star, had later married Rosita's father, The Honourable Victor Beconsford. Sadly, Victor couldn't cope with life after the death of his first wife and took to the drink. Even his marriage to Margarita and twins Louis and Violet being born did not heal his soul. He passed away, a very young man, after the stress of the long years of the Irish Famine took its toll on him. Because Fleur had died giving birth to Rosita, Victor's mental health suffered badly due to fear that he could lose any of his children during the Famine. It robbed him of his sanity and alcohol became his only succour. Her step-mama, whom she always called just "Margarita", later went on to marry Laurence Flaherty, a renowned tenor from New York. That had pleased Rosita very much.

Now Rosita prepared to enjoy the latest family news from Margarita's mother Eliza.

My dearest Rosita,

I'm writing with some upsetting but not unexpected news. My beloved husband Jack's mother Molly, who was in her nineties, sadly passed away peacefully last week. She had a long life and loved living most of that life near her beloved son, my Jack. May she rest in peace.

I know that for you, Rosita, the biggest sadness was the untimely passing of your grandmother Deborah two years ago. She never truly recovered from the passing of your father Victor, all these years ago. Yet her memory still lives within the beautiful walls of Deborah's Secret Garden, in the grounds of the Beconsford Estate in Midleton. Everyone who enters that space feels its calmness and tranquillity, and think of her.

I know that you are loving your life in England, but we all truly miss you, especially your grandfather Isaac who does nothing but work, trying to fill all the empty spaces in his life.

However, I have another surprise for you. Jack is retiring from managing the estate as he says it needs new blood. We are shortly moving back to Rose Cottage where we started our married life in 1818. From now on, Jack is going to help with the accounts of the estate, which will still give him an interest. I don't think Jack is the kind of man that could stay totally idle for long.

I have a feeling also that my Margarita, who is singing somewhere in Europe with Laurence, will not always live in Ireland. Their young son Theodore stays with us when she is away, but she has hinted that sometime in the future they would like to go to Laurence's native New York.

Will you please send my regards to all our relatives in England?

Keep up the good work nursing at the hospital. You truly are doing a fine job and I know the joy you get helping people but, as I always finish – please make sure to take care of yourself also.

All my love,

Eliza

Rosita sat back in her chair, remembering the many cakes that Molly had given to her during her childhood. It was good that she had such an easy passing, she thought.

This brought Rosita back to the day that her grandfather, Isaac, had entered the lounge of their home in Midleton and found his wife Deborah had died during the short time he'd been gone from her side. He was so distraught that the doctor had to sedate him, assuring him over and over again that it was her heart that failed and nothing could have been done by anyone to save her.

Rosita also recalled, with a shudder, the day that Deborah was buried. Isaac kept repeating that she had died of a broken heart because of the early death of her son Victor. Now Grandpapa Isaac was waiting and hoping that Rosita's younger brother Louis would return from the university in Oxford and run the estate. As far back as she could remember, Rosita had emphasised that she did not want any part in the running of Beconsford Estate. However, she knew that Louis had his eyes set on becoming a military man. Yet he was the heir. He was burdened by duty far more than she was, Rosita knew that, and thankfully she could just focus on her own life and let them do whatever they had to with the estate in Ireland. She knew she was lucky because she had a financial cushion, as she had acquired a large inheritance when she was twenty-five, left by her mother Fleur, as her only biological heir. Thanks to that, she was a very wealthy woman.

As she shook her head out of her thoughts of Ireland, she set about getting ready for work. She loved nursing and was proud of following in the footsteps of her idol, Florence Nightingale. The way Nurse Nightingale had transformed how injured soldiers were treated in war, having been sent to increase sanitation in the British military infirmaries abroad, was remarkable. At the time, the French had a good system of light ambulances that worked for them but Nurse Nightingale was a lifesaver for the British troops, especially during the Crimean war. Rosita was still in awe of her when Nurse Nightingale made occasional visits to the infirmary and always proudly recalled the day that she had been personally introduced to her idol.

Rosita was still mulling over the contents of Eliza's letter as she got her bike from the shed in the back yard and cycled to the hospital. As she cycled, she smiled at the locals, many of whom she had befriended during the five years she had been in residence. She was looking forward to her day's work and thought that there were not too many dark clouds in her life at the moment and she hoped things would continue to stay that way.

Doreen had to attend the upcoming dance as her friend Nurse Greene had organised it. She kept insisting that she was not looking for a husband – in any case, she said, the men who went to the nurses' dances wanted only a well-trained housekeeper to marry and take care of them for life. Rosita agreed that she wasn't looking for anyone either but they both agreed that they should have some fun.

"Remember that it's raising much-needed funds for the hospital, so we might as well enjoy ourselves," Rosita said.

On Saturday, in the early evening sunshine, they set off on their bicycles to the village hall, three miles from their home. They were pleased to know that a full moon would later help light their way back. When they arrived at the hall and parked their bicycles, they were greeted warmly at the door by Joanne Greene, who was especially delighted that Rosita was attending, as she usually gave a generous donation.

"Come with me, please. I have a couple of army men in from a London barracks on their way back to their base who decided to stay locally overnight when they heard about the dance. I bet they didn't expect to meet such beauties as you two tonight!" She laughed as they arrived at the table where the men were seated.

Rosita had already warned both Joanne and Doreen at the entrance that they were not to mention her title.

"Gentlemen, I'd like to introduce you to Rosita and Doreen, two of our very best nurses."

Two tall, handsome men stood up and smiled as they stretched out their hands in greeting.

"I'm Lieutenant Marcus Nicholls and this is my batman Noel. Please come and sit down."

"Delighted to meet you two soldiers, but for the moment I'll be helping the organisers and hopefully my boyfriend will be here later," Doreen lied. "If you'll excuse me, I'll leave you for a while and help Joanne greet the new arrivals, but I'll see you both later."

As Rosita sat down, she gave Doreen a look that would kill for leaving her alone, but Doreen just grinned and returned to join Joanne at the door.

As Doreen left and Noel made a beeline for a group of nurses eager for a dance partner, Marcus looked at Rosita. "I will take good care of you until she returns," he said, "especially if you will save at least a few dances for me before the evening ends." He smiled, his eyes full of amusement. "But first I must get us both a drink."

Rosita, suddenly realising that she would be alone with the lieutenant, painted a smile on her face, hoping that he wasn't the usual type of army officer she met who thought she should feel lucky to be in such exalted company. Maybe he's different, she thought, deciding to give him the benefit of the doubt and engage with him, as by now Noel the Batman had caught the attention of a pretty nurse and they were already waltzing around the dance floor.

Rosita's companion turned out to be full of charm and sincerity as he heaped praise on the nurses who cared for soldiers injured in India who needed support for both body and mind,

He suddenly looked pensive. "It could be any one of us, when wars and skirmishes happen abroad, and I think that luck plays a part. No matter how good your men are, we all know that in any battle or skirmish it could be our last day on earth. I think that's why we enjoy evenings such as these so much."

Rosita watched and listened and soon had to admit that he really was lovely. As she finally relaxed in his company, she decided to enjoy the rest of the evening.

Marcus danced and talked with her for most of that night, as Noel had abandoned his nurse and befriended a local girl who looked to be in awe of his soldier's uniform and his good looks. Meanwhile, Doreen had decided to make herself busy for the evening helping the organisers and allow Rosita space to enjoy the company of the lieutenant.

"Noel will have a good night, without any concerns for the consequences," said Marcus. "I'm always telling him to be more respectful of women but he just laughs and says he's having fun."

Before the evening ended, Rosita was enthralled by the lieutenant and when he offered to take her and Doreen home in his carriage, she happily agreed.

"We can easily fit the two bicycles. The carriage driver is coming to collect me at around half past ten and I'm sure the trip to your home will be just fine with him."

Doreen was delighted that Rosita had enjoyed the evening so much. To see a smile on Rosita's face in the company of a man gladdened her heart, as she always seemed on her guard when men got too close to her.

Rosita had to wait until she was alone in bed that night before she could work out what had happened to her. The Ice Lady, as Doreen sometimes jokingly called her, was gone.

She was very attracted to Marcus and, she realised, for the first time she had met someone who seemed to both respect the opinion of a woman when discussing politics and was also interested in music and literature.

When he'd asked her to meet him to view the National Gallery in London on the following Saturday, she had agreed without any reservations.

The following day, once Doreen knew all about the proposed trip to London, she could be seen raiding Rosita's wardrobe, insisting on helping her pick a nice outfit for the outing. By the time Saturday morning arrived, Doreen was satisfied that her friend looked truly elegant. She wore a dark-blue dress over the new fashionable crinolette, with a rich wine-coloured cloak, and a small black satin hat with dark-blue flowers perched on her head.

"I've never seen you look so nervous in all my life, Rosita. You must really care about today. He's so handsome and he does seem like a lovely man. I can't wait for you to get home tonight. I'm not going to sleep until you return."

Doreen shooed Rosita out the door on her way to catch the train to London, wishing her luck.

On the train Rosita felt as nervous as a young girl. Earlier, when Doreen had asked her why, she didn't have an answer. Maybe it's because for once

I don't feel in control of my emotions, she thought, but I can't let him think that I'm a simpering female, which I definitely am not.

She shook her head to clear her thoughts as the train pulled into the station. As it slowed down, she spotted Marcus on the platform, raising a hand in greeting.

"I'm so pleased you came today," he said when he had helped her alight. "I was having butterflies in my stomach wondering if you would change your mind. Thanks for turning up. It's not often that I meet a lady and invite her to meet me again quite so soon." He offered her his arm to link.

She felt like a young girl, and an awkward one at that, as she took his arm and only began to relax when they were sitting in the carriage on their way to the gallery.

They spent over two hours there, during which Marcus displayed his extensive knowledge of art. Rosita was interested in the paintings of Raphael but she was most taken by the richness of *The Raising of Lazarus* by Sebastiano del Piombo, which Marcus told her was one of the gallery's first acquisitions.

By the time they finally left the gallery, Rosita felt really relaxed in Marcus's company and enjoyed the carriage trip to Claridge's in Brook Street where Marcus had booked a table. She did not disclose that she had been in this exclusive hotel in the past with relatives, as she still wanted to keep her title a secret. Too many men in the past had looked at her title and not at her as a person. Today is different, she thought, as they spent the time over lunch discussing art, the theatre and the opera.

Afterwards they walked around Mayfair, until it was time for her to get the train back to Hertfordshire.

As she was about to step onto the train, Marcus laid a hand on her arm and she turned back to him.

He hesitated, then took her hand. "Would it be presumptuous of me to ask you to join me again in London next week? I never know when I'm going to be called overseas and I haven't enjoyed a day as wonderful as this for a long time."

Rosita smiled brightly in return. "I would love to meet you again, Marcus. I'm free next weekend if you are. I really enjoyed coming to London today."

He helped her board the train, keeping hold of her hand and pressing it to his lips before letting go and closing the door of the carriage.

When Rosita returned home, from the moment she entered the house she could hear Doreen's voice from the kitchen.

"I want to know everything about your day! I think I deserve to know every detail, considering the effort I made to dress and groom you!"

Rosita went through to the kitchen where, as she sat down, a cup of tea was placed in front of her.

"There is only one thing I need to tell you and that is that I enjoyed every part of the day. He was incredibly pleasant company and he conversed so eloquently on diverse subjects that I can't wait to meet him again."

Rosita had a dreamy look in her eyes that Doreen had never seen before.

"I don't want to know what he talked about. I just need to know where you went and if he kissed you?"

Rosita laughed and admitted that he kissed her hand. Then she admitted that she did want to kiss him back.

Doreen let out a roar of laughter. "Are you falling in love with him?"

"I think I could be, but it's early days. I'm meeting him again next weekend and I'm imagining it already."

"Where's he from?" asked Doreen, but was very surprised at the answer she got.

"We haven't discussed families yet and if you meet him don't dream of letting him know my title. I want to be sure of how I am really feeling about him before we get into families. Thankfully, he didn't mention anything about his either and I'm glad that's the way things are for the present."

"Alright, I agree for the moment, but don't keep him in the dark for too long – he might not like the deception," Doreen warned.

During the weeks that followed, Rosita and Marcus spent as much time together as their jobs would allow. They took train rides to the sea and watched fun theatre performances on the seafronts.

Almost six weeks after they had met, they were finishing a late meal in London, in a hotel where Rosita sometimes stayed overnight. They had enjoyed another delightful day together.

"Rosita," Marcus said, with hesitation in his voice. "I have something I need to tell you."

Rosita looked at him, raising her eyebrows. "Why the serious expression," she asked, slightly alarmed.

"I'm leaving to go to with my regiment to India shortly," he answered, squeezing her hand gently.

"Shortly!" Rosita said, showing the shock she felt as she stared at Marcus.

"There's nothing I can do to stop it, but from what Sir John Laurence said to our commanding officer, this particular territorial skirmish shouldn't last long." He looked around. "Would you like us to go to a quieter area than this dining room and just talk for a while before I leave? I didn't want to spoil the day by telling you this morning, but I'm in no rush home tonight, I can assure you," he said, looking straight into her eyes.

Rosita nodded in agreement and they walked down the corridor to the by now deserted residents' lounge where a fire was burning brightly, although it had been a warm day.

They sat side by side on a chaise longue, so that they could stay close to each other. As Marcus held her hands, Rosita thought that she had never felt as miserable as now and, as he spoke words of love and comfort, she just felt that she never wanted him to leave. She knew what could happen as she often wondered about others who were loose with their morals and whom she usually despised. Yet tonight she felt so close to Marcus that when he suggested that he'd walk her to her room, she knew that what was about to happen went against all her previous beliefs and convictions.

Rosita finally fell into a deep sleep with Marcus still holding her close to him, making her feel together with him in mind, body and soul. She had no regrets about her decision to spend the night with him.

When she awoke, she had to think for a moment, as she wondered where she was. When she remembered, she put a hand out to touch Marcus, but rose quickly when she discovered that he was gone. Still slightly disorientated, she walked around the room.

Then she saw a letter on the dressing table, addressed to her.

Snatching it up, she returned to her bed and sat up to read its contents.

My dear Rosita,

As dawn broke this morning, I was lying awake in bed, looking at your beautiful face and watching the brightening shafts of light shining through the crack in the curtain. I looked at it lighting up your curls of gold, as you lay sleeping peacefully beside me. I could not allow myself to wake you up and watch your face while telling you that I'm actually leaving for India today. I was going to tell you that at the end of the evening, but love and life got in the way. It was a glorious day and night for me but tinged with so much regret that I was leaving. Last night felt for me like the coming together of two shining stars.

If you have regrets about last night, I am truly sorry. Perhaps it shouldn't have happened? Yet the last month for me has been a truly special time in my life as I hope it was for you also.

I will write to you when I first reach dry land and hopefully we can communicate with each other during my time abroad.

Sincerely yours,

Marcus

Rosita read the letter over and over again. It was beautiful, poetic and sensual – but nothing much in it was pointing to a future together. He thinks that he may die in battle, she thought, or even lose his life in a raging storm. She had to shake her head a few times to return to reality.

She washed and dressed quickly and soon after eating breakfast took a carriage to the train station. She wanted to get home as quickly as possible.

When she got to the house, she was very grateful to find that Doreen had not yet returned from work.

A couple of hours later, when Doreen opened the front door, her first question to Rosita was, "How did yesterday go? I want every detail and leave nothing out. I'm sure you must know by now that since you met Marcus I've been living my life imagining myself like you, having nights in hotels, dining out and seeing any concert or play that I want to see. Not with a man though! I'm very happy with my own company but I'm not rich enough to indulge in such extravagance!"

She sat, smiling as she waited for Rosita to answer.

"Not so fast, please. Take your cloak off, at least, and I have tea ready in the front parlour. I knew I'd get this type of inquisition, so I am prepared to tell you everything that happened."

"That's not like you, Rosita. You're always keeping things to yourself. In the past I've watched the way you are with people. I see it in your expression when you're talking to people who are speaking rubbish and yet you smile sweetly while all the time you are probably thinking that they are all just spouting hot air, especially the men who fawn over you when they know that you're a titled lady."

Rosita had to agree with Doreen. "You're right, of course, but this time it's different. I really like him."

As they sat by the fire eating hot muffins and drinking tea, Doreen was, for once, speechless and slightly in shock when Rosita finished telling her about the weekend. It was a while before she asked the first question.

"Are you still happy that you allowed him spend the night with you?"

When Rosita answered yes, Doreen nodded before asking, "Would you mind allowing me to read the letter? Perhaps I could read more into it than you can?"

Rosita agreed and handed it to her.

Doreen read it at least three times before handing it back. "I would have expected more assurances in that letter that you might have a future together. A kind of early proposal, perhaps?"

She was trying to work out how her friend had given herself to a man she knew only for a short while. She shook her head in amazement, while closing her eyes, unable to comprehend how complacent Rosita appeared to be.

"Well, as I said, I think he's really worried that he may not return," Rosita said in an effort to reassure herself, hoping Doreen would agree with her. "He has often spoken of the perils of war for soldiers."

"I agree, Rosita, but usually officers are far less likely to die than the ordinary foot soldiers. Maybe you're right. I hope so because I've never seen you so happy and alive as since you met him. I think we should wait for his first letter. By that time he may realise how important you are to him. Hopefully by then he'll reassure you of his intentions. You would like to marry him, wouldn't you?" Doreen looked Rosita straight in the eye.

"Yes, I would!" Rosita announced, even surprising herself.

"Well, that's good enough for me," Doreen said, somewhat reassured, as she rose from the chair and put her arms around her best friend. "I hope it all works out for you, love. You deserve happiness and the love of a good man."

They prepared for bed, each with a different scenario in her mind.

Chapter Two

Back in West Cork, in Ireland, families were still struggling to earn a living. One such family was the Cahills, who lived at the end of a lane behind Main Street in Bantry, in a small two-storey cottage which originally housed seven children and their parents. Two of their children died during the Famine, and another a few years later from consumption. Their father had been a belligerent agitator and a drunkard, and his wife Eithne had always struggled to put food on the table. By 1853, her husband had died in jail and she was worn out from worry and exhaustion. By then her eldest two boys had left the country. They never sent a penny back to her, and she never even knew where they were. She excused them because their father had really left his mark on all of them. The boys had left West Cork just as soon as they had earned enough money for the ticket to Canada. Her remaining son, Finn, was a nasty man who had learned too much violence from his father. Eithne despised the way he treated her when in drink.

However, she'd go through all she had gone through in the past over again because of her great love for her only living daughter Bridie. At seventeen, Bridie was a strapping young girl with flaming red hair and a heart of gold. She diligently brought home her wages each week from the haberdashery where she worked in the town. She was well liked by all the customers and the people who came to the shop from the surrounding countryside. Her mother's only sorrow for her was that the girl also, on occasions, took beatings from her brother Finn, whenever she disagreed with him. Yet her mother couldn't stop him because of fear of what he was actually capable of.

One day it all came to a head when Finn stole Bridie's wages and the girl told her mother that she was moving out of the house to share a room with her friend Holly Desmond's family. Bridie promised to bring over a good bit of her wages each Friday. Sadly, because her mother placed no value on her own life anymore, she was pleased and relieved that Bridie was leaving.

"That's the best news ever, love. Go and make a good life for yourself."

"I'm not leaving you to suffer, Mam. I'm going to give you the money just for yourself every week and we won't let him know about it. Holly Desmond's brothers have said that they're going to warn Finn that if he ever touches you again, he'll regret it. Her brothers are good lads and look out for their family. I think that Finn must have some screw loose in his head or something because he can't control his temper like most people. From now on I'm going to meet you every day in the town and, if I see anything amiss with you, he'll soon pay for it."

Eithne Cahill put her arms around her daughter, before saying, with tears in her eyes, "I've often had thoughts in my head wishing that he had died and not his other brothers and sister. That's not changed, lass, but I'm happy that you're going to make something of yourself. I'll die happy if that happens."

"That's silly talk, Mam. I'll help take care of you now like you did me, teaching me all that sewing and knitting when I was young. Sure, I'm able to make a living now because of you."

At that time the Irish Fenian movement was gaining ground around the town of Bantry. In 1863 Finn Cahill was one of the first to offer his services if anything was being planned. That didn't please the more educated members of the local organisation but others said that they needed someone like him with the nerve to carry out planned actions.

One remarked that, even though he disliked him, he was happy to allow Finn to carry out difficult jobs when required. "Fellows like Finn Cahill are dispensable, although I wouldn't like if people heard me say such a thing about anyone. But life is tough and you sometimes need madmen like him."

Another said angrily that they weren't an organisation for thugs – they just wanted more rights for people, especially farmers and workers.

They finally agreed to allow him to get involved. They would not let him be privy to many actions, but would use him if and when it was necessary.

Bridie loved working in the haberdashery shop in the town but she had ambitions to learn how to make good ladies' clothes, even wedding dresses, and to get out of Bantry and go into Cork city to work. But fate took a hand and, six months after leaving her mother's home, she met Gregory Saunders and he turned her world upside down. He was from a really good family and Bridie had never thought that she would catch the eye of such a boy. Unfortunately, Gregory told her that his family were considering a move back to Midleton in East Cork where his mother Alice was born. Bridie thought that if this happened it would be the end of their friendship, until Gregory made a suggestion.

"Perhaps, Bridie, it could be a chance for you to follow your dream to work in a smart shop in Cork city. That would mean that we'd be living quite close to each other and could continue to meet."

Bridie squeezed his hand tightly and, smiling with delight, she told him that if he moved she'd do just that, once she had sorted out the problems of her mother, making sure she was safe from the aggression of Finn.

Gregory's mother, Alice Staunton, as a younger woman had travelled Europe before the Famine as support to her opera singer niece, Margarita Beconsford. Although they were aunt and niece, they were almost the same age.

Today the family were engaged in a family round-table meeting. This was taking place in the prosperous Staunton farmhouse in the townland of Ballyeoin in West Cork.

Alice and her singer husband Richard were discussing their future. Thankfully, Richard's brother Barry had finally returned from America to look after the family farm. His return had been prompted by the unexpected death of their father Jerome and Alice's mother Meg. Barry, his wife Elsa and their growing family, seemed happy to live in Ireland and take over the farm. This would finally allow Richard and Alice the freedom to leave West Cork. Alice also saw it as a chance to join some of her husband's singing engagements abroad.

Now she, as usual the organiser of the family, addressed them.

"I am so pleased that you are here, Barry, and that you and Elsa are happy to raise your family in Ireland. This really is a prosperous farm again, after the devastation brought to our doorstep during the dreaded famine years. Our two, Gregory and Emily, are delighted with our idea of moving back to the farm in Midleton which my late mother Meg owned." Tears sprang to her eyes as she thought of her mother. "I have loved my years in Ballyeoin but my heart is in Midleton where my father Robert worked all his life for his family. I want to spend the last days of my life there and, Gregory, you will have a fine farm there to work. The Beconsford Estate, which rented it after we all moved here, has looked after it well for the last twenty years and you'll make a good job of it too. And, young Emily, you will get a job teaching anywhere in the county. I just want to begin to live my life more fully and have fun while myself and Richard are still young enough."

They all began to nod their heads until Barry put his hand up for hush.

"I'm delighted for you all," he said. "Go back to the home where you lived and loved in the past. You are always welcome here and our Richard will, I know, return to West Cork very often. Go off and make your fortune, brother, and don't forget us when singing finally brings you fame and fortune!"

Everyone laughed, and Alice said, "I assure you that all the money we make will be spent touring as much of the world as we can. I've done my bit for society and from now on I'm going to spend my husband's hard-earned money! So let us toast with a cup of tea – to the future!"

Before the family moved from West Cork, Alice received a letter from her oldest sister Eliza. As she read it aloud to the family at breakfast, she could not keep the happy smile off her face.

My dearest Alice,

I am beyond delighted to hear the news that we are going to be neighbours again shortly, but what you don't know is that we will be even closer that you think!

Jack has finally decided that the time has come to retire from the estate. He's trained the carriage man Austin's son very well and Jody, like my Jack, has a love of exotic plants as well as the forest and the rest of the farm. Jack taught him well and apart from his growing up on the estate, he is also a hard worker. It pleases my Jack very much to have a manager who grew up on the estate!

What we propose to do is to return to our first home, Rose Cottage, which Jack bought for us before our marriage and where his mother Molly lived until her death. Therefore, Alice, we will be living on your doorstep, and I hope that if I ever need a couple of spoons of sugar or a drop of milk, I can walk around to your farm and borrow them!

I can't wait to see you all soon and I'm sure with your organisational skills that you will help re-organise our new home when we move?

Your loving, much older sister,

Eliza

Alice and Richard were delighted with that news and Alice shed some tears of happiness with the knowledge that she would spend many years in the home where she was born. She had been the surprise late baby born to her father and his second wife Meg.

Chapter Three

Sitting pensively each evening in her Hertfordshire home, Rosita spent her time wondering if she would ever hear from Marcus again. Then, finally, she breathed a sigh of relief as the eagerly awaited letter arrived. She tore it from its envelope, feeling a calming in her stomach.

My dear Rosita,

This is just a quick note to let you know that we have stopped at Aden and will be continuing our journey in a couple of days. I still think of our time together and miss the feeling of connectedness I felt when I was in your presence. I'm hoping that our time in India is short but I have to accept whatever is ahead for me over the next few months.

I will keep in touch, and please send also my regards to your good friend Doreen.

I remain,

Sincerely,

Marcus

As Rosita walked back into the kitchen, she was frowning as she found that she suddenly felt no great sense of comfort from the short letter. She placed it in front of Doreen to read, sat down and lifted a cup of tea in her now shaking hands.

"That's an interesting letter, Rosita. It reads to me like 'I just said nothing', but I'm wondering what you are thinking?" Doreen paused, waiting for a reply from her friend.

"Well, it didn't inspire me either, but maybe he's not as comfortable writing when he has so much ahead of him," Rosita said, trying to convince herself that everything was still good.

"Alright, Rosita, but is that the only thing you're going to say to me? Have you anything else you want to share with me? I'm not working tonight or even tomorrow, so I can sit all day and night waiting for you to tell me," Doreen said, raising her eyebrows.

Rosita took a while before answering.

"I believe his intentions were honourable when we were together," she then said, tears glistening in her eyes. "But I must admit that I've been petrified for the past few weeks, but now I'm somewhat reassured by his letter."

"So, I'm right. You're pregnant by a man who has left the country, aren't you? And if you are, what in God's name are you going to do about it?"

"I knew that you'd probably already worked that out and the answer is I just don't know! I've been terrified as well as sick for the last couple of weeks."

Doreen put out a hand to touch her arm.

Rosita pulled back. "Have you any suggestions instead of just stating the obvious to me?" she said angrily.

"Alright, it's done. Now we need to decide how to deal with it," Doreen said, practical as always.

"I was hoping if I don't show for a long time then he'll maybe be home and we could marry."

Doreen had never before seen Rosita so lacking in common sense to the point of naivety. She took Rosita's hand and patted it. "Look, get yourself off to work and we'll talk again later. Between our two heads, we will come up with something and work out a plan of action. Perhaps we could contact his regiment or something like that. We'll surely come up with something that will work."

Over the following weeks, it was agreed between the two that Doreen would make discreet inquiries through various regimental officers, but her efforts came to nothing. She was told in no uncertain terms that information about specific serving officers could only be disclosed to close family members. Unfortunately, when asked why she was looking for information, she had to refuse to give a reason.

They both were still going around in circles trying to work out a solution, but could think of none.

Rosita was nearly three months pregnant and hitting a brick wall when out of the blue a large envelope with a stamp indicating it had come from Aden, was given to her by the senior staff administrator at the hospital.

"This letter arrived for you yesterday, Nurse Beconsford. Obviously, the sender didn't know your home address. Please let me explain that it is frowned upon to have private post sent through the hospital." She handed the letter to Rosita and said, with disdain in her voice, "Perhaps you will remember that in future, Nurse."

"I apologise and assure you that this will not happen again," Rosita said, anxious to leave the woman.

"Please make sure it does not," she replied, as she opened the door and dismissed Rosita.

As she stood in the corridor, Rosita had to put her back against the wall as she began to feel quite faint. She tried to pull herself together, realising that she had two more hours of work. She made the decision to wait until her work day finished before opening the envelope.

When she arrived home, she was exhausted. She was trying to stay optimistic in the hope that the letter contained good news. Doreen was preparing dinner in the kitchen, as Rosita ran straight into the parlour and tore open the envelope. As she did so, she felt far sicker in her stomach than she did from her pregnancy because she had realised that it was not Marcus's handwriting on the envelope. *Dear God*, she thought, *don't let me read that he's dead.*

Doreen was still in the kitchen but Rosita decided to share the letter with her. She called Doreen into the parlour and sat down, feeling weak.

"Rosita, you're white as a sheet!" Doreen exclaimed and began to fuss over her.

When Rosita finally opened up the letter, inside she found several pages, but not from Marcus. She lifted the last page to see from whom it came, but she found that it was signed by '*The batman*'.

Her hands shook as she decided to read the letter out loud so that both of them would know the contents at the same time.

"It's from his batman," she said to Doreen, sick with the thought of what she was about to read.

Dear Miss Rosita,

This is the most difficult letter I have ever written in my life. It pains me greatly to impart what I'm about to write.

I will start by stating that the love shown to you in England by Marcus was real. I had never before seen him so besotted by a lady. When he wrote to you in Aden, he told me that the only thing he would like to do in his life was to see you again. He was crying as he posted the letter and I felt sorry for him as he was a good friend of mine. He left the ship later that evening to drown his sorrows in a drinking establishment in the dock area. When he didn't return to the ship by midnight, some of us got permission to go and see if anything was wrong. We later discovered that he had got into some type of altercation in the establishment and someone waited for him after he had left and kicked him brutally before leaving him on the footpath. He had been brought to a hospital just before we arrived on the scene. He stayed there for a few days and he was then put into a medical unit on a ship returning to England with his batman to escort him to his home to help his family take care of him. I believe –"

Doreen interrupted Rosita. "Wasn't *he* his batman, isn't that what you said?" she asked, puzzled.

"Please, Doreen, would you finish reading it for me? I'm feeling very faint."

Doreen took the letter from her friend's shaking hands and read aloud. *"I believe that he was diagnosed with acute injuries to his body and a severe injury to his brain. I'm sorry I have to inform you of that.*

Yet, what I now have to tell you is much more difficult for me to write and will be very painful for you to read. I can but apologise to you on my own behalf and on behalf of my friend. I hope you can find it in your heart to forgive him and I hope that your friend Doreen is close by when you read what is to follow."

Doreen stopped reading and stared at a shocked Rosita in consternation. Then she took a deep breath and continued.

"Marcus Nicholls is not his name and I was not his batman. We are both officers in the army and during the few years we were together we decided to have a game when we went out to a dance or event. We both used fictitious names. Sometimes he would be Marcus and I would be the batman but the following week that might change and I would be Marcus and he would be the batman. We both thought it was funny and it allowed us enjoy the company of women without any repercussions. I bow my head in shame now as the truth is that we are both married men."

Rosita gasped, her eyes widening in horror.

Doreen continued. *"He has a wife and three children under the age of ten and they live in the north-east of England. I never asked if he was happily married and I don't know the answer to that. What I do know is that during the whole journey to Aden he obsessed about you and how you were soulmates and that he had never felt like that about any woman he had ever met. I truly believe that if circumstances were different, you could have been the love of his life but, instead, he has now returned with his actual batman to live in the care of his wife, children and extended family.*

I am so, so, sorry for the hurt this has caused you but I beg of you never to try and find him, as the pain that would cause would extend to too many people. That is why I haven't given you his real name. His family have enough in their lives now with caring for a man who remembers nothing and doesn't even know his own name.

As I said previously, I am full of shame writing this letter. It all seemed such harmless fun when we did what we did, but I can now see what idiots we really were.

If this upsets you, as I know it will, I can offer no comfort except to say that he loved you.

Sincerely yours,

The batman"

Rosita sat in stunned silence and in complete disbelief as her brain failed to process what she had just heard. Doreen had the same reaction and for once was lost for words.

As they sat in the room in the fading light of the evening, they were both feeling as if the world had stopped moving.

Then Rosita suddenly stood up and in a fit of anger tore the letter into fragments and tossed them into the burning coals.

"What a stupid foolish woman I was to fall for that despicable excuse for a man! How could I have done it, Doreen?"

Doreen had never seen such anguish before on Rosita's face.

"I always thought I was so in control of my emotions. Even as a child, when I knew that my father was dying and everyone else was falling to pieces, I was the stoic and sensible one. Where the hell has that person gone?" There was desperation in Rosita's voice.

Doreen stood and went over to put an arm around her friend.

"You are not a stupid woman – you made a mistake. I know it's a big one but you won't be the first woman to fall in love with a cad and you won't be the last. For now, I just want you to sit down by the fire and I'm going to make something for us to eat, because we have a lot to talk about and wasting your anger on him is fruitless. He's not worth it."

Doreen left and returned about fifteen minutes later with a tea tray. While the kettle was boiling, she had gone into the back garden and thrown several loose rocks at the back wall, as she muttered, "*I'd like to kill that loathsome excuse for a man! If I had him here now, I'd throw all of these and more rocks at him!*" Yet she knew that she too had to let go of anger as they both had big decisions to make fairly quickly.

"Let's both have some food inside us before we calmly discuss what we need to do about the baby. Remember I'm with you for the long haul if you want that, so we'll try find some way of dealing with it. We may not have solutions but perhaps some resolutions might do for now."

As Rosita lifted her head from her hands, her face was blotched and her eyes were brimming with tears. "Thanks, Doreen, of course I need you, but I don't think God nor man would have an answer to my predicament. If word gets out about me, I'll lose my job and I'll be shunned by society, apart from the fact that I'll bring massive shame on my own family."

"Rosita, eat and drink your tea," said Doreen calmly, "and then we'll put our heads together and come up with something. Sure, we have at least two or three months before a slim person like you will be showing."

Having eaten in silence, the girls spent hours going around in circles and resolving nothing. Doreen finally suggested that they sleep on it and talk again on the following day. Rosita agreed, but they both knew that very little sleep would be had by either of them on that long dark night.

It was close to sundown on the following evening when Doreen made a suggestion that threw Rosita completely.

"Are you out of your mind to suggest that? How do you think it would work? It certainly is not something that even crossed my mind last night as I tossed and turned," Rosita said in an annoyed but still anguished voice. "Nor would it ever!"

They had been consuming copious mugs of tea as thankfully, being Sunday, they had no work. Neither attended church as Rosita was sure people would have passed remarks on her ravaged face. They had, by now, exhausted all the possible options open to Rosita.

"Don't throw the idea out so quickly, Rosita. I realise that I haven't thought through the ins and outs of it yet, but can't we at least discuss it?"

The only thing they both knew for certain was that Rosita would never go down a dingy back alley in London to rid herself of her unborn child.

"Alright, then let us discuss your mad suggestion," Rosita said with exasperation and disbelief in her voice. "I know that you're more streetwise than I am, but what you are saying is preposterous. You're suggesting that we should go away somewhere we are not known, that I should have the baby using your name, and that you will help me bring up the baby who will have your surname. Why in God's name would you land yourself in that mess, Doreen, when this is my mess to sort out?"

"It's not as daft as you think. I have always said that I would never marry. My mother died from sheer backbreaking work so that I could go to school and get an education for myself. I did that and have a good career as a nurse. I haven't a single relative in the world that I know of, so I have no problem telling anyone that I've had a child out of wedlock. I have seen during my training girls hiding pregnancies and later their relatives bringing up the child as their own. It happens, so why couldn't we do it? I could drop some of my nursing work and mind the child until it goes to school. You've always been saying that you'd have loved to have me as your lady's maid. Well, that was the career that my mother thought would be a great position for me. So, just think about it. Look, Rosita, I'm exhausted now and I need my dinner. The chicken is nearly cooked so I'm going for a short walk in the fresh air to clear my head before serving our meal. So why don't you just sit here and calmly think about what I am offering you?"

Doreen walked out before Rosita could answer.

It was over two hours later that they returned to the subject. They had both calmed down slightly, having enjoyed a meal of vegetable soup and warm buttered bread followed by roast chicken, apple pie with cream and some strong tea. They almost felt normal and were reluctant to come back to the subject, but Doreen started off again.

"Rosita, you've often told me about the fact that you loved travelling and visiting new places. Contradict me if I'm wrong, but you have always said that you have enough money on which to live without your nursing job. So maybe now is the time to do that. However, if this sounds like a good plan, don't expect me to work out what we can actually do for the next year. You have far more knowledge and experience than me about planning things but I'll go along with whatever you decide." Doreen had an anxious look on her face, worried both about the responsibility that she might be taking on or that she might have crossed a line with Rosita that she should not have done.

Rosita smiled wryly, acknowledging to herself that nursing was never about the money for her, but her desire to live her life as she saw fit and not be burdened by duty. Now she admitted that duty had come back to bite her as the reality of her situation began to dawn on her.

Later that day, they decided that Rosita would not go to work on Monday. Doreen would go in and make an excuse for her absence. This would give Rosita a whole day to think of a way of dealing with the next year.

Rosita spent the next morning making notes about how she could account for her long absence, should they follow Doreen's plan. Her biggest worry was how she could reasonably organise the future without visiting any of her family during that time. That needed a lot of thought. Her brain felt overloaded and she was afraid that her decisions at this time would be flawed by bad judgement. Yet she knew that she had a good friend and a survivor by her side and that was important at this moment. A best friend, who was also a trained nurse, and had carried out lots of deliveries when she spent six months of her training at St. Thomas's Hospital in London. Yet she knew also that whatever choices she made, they would have implications for the rest of her life. She wasn't sure if she had the courage for that sort of thinking.

During that long and stressful day, she often came back to what her father and grandfather used to say and she felt was reassuring. "*Rosita, love,*" they would say, "*whatever decisions you make, even if they prove to be wrong in the end, don't have regrets. You can only do the best you can given the circumstances in which you find yourself at any given time.*" She just hoped that this reassurance was wise as she made a decision and began to plan the next year of her life.

Chapter Four

Alice, Richard and their two adult children finally moved into the farmhouse in Midleton, where Allice found that everything was almost as she had left it in 1843. She felt as if she had never left. However, it now had two additional rooms added to the back section of the house. That meant it was roomier and the back of the house now received more of the sun as it shone through the large windows of the new extension. This home had always been a happy place for her and her family, and she looked forward to them living out many more years in this special place.

Her older sister Eliza and her husband Jack had already returned to Rose Cottage, just a stone's throw from the farmhouse. With the Beconsford Estate and the town of Midleton within walking distance, they were all delighted with their decisions.

A happy reunion took place when both families had their first meal together in the farmhouse. Alice and Eliza had insisted on cooking together "for old times' sake".

As Alice looked at her family, all sitting around the table having Sunday lunch, she couldn't have been happier. She smiled as she watched her son Gregory and daughter Emily conversing happily. Emily was shortly to take up a post in a Cork school as a teacher. Alice hoped that she would soon find a nice young man and settle down. As she looked at her son chatting with his sister, she thought that while he was not as easy-going as his father, he was a young man who knew his own mind. He was serious-minded and sometimes appeared as if the weight of the world was on his shoulders. She often wondered if going through a famine during the first five years of his life had affected him. He had always loved his Auntie Sylvia, as he had called her, in Ballyeoin, and when she left for America during the Famine, he was forever asking why she left. Only later did he realise that she had been married to the most hated man in the district, Toby Ramsay, who was killed by Irish nationalists during the Famine and the estate burnt to the ground. Gregory was always smiling and happy when Sylvia and her two boys came on holidays from New York. Maybe the number of bad experiences his young brain had absorbed dampened the sunny, relaxed, cheerful little baby who was born just before the Famine.

Alice was reflecting on all this, knowing that she had a good, serious-minded son, who loved his work on the farm, when she realised that Gregory was speaking to her.

"Mam, I think you know already that I'm seeing a girl called Bridie and I want to invite her to our home to meet you and Father. I was thinking of next Sunday when she's off work. Would that be alright with you both?"

Alice was prepared for this and, with a smile and a warmth of expression that she was suddenly not feeling, she answered, "Of course she's welcome to come. We'd all love to meet her, wouldn't we, Richard?" She looked at her husband, gently kicking him on the leg under the table.

"Yes, of course we would, son," the always amiable Richard agreed.

When their meal was over, the family stayed talking for the rest of the evening and it reminded her of some of the family gatherings when she was a child. This was one reason why she was so happy to be back in Midleton.

When Alice and Richard retired to their bedroom, his first question was why she had kicked him in the leg earlier.

Laughing, she reminded him that she was concerned about Gregory's choice of girlfriend.

"I had told you I was worried because her brother Finn is a nationalist troublemaker," she responded.

"And didn't I tell you at the time that none of us have control over our adult siblings behaving badly, so give the girl a chance and we'll have this conversation again after we meet her," Richard said, smiling at his still beautiful wife.

"Yes, of course, but you know me, I want to organise everyone and make things good for our family and I don't want our son marrying the wrong woman."

The following Saturday Gregory waited at the railway station for the arrival of Bridie on the train from Cork. He had paid for her to stay at the Haven Inn, now run by the Swan family. When the carriage door opened, he was proud to see his well-dressed girlfriend alight, her face beaming.

As she took his arm, he said, "I've dinner booked at the inn. It's in the beautiful Regency Room at the back that all the rich people who visit the Beconsford Estate use if they want to dine outside the estate."

"Oh, how grand!" said Bridie, laughing.

"I'm glad you're impressed!" he said with a grin. "You see, because I'm related through marriage to the Beconsfords I have permission to use the room." Gregory was still not sure how the locals felt about him and his sister using the perks of the estate. But he had fond memories of enjoying cakes and lemonade there when he and his sister visited Midleton in the past.

Bridie was indeed impressed with the food and her surroundings and couldn't stop smiling all evening. She couldn't wait to tell her mam and her friend Holly when she next visited Bantry. Nowadays Bridie sent money to her mother each week, through her friend Holly, who assured her that Finn was always out when she handed over the money.

After church on Sunday morning, Alice rushed home to put the finishing touches to the dinner that was cooking in the oven. She didn't know why Bridie didn't attend church but decided she wouldn't ask.

At two o'clock Alice opened the front door and watched as Gregory entered the house accompanied by a tall, well-dressed girl with flaming auburn curly hair you could almost call unruly, and a beaming smile on her freckled face. She surprised Alice because she had an air of confidence about her that was impressive.

What Alice didn't see was the bundle of nerves Bridie was before she left the inn with Gregory. She had to keep telling herself, while looking in the mirror, that his family were only people and she was as good as any of them. At least that was what her mother had always said to her and now she decided that she had to believe it.

Bridie having been introduced to the family, they all sat down to eat. As the meal progressed, Alice and Richard were more and more impressed by Bridie. She had good manners and was knowledgeable, especially about fashion and clothes, which pleased Alice. Also, Alice was delighted with her appreciation of the food and enjoyed the enthusiasm of the girl, especially her ambition to make high-end clothes for those with money.

Richard interrupted their conversation as he put his arm around his wife's shoulders.

"Do you know that my wife designed and made lots of dresses for opera singers?"

"Don't exaggerate, Richard! I haven't done anything except make functional clothes for years now. However, Bridie, if you ever want some help, I will be delighted to be of service." She smiled, thankful that the girl had a bit of ambition. She might be just what Gregory needs, to help him settle down and lighten up, she thought.

Chapter Five

Back in Hertfordshire, Rosita sat down at her desk, overlooking the vast estate beyond, and put pen to paper. This was a letter that she was not looking forward to writing. She had always hated people who were deliberately deceitful and now she felt like one of them herself.

My dearest Margarita,

I'm writing to tell you that myself and Doreen are taking time out from work and we hope to travel around England and even Europe over the next while, but we won't be going over to Ireland on this occasion. Where we will make our stops, I am not yet sure, but I will keep you informed of where I am. Doreen has some business to attend to, which I will tell you more about when we meet in Ireland next year.

I'm quite looking forward to a break! As you know, I love seeing new places. I have written to Louis and Violet and they seem delighted that I'm not nursing. I expect you will tell the rest of the relatives and when you're doing this, perhaps you could apologise to them if I don't write too many letters to them during my long overdue vacation.

I'm so pleased that you're having success singing around Europe with your equally famous husband! Like your papa, Jack, always said, 'everyone deserves a second chance' and I'm glad that you got that after the death of my dear papa Victor.

Send my love to your handsome husband Laurence and my beautiful very young, sort of half-brother Theodore!

Love for now,

Rosita

Rosita and Doreen were at last ready to set out from Hertfordshire on a bright sunny morning.

Rosita handed over the keys of the house to Mrs. Randle who worked for the Hatfield Estate as the housekeeper for the workers and guest properties. Rosita assured her that if an overspill of guests arrived in the estate, they could use the house over the autumn and winter months.

"It would help keep it fresh and aired," said Rosita. "Also, if at the end of each month you could forward any post to the postal office I have written down – I've left that and other notes on my desk – I have arranged to have it forwarded to me."

Mrs Randle assured her that good care would be taken of everything and Rosita was happy that their home was in good hands.

Then Rosita sought out Doreen.

"That's everything put in place now and, you know, for the first time in months, I feel almost normal, like we were going on holidays," Rosita announced and she smiled, which was something she hadn't done in a long while.

Doreen beamed at her, glad to finally see some positivity in her friend's demeanour. "I hope that we can enjoy some sun before we have to put our plans into action. So, let's just pretend that we really are going on our holidays. Thankfully, your sickness seems to have disappeared and your cheeks have a bit more colour in them. I was beginning to think I'd never see the old Rosita again, so I'm relieved."

Leaving Mrs. Randle to lock up the house, Rosita and Doreen made their way by carriage to London, to board a train that would take them to Brighton.

Earlier they had agreed that Doreen's name should be on all the bookings, but then decided that instead of *Trent* she needed a false surname. Doreen suggested that she should be called Mrs. Nicholls. Rosita smiled wryly as she approved the decision after Doreen said they might as well get some use out that odious man Marcus who had used Nicholls as his made-up name. They laughed at the irony of the situation when they finally put their plan into action.

Doreen had given her notice at the hospital, telling them that she was going to become a full-time housekeeper and companion to Lady Beconsford. Many of the nurses said they envied her the soft life that she had opted for and Doreen just agreed with them.

Rosita had informed the hospital that she was taking a break with Doreen, both for holidays and to attend to some urgent business matters. However, she would hopefully be returning to work in the hospital the following year, if they still had a vacancy for her. She apologised to them for taking Doreen with her but assured them that Doreen had made her own decision about taking up her new position as companion and housekeeper. The matron had wished her well, saying that she always expected Rosita would leave when the time was right. Rosita assured her that she was definitely going to return and they shook hands, as the matron again wished her all the best.

The hotel room in Brighton had a view over the harbour and they immediately fell in love with the lively holiday spirit in the town.

"The first thing I want to do," Doreen announced, "is to walk along the prom and check out the ladies' fashion shops."

Rosita agreed, while insisting that they first eat a hearty meal, now that her appetite had returned, having lost so much weight during the first three months of her pregnancy.

The sea view from the dining room was soothing and they both began to feel relaxed as they watched the boats bobbing about in the sea beyond. The room was ornate and had numerous chandeliers and brightly shining oil lamps adorning the walls. It gave light and colour to the room and Doreen was overcome with the grandeur of it all. On the stage in the centre of the room, a small orchestra played. It comprised a pianist, a violinist and a harpist, who played gentle music that almost had Rosita asleep before their meal ended.

"I think you need a bit of air and exercise before bedtime – it will make you sleep better," Doreen said, coaxing Rosita to leave the warmth of the room.

Rosita laughed. "I agree I need some exercise, but I could fall asleep standing up right now, so we'll just take a short stroll and check out some of the other establishments on the promenade where we can also go to eat while we are here."

The girls liked Brighton so much that they opted to stay on for over a month. They attended a host of eateries where often they were entertained by orchestras and singers. They both found that the sea air was very bracing and it must have helped them sleep as neither suffered like they had during the past couple of months in Hertfordshire when sleep was a luxury. They both agreed that they were lucky that so little rain fell during their time walking along the promenade.

But planning had to be done and Rosita sent Doreen to the shops to get the kind of clothing they would both need for the winter. Rosita in particular needed clothes that would not reveal an expanding waistline.

Finally, Rosita announced. "I think that we should move on to Paris now as I can then put a blur on our next destination when writing to Margarita, suggesting that we're going further into Europe."

"I agree, and we'll have a good time there before settling down quietly for a few months," Doreen said with a smile of delight on her face.

Rosita was five months pregnant when the ladies arrived in France. She now had no sickness, was still not showing her condition, plus she felt energised with no illness to worry her. For Doreen, all of this was new and exciting and she relished every moment, as she tried to put the enormity of what she was about do in the years ahead out of her mind. It felt daunting to her but she didn't dwell on it. Instead, she trusted Rosita to make the decisions that would smooth their future paths.

Paris and the French people were an eye-opener for Doreen. Their hand gesticulations, the fashionable clothes they wore, plus their air of superiority made her feel like a country bumpkin in their midst. Rosita told her not to take them too seriously and, thankfully, Rosita spoke enough French to put them in their place if she thought they were out of line or dismissive of their Britishness. They spent their time there taking boat rides on the Seine and dining in elegant hotels. The highlight of their trip was when they visited Versailles to see the palace where Margarita had sung with Alice's husband. Rosita told Doreen that Margarita had worn a tiara belonging to a countess on the evening of the concert. Doreen was suitably impressed.

However, Doreen was almost grateful when, at the end of September, Rosita agreed that it was time to face reality.

That night, before retiring, Rosita wrote a letter to Margarita and hoped that it was vague enough to reassure her insightful stepmother.

My darling Margarita,

I hope that you and the family are well. Myself and Doreen are having a wonderful time on our travels. We were in Versailles over the weekend and I told her all about your exploits when you were there all those years ago. You know how much we enjoyed Brighton, but now we are seriously considering going to warmer climes over the next few months. This break from work is doing me a power of good but over the winter I must guard against getting too immersed in the European culture and climate! We shall be returning to England well before the spring and if you don't hear from me for Christmas, it will be because we will be enjoying some good weather in some remote exotic place!

When you receive this, please let Louis and Alice know, and when we next meet up we shall have much catching up to do.

Best wishes to Laurence and kisses to Theodore,

I remain,

Your loving Rosita

Rosita posted the letter in Paris before they finally set out for Dover.

Both Rosita and Doreen were tired and almost looking forward to resting up for a while. As Rosita sat down in their hotel suite later that evening, Doreen kept her supplied with tea and scones, while she composed the letter that needed to be written.

My dear Mr. Wilder,

As agreed with you some months ago, I am today organising the payment of six months' rent for your house overlooking the bay beyond Saunton Sands, near Croyde in Devon. I shall leave said six months' rent in an envelope with the postmaster in Croyde, as requested by you, where I believe I can then collect the keys of the house from the postmaster.

As you know, myself and my friend are hoping to paint some winter scenes during the next months. If we decide to vacate the cottage before the end of the rental period, we shall inform the postmaster in advance and you can then re-rent it without any need to return the monies paid by us.

Thank you again for facilitating me,

Yours sincerely,

Doreen Nicholls

"Is that okay," Rosita asked, looking anxiously at Doreen. "We'll stick to that name until such time as we have to register the birth."

"Rosita, you know that if you change your mind at any time before the birth is registered, I'll still support you for as long as I have a breath in my body," Doreen assured her friend.

Rosita had tears in her eyes as she put her arms around Doreen.

"Thank you, but, sadly, I know what I have to do," she said as she held Doreen's shoulders and looked into her eyes. "Are you having second thoughts?"

"No, no, definitely not. I just want you to know that you have my support no matter what you end up doing. I have in you the best friend I could ever have imagined and you've given me a life that I would not have expected. I'm here for you, Rosita, no matter what the future holds."

As the carriage finally drove into Croyde, Rosita had very conflicting feelings about her decision to come to a place that had in the past been traumatic for her. Back at the time of the Famine, her sick father Victor had taken herself and one of the maids, Florrie Bowe, from Midleton to a cottage there, from where later Margarita had to rescue them. Yet she knew that it was such a remote spot in the winter that it was safe for her to be there. Nobody would imagine that she would ever return to that place.

Doreen collected the keys as agreed and bought some provisions for the next few days. As they passed a tall green gate, Rosita pointed it out to Doreen as the place where she had previously spent close to a month when she was little more than a child.

When they arrived at the head of the peninsula, on their right side a large wrought-iron gate painted in white was already open. Beyond, nestling into the hills sat an imposing two-storey house with a slate roof and a wide driveway with well-cut lawns at either side. A large oak front door had two windows on either side and above the door a wide balcony sat between windows on either side of the upper story. This house was a mansion in comparison to the one in which she had stayed in the past. As the ladies stepped from the carriage, they turned to look at the breath-taking views of the seas below.

"I definitely will resume my painting career while I'm here. I was always sketching and painting when I was a child and this might be the time for me to restart," Rosita said as Doreen opened the front door of their new temporary home.

When Rosita stepped inside, memories of more than fifteen years before came flooding back. She recalled passing this beautiful house and had wished they were staying there instead of in the dingy hidden-away cottage. She had looked at its Alpine style roof with the balcony above the hall door and had wished it was theirs.

She immediately walked up the stairs and when she turned left and walked inside the bedroom, she was captivated. The room was huge. It spanned the full width of the house with the balcony door in the centre between the two windows. The large bed was a four-poster. Both the canopy and bed coverings were in rich navy blue and matched the pale-blue printed wallpaper.

She opened the door that led to the balcony. The sea stretched out below as far as the eye could see and a few boats bobbed in the waves in the distance. She stood there, entranced by the view. She reflected that the overhanging eaves from the roof and the waist-high balcony would both help keep the winds at bay during the autumn and winter to come. As she stood gazing into the distance, she felt a certain peace there, unrealistically perhaps, but she was truly captivated by the house. She knew that she would return to her painting in this quiet space and perhaps for now stop worrying too much about her increasingly noticeable pregnancy. As yet she could not deal rationally with her outrageous decision and still held it to the back of her mind, deciding to still live for the time being just one day at a time.

As she sat in the balcony, Doreen came into the bedroom and smiled when she saw how relaxed Rosita looked.

"This is quite a place, isn't it?" Doreen said.

"Yes, it must be beautiful in the middle of summer."

"I'm presuming that this is your bedroom," Doreen said jokingly, "because I hope it is! I've discovered a room at the back that has a view of the lovely hills in the distance. I couldn't be having the sounds of the waves and the wind while I'm trying to sleep." Doreen already knew that Rosita was very happy with her choice.

"Of course I'm choosing this one! Can't you smell the sea salt? It will do our health a power of good."

"I hope so because I'm going to have to do a lot of walking to the village shop over the next few months," Doreen said, glad that the road to the village was without hills.

"You can maybe walk there for the first day but then ask the shop owner to bring our provisions or send them by carriage. You can give a list to the shop. I have no intention of letting you wear yourself out tramping the roads during autumn and winter. I need you too much for you to exhaust yourself while you are here looking after your reclusive artist friend."

"Well, that's grand. I'm off now to get the fire and the range started and I'll let you rest until we both get food into ourselves," Doreen said, leaving the room to get on with her work.

Over the following months, Doreen got to enjoy walks along the clifftop as she didn't have too much housework because, much to her relief, the house had every convenience, with indoor plumbing for baths plus water closets.

Rosita started painting landscapes and insisted on Doreen standing while gazing out to sea, as Rosita endeavoured to capture her, with the wind blowing her flaming chestnut hair. Even Doreen was surprised at the finished painting and had put it on her bedside locker.

Soon, Christmas was upon them but thankfully the weather wasn't too severe. They began to spend most of their time indoors. Doreen cooked a veritable feast for the two of them on Christmas Day and they laughed as they both had given each other almost identical scarves and gloves as surprise presents, bought months ago in Brighton. The turkey and plum pudding lasted them nearly up to New Year.

They found that Croyde in winter could be a very cold place and Doreen prayed that the weather would have eased before the baby was due at the end of January.

As 1867 dawned, Doreen did not get her wish. Icy rain and chilling winds were followed by scattered snow showers. This turn of events had her concerned. With that in mind, as a precaution she called to the village doctor and told him that her friend sometimes had problems with breathlessness. He instantly assured a relieved Doreen that he would come out to the house at any time of day or night, if his services were required.

"Rosita, I'm covering all eventualities. We have everything ready for when I help you deliver the baby and I've already stocked up on food because if bad weather continues the provisions may not be delivered and we can't take that risk. You'd better have an easy birth or else we'll need a doctor. I just hope and pray that it all goes well. I'm not trying to worry you but I need to let you know that I'm not taking any chances with this birth. I'll call a doctor if there is any issue, alright?"

Rosita saw that she meant business. "Alright, I agree. I know enough to not do anything foolish. But let's just wait and see. Hopefully, it will be an easy birth." Rosita was happy that she had a good nurse by her side.

Heavy snow began to fall in mid-January and they were stuck indoors for the week that followed. Thankfully, as the month came to an end, the harsh weather abated and after a few days of soft snow it began to turn to slush. Doreen had earlier warned Rosita not to attempt to walk outside, while even a hint of slippery ground was in the yard.

It was coming up to two o'clock, on a bitterly cold morning in early February, when there was a loud knock on Doreen's bedroom door.

"*My waters have just broken!*" Rosita cried out.

Before she had finished the words, Doreen was with her, determined to stay calm.

"Take this nightshift, Rosita. Go back to your room and change while I prepare everything. Don't worry, we're both ready for this," said Doreen, trying to convince herself as well as Rosita.

Doreen put on a comfortable dress and went swiftly down the stairs to the warm kitchen. While she was stoking the fire and putting the prepared bed into the centre of the large room, she just kept praying. *Please, if anyone is up there, will you pray that today will go well?* She beseeched her own mother, and Rosita's parents to keep Rosita and the baby safe. If anything goes wrong today, she thought, I'll never forgive myself. She knew she had to stop her negative thinking and concentrate on the job ahead. When she had the bed ready, a kettle boiled and towels heaped up near the cradle that stood ready by the fireplace, she went up to bring Rosita downstairs.

"Hold onto my arm going downstairs. I have pillows on the bed and I want you to sit up while I make you some tea and then we'll both eat some breakfast. We could have a long day ahead of us," Doreen said as she carefully walked her friend into the kitchen.

When Rosita was settled in the bed, Doreen began to make tea and toast.

"How much pain are you having?" Doreen asked.

"I woke sometime in the night and I've been having pains ever since," Rosita said, with a petrified look in her eyes.

"How frequently? And what time did you wake up?"

"I don't know – I didn't check." Rosita had forgotten all her nurse training because all she felt in her brain was a blind panic.

"Don't worry, Rosita. Please relax. We might have a long day ahead of us unless this child is anxious to see the world!" Doreen laughed, in an effort to put a smile on Rosita's pale face. "Childbirth is a very natural occurrence for someone as fit and well-nourished as you. Remember to relax and just keep breathing out through your mouth when you feel a pain." Doreen was trying to sound in charge, as she handed Rosita tea and placed hot toast with her favourite honey within reach.

Doreen had looked out of the house on several occasions during the previous day to check and recheck the weather and thankfully no snow had fallen and she thanked God that she could see green grass beginning to appear in the garden outside.

The carriage again arrived with deliveries, which cheered her considerably and her only worry was now related to the actual birth, because if a big problem arose they had no better plan in place except for Doreen to run to the doctor's house in the village.

It seemed to Doreen that this day was the longest ever in her life as she sat by a groaning Rosita's bedside while the pains increased in frequency and became ever stronger. By half past five Rosita was screaming with so much pain that Doreen gave her a damp washcloth to bite on. Soon Rosita's pains were three minutes apart, with each one lasting up to a minute. Doreen knew that the birth might be imminent.

"I feel an urge to push," Rosita gasped sometime later.

"We're nearly there," said Doreen.

At seven o'clock in the evening of the 7th of February, 1868, a head slowly emerged into the world. A blue-eyed boy was born, with a head of black hair, and the image of his father, for which Rosita was grateful.

Doreen held him very close to her heart. Then she cleared his airways and, as he gave his first healthy roar, she wrapped him in a towel and laid him on his mother's breast.

After she tended to Rosita's needs after the birth, she sat by the bed and both ladies gazed at the baby. They had no words, lost in the wonder of the baby and a certain fear of a future that would unfurl.

"You will need to feed him soon, love. I'll give him a few sups of water for now and help you to start his feeding," Doreen eventually said gently to Rosita, who had still not uttered a word.

Doreen gave him some boiled water that she cooled, before placing him in the crib.

"I'll put the cradle near you and we'll both have a bite to eat while he's quiet. I am also going to say a prayer of thanks to whoever made today go so smoothly."

"But, now that this beautiful boy is born, our problems start," Rosita said.

"We're discussing nothing about the future," Doreen said firmly, "until such time as you have given this child nourishment for the next few months. Only then will we speak of the future."

Doreen was true to her word. Rosita had little difficulty feeding the baby they called Benjamin. Doreen was proud of the way Rosita fed him, even when woken every few hours during the night.

He was a contented boy and they both enjoyed playing with him indoors and on dry days walking him around the back garden of their house in the small perambulator that Doreen had told Rosita was necessary. It had been delivered by a company in Ilfracombe along with the cradle that was standing beside Rosita's bed and both were put to good use over the months that followed. Benjamin seemed especially to love being wheeled around the garden and even seemed to smile as the two happy faces gazed down upon him.

Finally, Doreen broached the subject that since the birth had been unsaid. In her head she was happy to continue as agreed, but was prepared for whatever Rosita wanted.

"Rosita, it's time for decisions. It will be nearly summer soon and we both need to go back to some form of reality. In another month the baby can be weaned and then I'll start to feed him, if that's what you want. However, I will accept whatever decision you make about Benjamin's future. Is he going to be a Trent or a Beconsford?"

Rosita sighed heavily before answering. She had spent many hours and days in the past months trying to work out every different scenario regarding the future of her son. She knew that she did not regret his birth but everything else was turning out to be almost too complex. During the last week she had spent her entire time coming to terms with her decision and now she had to say it in words and it was proving difficult.

She sighed as she answered Doreen. "Will you join me on the balcony later, when Benjamin is napping in his cradle, and we can then talk?"

Doreen agreed, and arrived with tea for them both at twelve noon as the sun streamed onto the balcony where they sat. As they drank their tea, Doreen didn't speak.

Rosita placed her cup back on the tray, turned to Doreen and held her hand.

"I have already set the future in train by writing a letter to Margarita. I'll let you read it before I send it in a week or so but, first of all, I want you to agree to its contents."

Rosita handed her the letter to read.

My dearest Margarita,

We have finally neared the end of our travels and are now in Exeter, before returning to Hertfordshire soon. Do you remember I told you that we were going further into Europe? Well, we enjoyed our time there but later returned to England. You may recall when the "holiday" started that I told you I would fill you in sometime in the future about some business that needed to be attended to. Well, the future is now! So here goes.

Early last spring, Doreen began to walk out with a soldier on leave from the army. She was enjoying his company and after a few weeks, on an evening out in London, he told her that he was due to sail to India the following week. They spent the evening drinking too much and crying too much to take account of their actions.

The following month Doreen found that she was pregnant. She heard later from a friend of that soldier that he sustained a serious head injury shortly after arriving in India. It now appears that he has little or no memory of the past and is being cared for in India and has no prospect of ever getting better. Doreen had never seen herself as the marrying type anyway, due to her father deserting her mother before Doreen was born. However, she quite liked the idea of having a child. So, the news is that Benjamin Trent was born in Devon at the start of February. I had agreed in advance of the birth that she could begin to work for me full time as a companion/housekeeper. Now I'm actually quite happy to see a young life entering our home in Hertfordshire. He's a beautiful little boy and I believe that he smiled at me last week!

If you wish, you can go ahead and inform the family members that Doreen has had a child but that she has no husband. It does not worry her and I'm proud to still call her my friend. I am already enjoying the prospect of being Benjamin's Auntie Rosita! Assure them all that I will write copious letters to them when I'm back in my home.

I'll write to you again when I return but, rest assured, I am not going to miss my planned visit to the family in Midleton at the end of the summer. I'd love to stay in the Dower House with you if that's alright. I've got used to living in smaller, cosier accommodation than is available in the Big House!

As Doreen will not be travelling with me on this occasion, I hope you won't mind taking care of your adult stepdaughter, when I come to Ireland.

I remain, your loving stepdaughter

Rosita

When Doreen finished reading the letter, her hands were shaking.

"So, you've definitely made up your mind about me being Benjamin's mother?" she said, waiting for a reply.

"Yes, and I believe that I would never have the level of dedication and patience that you seem to have, for me to take on the sole responsibility of caring for him. Maybe I actually was pampered as a child, but I will be the best auntie he could ever have."

Doreen was stunned by the suddenness of it all and the fact that she now was going to be a mother of a child. In the past few months when she had washed and bathed him, she tried to hold a bit of distance from him because Rosita might have wanted to keep him. What was now happening was what her heart wanted. She loved the little boy and wanted to care for him and watch him growing up.

There were tears in her eyes as she went over to Rosita and put her arms around her before walking to the cradle, lifting Benjamin and holding him close to her heart.

"I will care for you, my sweet boy, forever, and myself and Auntie Rosita will make sure that no harm ever comes to you."

Rosita felt a pang of regret when she heard the words of love spoken by Doreen but she realised that whatever her own feelings were she was doing the right thing.

That boy and myself would have been classed as outsiders in the upper echelons of society, she thought, but with Doreen as his mother and me supporting them, he'll find his path in life. I'll make sure of that.

"Thank you, Doreen. You'll make a wonderful mother and I agree that we should leave this beautiful place shortly and return to the real world. I have already written to a carriage company in Barnstable to send the largest carriage that they have to take us up to that town and we can get a train from there to Exeter. I know of a good hotel there and when we've settled in, this time in my own name, we'll go to the town hall and you will register the birth with father unknown."

Doreen nodded.

"So, are you happy that I send this letter to Margarita?" Rosita asked, already knowing the answer.

"Of course I am and I'm so grateful that you have all these arrangements in hand. I was just about able to cope with the birth and I certainly can cope with the needs of a young baby, as he'll need to start on solids and bottles of milk when you stop feeding him. As I said, I can do all that but don't ask me to organise hotels and trains and the like. So, thankfully, I'm happy to go along with whatever you arrange."

Within a week, they had returned the key to the postmaster and quietly left the village where nobody ever found out who Miss Nicholls and her friend actually were. As they drove away in their large carriage, they felt sad seeing the last glimpse of the sea way below them, with its myriad colours from blue to green and then the white surf washing onto the sand below.

"You know, Doreen, I would have loved to paint the sea here in summer with people wandering along the beach, but I'm not too sure that I ever want to return here again," Rosita said, casting a last glance at the sea below.

Doreen nodded in agreement. She too wasn't sure if she would ever want to revisit the trauma that she felt when Rosita began her labour. She still went to sleep each night saying prayers of thanks that the mother and baby both survived the ordeal.

When they finally arrived in Exeter, the carriage took them to the magnificent Royal Clarence Hotel. Rosita informed Doreen that the composer Mr. Franz Liszt performed with six other musicians in the hotel back in 1840. Rosita laughed when Doreen asked who Franz Liszt was. However, Doreen was impressed with their accommodation which comprised three hotel bedrooms. One for each of the ladies and in the centre a room where the baby could cry and not disrupt the sleep of other hotel guests.

They spent a blissful month there wheeling the perambulator around the town and along the banks of the River Exe. Doreen duly registered the birth and they both drank some wine to celebrate on the day when Doreen was handed the certificate.

Finally, on a bright summer's morning, they boarded a train at Queen Street in Exeter and made their way back to London on their way to, what was for them, a new norm.

Over the following couple of months, Rosita got her energy back and both Doreen and Benjamin thrived. Rosita returned to the hospital and explained to the administrator that if they wished her to return to work at the infirmary, she would be free from late October.

"I have some business to attend to in Cork but, until that time, I am assisting my good friend Doreen take care of her young baby," Rosita announced to the administrator, as she looked her in the eye with a defiant expression.

The administrator looked back at her with what appeared to be disgust on her face.

"I have been informed that Nurse Trent will not be returning to her duties but I did not realise when she took time off last year that she was with child," she said with a nasty look in her eyes. "Surely, Nurse Beconsford, you are not having your reputation sullied too by letting her live with you?"

"Nurse Dawson, the one thing I would never do is turn my back on a friend who needs my support. It was drilled into me during my training to become a nurse not to judge patients, but to help anyone who was sick to return to full health. If this hospital is uncomfortable with my decision to live with my friend and her son, please let me know and I can look out for another post."

"There's no need to take that attitude, Nurse Beconsford. I will inform the relevant authorities of your new circumstances and leave it to them to decide if they want you to continue to work in this hospital," Nurse Dawson said, looking thunderous.

Rosita nodded her head and left the room. She closed the door quietly and only then let her mind give way to her fury. There is no sympathy in that women's heart, she thought, and if they decide not to have me back, then it will be their loss.

When Rosita returned home, Doreen opened the door with a smiling Benjamin in her arms.

"What's making you look like you have murder on your mind?" Doreen asked, as they went into the kitchen.

"It's that damn administrator Dawson. She made insulting remarks about you and I put her back in her box and we didn't part on the best of terms."

Doreen burst out laughing. "Rosita, I've told you enough times I couldn't care less what anyone thinks about me. I have a good job with you, I'm living in a beautiful home and I have a handsome son to raise. Don't fight with anyone, trying to defend me. Just smile sweetly and bite back your words. We don't want to make enemies and have it affecting you getting on with your nursing."

"Well, I did what I did and if they don't want me to return it's their loss."

"Well said, girl, but in future learn to keep your mouth shut. We both agreed that we would present Benjamin to all our friends and acquaintances as my baby and offer no explanations. It won't take long to know who our friends are." Doreen handed Benjamin to Rosita. "I'm going to make lunch and you can give this young man his bottle."

Doreen was right. Some people avoided them but mostly they met with either kindness or pity. And Benjamin was such a sunny baby that people were drawn to him. Doreen knew that some of the locals admired Rosita for sticking with her friend and she hoped that attitude would prevail.

Just before Rosita left for Ireland, she received a letter from the hospital stating that they would look forward to Nurse Beconsford resuming her duties at the beginning of November. Rosita was delighted and Doreen smiled as she commented, "That must have felt like a slap in the face to Nurse Dawson, the old cow!"

Although Rosita scolded her for such remarks, she agreed, but was also relieved and grateful and looking forward to resuming her career.

Chapter Six

Hertfordshire 1877

Rosita had resumed her career in the hospital on her return from Ireland and their life in Hertfordshire was enriched with the presence of the delightful little boy who was growing up with confidence, responding to the love bestowed upon him by the two women who cared for him equally. Each evening, when Rosita returned from her hospital work, she spent at least an hour playing with him, teaching him, or watching him play in the tree house in the oak tree that the estate maintenance man had erected for his sixth birthday.

By that time, Rosita had risen to the rank of Matron in the hospital and her job took over more of her time than she cared to give to it. Yet she could not see any way of changing that. It felt almost like she was on a treadmill, walking up the steps of a wheel that kept turning, with no way of stepping off.

Benjamin began to attend a school in the town with a few more of the estate workers' children. He thrived in the company of those other children and made both women proud of his achievements. He became very proficient at art but had not too much interest in subjects such as Geography and History. When he returned from school each day, he preferred to spend time watching the ploughing of the fields in the estate and helping out with any outdoor work being carried out by the gardeners, than what he called boring homework handed out by his teacher.

What he loved most of all during these years was the month's holiday they all spent in the Beconsford Estate in Ireland each summer.

When a loving, cheerful Benjamin turned ten years of age, they celebrated this milestone in his life with a party for his many friends both within and outside the estate.

A few weeks later, Rosita returned from her work at the hospital, feeling weary after a long day, where she now had to have a finger on the pulse of everything that happened. The day had been particularly harrowing, with the death of a young child who had influenza and a farmer arriving with serious injuries from a tree-cutting accident. Thankfully they had stemmed the flow of blood and she had put him in isolation to ensure he didn't get any infections. The farmer had a wife and children with only one old enough to help on the farm and she just prayed that he would make a full recovery.

When she opened the door, she saw a letter on the hall table. It was from Margarita and that lifted her spirits somewhat.

She entered the kitchen where her supper had been prepared by Doreen. Benjamin was enjoying a lesson at the home of a local artist who was teaching him how to paint landscapes. Rosita was delighted with his interest in art as she had returned to that hobby herself before his birth over ten years before.

She was glad Doreen was out, as lately, after years of harmonious living, they had differing opinions on Benjamin's future education.

Rosita would have liked him to get a good private education, but Doreen was adamant that, as her boy, she didn't want him growing into adulthood with upper-class children and getting notions above himself. She had insisted that when Benjamin was older she wanted him to learn a trade, because he wasn't a particularly academic boy. Benjamin would rather be out in the fields where he was happy. He loved the job of stacking wood that would be used for firewood inside the estate. Rosita had begun to realise that she had put him on a path from birth where he would never be seen as privileged and she was now having conflicting thoughts about the road he was likely to take from now on. Yet she knew it was not her call and that she had to let these decisions to Doreen and reconcile herself to whatever direction Benjamin took later in his life.

Having eaten her meal, she sat down close to the fire and opened Margarita's letter with anticipation, as always.

My dear Rosita,

You are often complaining that I tell you only of touring Europe and singing in so many nice places with our beloved young son. Well, I do have some news for you now. After much soul-searching, we have decided to return permanently to New York. We are both getting tired of the constant travelling and want a more settled life, especially as it's time for us to consider Theodore's future. Like his father, he has a wonderful tenor voice and has already been offered work in America. Therefore, we will leave after the summer ends. I'm hoping that before we leave we could have a musical event in the Big House. It would, of course, be for charity, but we will obviously sing and may even allow our son to make his Irish debut that evening. Let me know when you are likely to visit and we will arrange it for that time.

Finally, I feel that my time living in the Dower House has reached its end and therefore, Rosita, you are welcome to use it from now on. Violet is very happy and settled with her husband and two children in their estate in North Cork and she seems to have lost all interest in the Beconsford Estate. She now talks only of the way she hopes to improve her own home. Louis will miss us most, I believe. I wish he'd take a wife but he keeps saying that he has plenty of time.

Give my love to Doreen and her beloved son Benjamin,

With love, always,

Your loving stepmother, Margarita

Rosita sat back and frowned as she reread the letter. She knew that her brother Louis would really miss Margarita and so would she. As would Benjamin who loved roaming around the estate when they visited and especially talking to Louis about military history. It's a pity, she thought, that he never had the opportunity to go into the army, as he wished, after university. As she read the letter a third time, it got her thinking.

Shortly afterwards, an excited Benjamin arrived home with Doreen, not able to contain himself before he handed a framed picture to Rosita.

"I've been painting this for you, Auntie Rosita. I know how much you love paintings of seas and mountains and Mr. Jenkins helped me with some of the painting but I did all the drawing myself," he said proudly.

Rosita was almost overcome as she touched the texture of the oil on canvas. Although Benjamin was getting a bit too old for his aunt to be hugging him, on this occasion she drew him into her arms and held him tightly.

"Thank you so much, darling boy. I will treasure this for all of my life. I'm so proud of you. But I'll need you to help me put a nail on the wall to hang it. It will have a place of honour in the front parlour."

By now poor Benjamin was getting embarrassed and asked could he have his tea before they put the painting up on the wall.

"Of course – your stomach is more important to you! Go off and have your food and we'll hang it later before you go to bed."

While Doreen and Benjamin were bustling around the kitchen, Rosita left the room and went to sit in the parlour. She had been thinking a lot since she finished reading Margarita's letter and decided to share her thoughts with Doreen later, after Benjamin had gone to sleep. As she stared out the window of her parlour, she saw a dreary, late February evening sky, with raindrops streaming down the window. It seemed to match the mood of the day she had experienced at work.

When an excited Benjamin had placed the painting over the mantelpiece, the two ladies clapped as they showed their appreciation for his efforts.

After, when he had gone upstairs to his bedroom, Rosita called Doreen.

"Can you come in when you're free? I want to talk to you about something!"

"What's up with you? You're looking pensive," said Doreen as she came in and closed the door of the parlour. "You've got that brooding look on you and when you're like that it means that you're planning something."

"Sit down and let me tell you what I've been thinking ... but first ..." Rosita handed over Margarita's letter for her to read.

When she had read it, Doreen handed it back with a nod of her head.

"I expected that she'd eventually live in America," Rosita said. "Laurence's parents must be a good age now and he'd want to be near them and let Theodore have time in America with his grandparents. Jack and Eliza, his other grandparents, were lucky, minding him over the years when the singers were abroad."

"So, what are you about to tell me? Is it anything to do with this letter?" Doreen asked.

"Well, in a way it has – but also, today I had another very difficult day in the hospital and the whole thing got me thinking. You know the way you and I haven't seen eye to eye about Benjamin's schooling? Now don't panic at what I'm about to say. It is only a suggestion, but at least hear me out."

Doreen nodded, while frowning, as she waited for some bombshell to fall into her life. She just hoped it was nothing to do with the fact that she was not actually Benjamin's mother and Rosita was going to remind her of that.

"Don't look so anxious, Doreen. It's only an idea and I want your view on it. How would you feel about the three of us leaving and going to live in Ireland? As you can see from the letter, we now have a beautiful house in which we could live and Benjamin could go to the local school in Midleton and not go into private education. As you know he loves his Uncle Louis and, as he gets a bit older, he'll be able to help around the estate like he does at Hatfield House. What do you think?"

Rosita looked at Doreen's astonished face.

"Well, that's an awful lot of change you're suggesting in just a couple of sentences. Benjamin has spent his whole life living in England and I have never imagined myself going back to live in Ireland. Plus, what about your job? You've worked hard to get to become the hospital

Matron. Do you want to give all that up just because we can't agree about the boy's education?"

"Doreen, I know that I sometimes make quick decisions but I never regret them later, even if they're not always right. I believe that Benjamin would love to live in Ireland. You know how much he enjoys his trips there and he seems to hero-worship my brother Louis. Plus, paradoxically, since I've been in the top nursing job now for a few years, I have nowhere left to go and I'm not as enthusiastic about my job as I was in the past. Maybe years ago, if I had been allowed train as a doctor, I would think differently. Although now I could train as a doctor in London, I'm too old, and I also don't have the interest any more in returning to studying. However, regarding this proposed move, what's most important is what *you* think."

Rosita waited for a response as Doreen sat musing over this unexpected announcement.

"Well, you'd definitely find it difficult working as a nurse in County Cork, where you are known as Lady Beconsford. And I certainly don't want to live in a castle!" said Doreen, her forehead puckering as she thought of the downsides to such a move.

Rosita laughed. "You don't have to worry about living in a castle. The Dower House is down by the river and away from the main house, as you know, plus with Margarita and her family gone it would be for us three only. In the future, Margarita is only going to be making visits to Ireland, and she has lots of places where she can stay, including with us. Doreen, you will still be my housekeeper, companion, friend or whatever you want to call yourself, but you'll have fewer household chores because the staff from the Big House do the heavy cleaning in the Dower House. Esme Bowe would probably like to come down from the Big House as a daily maid to help. Doreen, what's really worrying me is that when

Margarita and her family have gone Louis will be left on his own. You know that he wasn't happy looking after all the affairs of the estate and since Grandpa Isaac passed away in 1870 all the responsibilities of the estate have fallen on his shoulders. Louis should have been allowed to join the military after university, but he's such a kind and gentle man he saw it as his duty to look after the estate and he's honouring that. Now, I would actually like to be there, as a support for him." Rosita was remembering her own position and how happy she was when she was young and was allowed take any path in life that she wished to follow.

"Alright, Rosita, maybe it would work and at least it would sort out the future education of Benjamin, but first I think we both need to speak to Benjamin and, more importantly, listen to him, to see if he has any fears about the move. We can discuss it again tomorrow, and I'll sleep on it tonight."

Rosita agreed. She was relieved to have a day to consider such a drastic move.

Two days later, when Benjamin returned from school in the afternoon, the people in Hatfield House could have heard the shrieks of excitement that emanated from his mouth when he heard he was going to live in Ireland. His only question was, "Can I spend time with Uncle Louis on the estate?"

When Doreen nodded her approval also, Rosita responded with a grateful thank you.

It was with a sense of great relief over the following two months that Rosita and Doreen made their plans to return to Ireland, with Benjamin constantly hopping around the house in high excitement. He was yearning for a life running around the open fields of the Beconsford Estate.

In early summer, his friends from school joined him to play in the treehouse that had been built for him years before. They always had great fun in that space and finished their play by rolling down the slope of the garden. Doreen would always know they were ready for refreshments when she heard their shrieks of laughter as they tried to be the first to reach the hedge at the bottom of the garden.

After one of these happy afternoons, Doreen asked Benjamin if he was sure he wanted to go to Ireland.

He looked puzzled as he replied. "But I've always dreamed of going to live near my Uncle Louis. He lets me roam all over his estate and tells me all about soldiers. I want us to go there as soon as I get my school holidays," he said, using his pleading voice that he knew got him his own way with his beloved mother and aunt.

"Yes, we will, but only if you give us help by getting all your own stuff into the empty trunks that are sitting with nothing inside them in your bedroom," she said, trying to be stern with him, but grateful that he seemed to be very happy and taking the transition in his stride.

By the end of May, letters of excited expectancy had been received by Rosita from both Margarita and Louis. It was a very happy group that finally boarded a train in London to travel to Liverpool, before setting out on the Irish Steam Packet ship for Dublin.

Later that day, as they watched the ship pull into Dublin port, Rosita felt in her heart that this decision was the correct one. She felt grounded once more as she stood on her home soil.

"England was good to us, wasn't it?" she said, turning to Doreen as they sat back in the large carriage for the drive to their hotel. "I really do intend to still keep our home back in Hertfordshire. We can go back often, because I don't want to forget the life we lived."

Doreen was relieved to hear that, as she still wasn't quite sure how she'd fit into her new life in Ireland.

When they finally arrived in Midleton, they were greeted by Louis, Margarita and the staff of the Big House. Then, after a lovely meal with Margarita and the family and a welcome rest, they eagerly went to their new home, the Dower House. Margarita and her family had already relocated to the Big House, where they would reside whenever they next returned from America.

The first thing Rosita did in the Dower House, as soon as they were alone, was to hang the painting she received from Benjamin on the wall. She smiled as she removed a painting of an ancestor and replaced it with Benjamin's seascape.

"This house is now our home and we will treat it as such," she said. "Doreen, I want you to put your stamp on it with any décor changes that you wish to make."

Doreen was delighted with that and, as she smiled and nodded reassuringly, she began to feel that maybe the move was the correct one. She was very pleased with the way Benjamin had behaved when in the company of the adults in the estate. He appeared excited but thankfully not overawed.

Having settled into her new home, it didn't take Rosita long before she made her way over to the farmhouse to discuss the idea of the upcoming concert with Alice.

"Margarita asked my advice and myself and Richard thought that it was a great idea, but I said that in order for lots of people to enjoy the evening, it needed to be in the grounds of the estate and not the ballroom," Alice said with eyes gleaming. "I know lots of charities who need funds here and in West Cork, plus I'm excited to have all the family around once more, even if Margarita is going back to America for good. This concert will be like the old days. I think it would be a good idea to hold it on Midsummer's Night. It has a good chance of being dry then."

"Will you hold your horses, Alice!" Richard interrupted her, while smiling indulgently at his irrepressible wife. "Knowing you, you'll be turning this into an event as big as the Arena in Verona, if you continue to have bigger and bigger ideas."

"Alright, alright, but it's an event I think the locals should also get to enjoy. None of them could ever afford to go to such a concert and a select group of the county set who will get front-row seats can donate all the money to give to the charities. The only problem I see is that you can never trust the Irish weather if we hold it in the grounds."

Her son Gregory, who was listening to the conversation, interjected, "My friend Lee Cantwell in Cork city supplies really large marquees to the gentry and I know he'd give me a good deal if he knows it's for charity."

This was greeted with delight by his mother. "Well, that's settled then! Rosita, go back to Margarita and tell her I'll be in touch soon, when I've made a few more plans around the event."

Rosita could only smile as she left the farmhouse, more than an hour later. Alice was a miracle worker when it came to organisation and this should suit her down to the ground.

Over the following days, Margarita met regularly with Alice and Rosita, but on one of the mornings when Alice and Rosita were alone they decided to go to the tranquil Secret Garden to relax and sip some tea. As they sat enjoying the summer flowers blooming in abundance, Rosita noticed that Alice looked pensive and asked her if there was anything wrong.

Alice nodded before answering. "We have a problem in the house and I'm not sure how to deal with it. Gregory's wife Bridie is, as you know, a lovely girl, and it's taken her a long, long, time to conceive. Recently she told me that she is finally with child."

Rosita smiled with delight as Alice continued.

"She has already given notice to the fashion house in Cork where she has worked for years. Now that she'll become a full-time farmer's wife, she says that she still wants to continue to make clothes. She's a great girl, is Bridie, and she's very talented."

"Yourself and Richard must be thrilled about the pregnancy. Another to add to Emily's two living over in Glanmire. It will be great for you to finally have a grandchild actually living in the house. So why are you looking so miserable?"

"The reason is because, as you already knew, she has an undesirable brother, Finn, and I'm being charitable by just saying he's an undesirable. He is actually a rather menacing character. Since their mother died last year, he has had nobody to sponge off anymore and he'd begun to call to Bridie at Mrs. Langford's shop, where she worked. The problem is that he actually turned up at our house about a month ago because he couldn't find Bridie that day at the shop. She had been feeling sick and hadn't gone to work, but Richard was home also and answered the door before sending him on his way as he seemed to be drunk. I know that he's mixed up with the Fenians and more dubious people in Bantry, but even they only use him for dirty jobs, I'm told on good authority. I'm at my wits' end over him and don't have any answers as to what to do about it. He hasn't committed any crime when he calls to Bridie at the shop but I'm seriously worried because I now know that he had been trying to get some of her wages while she worked, saying that he's entitled to it now that her mother is dead. I think that Bridie has been giving him money recently in order to keep him quiet."

"Oh, I can see why you're worried!"

"Have you any suggestions?" Alice asked plaintively.

Rosita thought for a while before saying, "He seems like a shocking bully but you would need him to break the law before you can call the police on him. How do you think Bridie would feel if he ended up in prison? Or maybe we could sit him down with the local sergeant if he comes back to Midleton and perhaps buy him a ticket to leave the country and give him some money. Maybe he could be persuaded to agree to that?"

"That might be something worth thinking about. If you have any other ideas let me know. Thanks, Rosita, for that advice. I'll talk to Richard again about it when all the festivities are over. Come on, let us get back to work or there will be no concert in this town on Midsummer's Night!"

The following week was a hive of activity around the estate. The three ladies linked arms as they walked down to "The Arena" as they now jokingly called the large field close to the Dower House where white marquees were ballooning up towards the clouds. Seating was being arranged both inside and outside, close to some smaller tents where Alice had organised food and beverages to be purchased by those with means. Free food would be available in other tents for all the helpers and those from the town without means. Oil lamps were being prepared to light up the driveway for those going home when darkness fell.

When Rosita woke on the morning of the concert, she told Doreen that she was relieved that the sun was shining brightly in the sky, with no suggestion of clouds or rain on the horizon.

"Rosita, you can worry yourself into the ground about the weather in Ireland but there is nothing about it that you can control. So, relax and save your energy for things that you can do. Even if it rains, we have enough marquees to shelter large numbers of people. The excitement that I have witnessed in Midleton since the concert was first announced is amazing. Just preparing for this concert is making people happy." Doreen was as ever practical in her approach to whatever life threw at her.

The weather was very kind to them, as the sun continued to shine throughout the day.

As the hour drew near for the concert to commence, the gatekeeper was kept extremely busy, with carriages arriving from all around the county. At the same time the locals were queuing up to enter the estate at the side gateway from the village.

At eight o'clock, the small orchestra, that had travelled from Cork, struck up Tchaikovsky's *1812 Overture* and as it ended with bells, cymbals, drums and trumpets, clapping and cheering could be heard all around the grounds. The musicians were very pleased to be playing to such an appreciative audience, both inside and outside the marquees.

Later, when Margarita walked onto the stage, the crowds outside asked for hush, as she began by singing her signature tune from the pen of Denny Lane from Cork, "The Lament of the Irish Maiden", known in Irish as "Carrigdhoun". This was followed by Margarita and her husband Laurence singing a beautiful duet from act one of Donizetti's opera, *Lucia di Lammermoor.*

Then there was an expectant hush when Margarita introduced her son Theodore. The sweetness of his tenor voice as it soared into the night sky belied his young age. He was asked to sing three encores before the public allowed him to leave the stage. Margarita again returned to the stage to sing a song called "Shenandoah". She explained that it originated with American and Canadian fur traders travelling down the rivers in canoes and became a well-known sea shanty, whose lyrics had been changed by many songwriters. This version mentioned the Oneida Iroquois Shanandoah who was a chief in central New York state and was the story of a trader who fell in love with his daughter.

As Rosita watched the proceedings from the back of the marquee, she was listening with fascination to the story behind the song, with a smile on her face, until a quiet but urgent voice from behind brought her back to reality. She was summoned hastily by the now elderly Brendan O'Leary, to leave the marquee.

Brendan was the local carriage owner, who was also helping with the security of the grounds for the evening.

"Miss Rosita, I need a word with you. There's a man causing trouble at the side entrance and the helpers are having difficulty stopping him from trying to force his way in. He insists that he is a relative of yours. I didn't know who to talk to as everyone else from the house is sitting too far up in the marquee."

"What did he say his name was?" Rosita demanded as she strode beside Brendan.

As Brendan was about to answer there was a commotion in front of them. Brendan was carrying a large oil lamp and he insisted on Rosita staying behind him, as they approached the miscreant. But Rosita was not to be stopped. She marched forward, confronting an overweight man who was trying to get away from the farmhands who were having difficulty holding on to him.

"Who are you and what are you doing on our land?" Rosita demanded.

"I have more rights than these fools. I'm related to the family."

"And how might that be?" Rosita said, now knowing exactly who he was.

"Me sister is married into the family," he answered, with a smirk on his face.

"Well, that may be so but this event is put on in Lord Beconsford's land and you have not been invited. Do you want to leave peacefully or do you want to be thrown out?" Rosita enquired.

"I'm going nowhere. I have a right to see me sister and I know she's here."

As he finished speaking, Rosita turned to Brendan O'Leary and asked him how quickly he could get his carriage and horses ready for a journey.

"Immediately, Your Ladyship. It's already in the grounds."

"Then, gentlemen, would you continue to restrain this man and escort him to the carriage – and, Brendan, would you and two others take him to Cork city – I'm sure he'll find his way home from there."

As she turned back to Finn Cahill, Bridie's brother, her tone was harsher.

"As for you, how dare you come here to upset your sister and the rest of her family? I'm warning you that if you ever cause a disturbance around here again, I will personally report you to the police."

As the lads gladly escorted him away, Rosita saw the look of venom on his face as he spat out his parting words. *"I'm warning your family, you'll all pay for this, you uppity Englishwoman! I have me ways of getting back at the likes of you."*

As Rosita watched him disappear into the distance, still screaming abuse, a shiver of fear shot through her. He's one bad egg, she thought. Alice was right, he needs dealing with before he does serious harm.

Although his presence cast a shadow over her as she returned to the gaiety of the evening, she was just happy that nobody else in the family needed to know what had happened. She would deal with it when the festivities ended.

Later, when all the family members returned to the Big House, everyone agreed that it was one of the best nights ever enjoyed by so many people.

Over the following days, Rosita spent much of her time in the company of Margarita. They reminisced about the past and they spoke about those who had passed on and who would have enjoyed the laughter and gaiety that enveloped the estate during the summer solstice.

It was on the last evening before Margarita's family were going to New York that the largest dining table was put in place in the ballroom of the Big House, as friends and family sat down to a dinner that included everything from venison to exotic fruits and sweet desserts and was enjoyed by all the diners.

Margarita and Rosita sat together and during the meal Margarita leaned over towards Rosita and whispered, "Do you think my mother and father are looking very tired tonight? Although I know they wanted to be here, perhaps it's too much for them. What do you think?"

"Well, Margarita, I have visited them a few times in Rose Cottage over the past few weeks and Jack's memory is certainly not as good as it was. Yet your mother does not seem to notice and says that everyone of a certain age forgets things. I think that we all forget how old people are getting and your mother and father have both reached a good age. You need to be grateful for that and the fact that they still have a great love for each other. Not everyone is that blessed." She reached out and squeezed Margarita's hand.

"I suppose you're right. I should be grateful, but I'm afraid I'll be in America if anything happens to them. Please, Rosita, let me know if either of them is really struggling. I'll come back, now that our Theodore is starting his own career as a singer and I'm close to retiring and haven't any recitals or concerts arranged for the foreseeable future. I can make the journey home more easily than in the past."

Rosita assured her that she would keep a good eye on them.

When Laurence stood up and said that it would not be a traditional dinner in Midleton if all the singers did not perform for the family, there were shouts of "*Bravo! Bravo!*" and everyone started to cheer.

As two guests who played piano and violin agreed to provide the music, the fun part of the evening began.

Margarita was the first to oblige. As she gazed around the room tears came into her eyes. She knew that this was likely to be the last night that all her family would be together and it left her with the feeling that life can seem very short but, while it's there, we must make the most of it.

It was two o'clock in the morning when the music finally stopped and everyone departed to their various homes and bedrooms.

It was almost time for another sun to rise when Rosita finally felt rested enough to sleep as she offered up a prayer of thanks for the fact that Doreen and Benjamin fitted in so well to their new family. It was a wonderful summer that she would cherish in her memory and hoped that the future would continue in the same way.

Chapter Seven

Margarita was not long back in New York before she received a telegram from Midleton. Rosita suggested that perhaps the time had come for her to return to Ireland and spent time with her parents, as Jack's health seemed to be deteriorating rapidly.

Over the previous few years, Eliza Ryan had witnessed the declining mind and body of her beloved Jack. As his illness progressed Doctor McNally, their friend from Cork city, had said to her that there was little they could do for him, especially with the increasing loss of memory he suffered.

When the doctor called to the house to visit on the day before Margarita arrived home, Eliza had a chat with him.

"Doctor McNally, I promised Jack many years ago that he would always have me by his side and I intend to keep that promise. He was a strong man, but the memories he has had to live with since 1816 on the fateful night in Tramore when the *Sea Horse* hit rocks and so many hundreds of people lost their lives, left its mark. Recently, he's had a return of the nightmares he suffered at that time and the anguish is still there. He wakes at night calling out for Angel, the name of the little girl whose life he failed to save. Yet since he survived the shipwreck, he has led a life where all he wanted to do was to take care of his family and those in his community. He did just that throughout his whole life. Lately I keep reminding him that it was because he survived the shipwreck that we met and then we had our own Angel when our beloved Margarita arrived. Of course, thankfully, after I reassure him and calm him down, he usually goes back to sleep. During the day he's grand and he forgets his melancholy and sits in his chair happily thumbing through books about herbs and plants that Old John left behind when he lost his life on the night of the Big Wind."

As Eliza's voice faded away, with memories of the past, Doctor McNally reassured her.

"Well, if you are finding things difficult, I'll send my youngest daughter Orla, who is a trained nurse, just like her older sister Jennifer, to help you care for him. So don't worry, we are all here to help. He was a good man and you're lucky to have a lovely family around you." He patted Eliza gently on the shoulder.

"Thank you, Doctor, I'm going to be fine," said Eliza, nodding, in an effort to reassure herself as well as the doctor.

As Eliza watched the doctor walk down the garden path, she said a silent prayer that she could keep her promise to Jack and make sure that he never ended up in the dreaded hospital.

It rained a lot during the following few weeks. Margarita arrived home from New York and spent much of her time sitting with her father and singing to him. It reminded her of the past singing to Jack's Granny Sheila in this very same cottage, before she passed away. Now she did the same for her father each evening until he nodded off. Only then would she say a prayer of thanks that she was back in Ireland with no other commitments, at a time when her parents needed her most.

As the first autumn leaves began to fall, Eliza Ryan woke early one morning and quietly went to the kitchen to make a pot of tea. She felt a nip in the air while the flames of the fire began to take and, as she waited for the kettle to boil, she could see the blue sky and a bright sun casting rays of light through the kitchen windows, the first bright day in a few weeks. While eating her breakfast, she hoped that today Jack would eat a little food.

Suddenly and unexpectedly, he appeared at the kitchen door, asking for some water. As she hurried to his side, he looked at her with confusion on his face.

As she held him, he looked helplessly at her and held her hand and spoke softly. "Eliza, my love, will you take me home, please?" he asked plaintively.

As she tightened her arms around him, tears flowed down her face. She gave him the water and guided him back through the door towards his bed. As she did, she knew in her bones that his hour had come and a shiver went through her body. It was the first time she had ever heard him utter such words.

Later that same evening, as a golden late autumn sunset dipped below the horizon, Jack Ryan breathed his last, his hands held by his loving wife Eliza and his daughter Margarita as he gently passed away peacefully into eternity.

Later that week he was laid to rest beside his mother Molly and his granny Sheila. After prayers were recited at his graveside, what followed was an avalanche of grief as every member of his extended family acknowledged his lifelong love of flowers, plants and the green fields of Ireland by each placing a fresh red rose on the coffin before his body was finally laid to rest.

As the weeks passed, Margarita spent many hours in the company of her mother. Margarita would collect her in the carriage and then they would take short walks through the estate. Eliza loved being by the river, looking at the trees in the forest at the other side, many that had been planted by her beloved Jack.

One day, as they sat in the summerhouse by the river, with warm blankets on their knees, Eliza spoke from her heart.

"You know, love, for more than fifty years my life has been organised. Looking after yourself and Jack and doing my teaching in Midleton and later helping my beloved grandchildren. Yet, over the past while since Jack's death, I have no need to get up in the morning, no need to structure my day and it's an uncomfortable feeling. To look around you and know that you can do anything you want while realising that there is nothing you want to do, is something I never expected to happen to me. I've even found myself wondering what day of the week it is. Indeed, I don't even notice the changing weather. It all seems such a blur in my head. I really miss him and I seem to have lost my enthusiasm for everything and everyone. Is that selfish of me when I have so many people like you and my grandchildren in my life?"

Margarita grasped her hand.

"Mama, you are still grieving. This feeling will pass, but you must give it time." As she put her arm around her mother, for the first time she noticed how thin she was getting. I must make sure she starts eating proper food again, she thought, as they left the summerhouse.

Before leaving the river walk, Eliza plucked a small branch from a fir tree and cast it into the flowing water. "I remember when Jack planted that tree," she recalled. "Look how serene the branch is, calmly floating through life. Just like my Jack. I miss him so, so much, love."

Sadly, Margarita could find no more words of comfort for her mother at that moment.

As mother and daughter walked slowly in the direction of the carriage, Margarita knew that her mother was unlikely to return to the river again.

Just eight weeks later, Eliza Ryan passed away peacefully, having for a long time past masked her own failing health in order to stay strong for her husband during his declining physical and mental state. Two days later, she was laid to rest alongside her beloved husband Jack.

As the year drew to a close, the world was a poorer place with the loss of two special people, when both Jack and Eliza Ryan went to their eternal rest.

Chapter Eight

In just a few years, following the deaths of Jack and Eliza, Rosita knew that a new era was evolving in the estate. Benjamin told his mother that when he turned fifteen, much to her disappointment, he wanted to leave his schooling and begin working alongside Austin's son Jody, who had turned out to be an excellent manager of the estate. There was little that Benjamin did not now know about plants and forests and he was particularly enthralled with the newfangled steam machine used by one of the farmers to help with the wheat at harvest time. His interest in the estate especially pleased Doreen as she saw it as maybe a career for him.

Also, the boy had always hero-worshipped Louis. That fact pleased Rosita enormously as Louis gave him lots of attention. The two of them spent many hours talking about military activity around the world and it fascinated young Benjamin.

After a few difficult years that had broken many hearts, following the deaths of both Jack and Eliza, another Christmas arrived and Rosita was hoping that this year mourning would be put behind them and she would try to make it as magical for Benjamin as she remembered from her own early childhood before the Famine.

"Can I light a candle, Auntie Rosita?" Benjamin asked, as the family gathered round the large Christmas tree, taken as always from the estate forest every year for the last fifty years.

"Of course you can, Benjamin. You are part of this family and we are proud to include you," Rosita said, giving him a hug that hugely embarrassed the growing boy, yet he couldn't hide his delight.

"If young Benjamin wasn't finally added to our growing brood," Louis said, putting an arm around a smiling Benjamin's shoulders, "I would have to adopt him myself, because he seems to be the only boy around these parts who listens to me talking about soldiers and military stories. Maybe he'll be an army captain someday."

As Doreen squeezed Rosita's hand, she could see that Rosita was visibly upset at the thought of Benjamin becoming a soldier in the future.

"Well, I think, young man, your head will be getting bigger with all this praise, so light that candle and place it in its holder and give the younger children a turn," said Doreen, knowing that Rosita would have a lapse into sadness that happened, thankfully, only very occasionally.

"You're right," Louis smiled, "Everyone is going to get cold out here and we want to go in to enjoy dinner and sit by the warm fires."

They all voiced their agreement and, as Violet's young daughter lit the final candle by the tree, Louis spontaneously said, "Let us sing a carol to absent friends and those who have gone before us, especially our beloved papa Victor."

As they all sang their favourite "Silent Night" Rosita's eyes welled up with tears. For whom she did not know? Was it for her father, her son, or was it just for herself? She just could not work out why this happy moment had made her sad.

Christmas turned into a great celebration and it was wonderful to see Doreen and Benjamin finally feeling fully integrated and comfortable in the Big House, as Doreen realised that they had been fully accepted as a part of that family. Up to recently, during her first few years, Doreen had felt somewhat intimidated by those up in the "castle", as she had called it. From the time they had arrived in Ireland, Rosita had explained to Louis and Violet's family that she had spent many years with Doreen and, since Benjamin was born, she had shared in his upbringing and she wanted this to continue with her own family embracing both Benjamin and Doreen. It warmed her heart today to find Doreen laughing and joking with the family members and she felt happy that another year had passed and none of them had regrets about the move from England.

A life of contentment followed for Rosita until late in the spring. One morning, as she and Louis were enjoying coffee in his office, he announced that he had something that he wanted to discuss with her.

She was surprised, but answered, "I'm all ears, brother. What's on your mind?"

"Well, you know what a great job Jody is doing as the estate manager," Louis said, pleased with his choice of replacement for Jack Ryan.

"Yes, I agree he's taken to the role like a duck to water. We're probably lucky that he grew up in the estate and has been learning about it since he was a boy," Rosita said, nodding her agreement.

"Well, I want you to remember that, after I tell you what's on my mind. Rosita, I'm hesitating to say the following but it needs to be said. When Violet married and went to live away from the estate, I knew that the full responsibility for the estate was going to be on my shoulders alone. Yet the only thing I ever wanted to do in my life was to join the army. I loved my time living near London when I was at university and, as you know, many of my friends from college became officers. I still correspond regularly with them and hear much about the regiment they joined. That's one reason why I love having Benjamin up at the house with me. That lad is obsessed with things military and I'm able to keep him updated on all the army manoeuvres and the wars around the world. I realise that you knew I wanted to join the army but, with my father dead, Grandpa Isaac needed me instead and I felt I had to do my duty by the family."

"So, what are you thinking now, Louis?" Rosita asked, by now alarmed.

"I've been informed by an officer friend of mine, with influence, that I could enter the army in an office-based position on a five-year commission, because I'm still under forty. However, I'd need someone I could trust to keep an eye on the estate. Alice's Gregory, who's a bright man said he'd help me with the accounts and that's going well. Yet the most important support I'd need is a family member to oversee affairs for me. Would it be possible that you, Rosita, would help keep an eye on the estate for that length of time, if I was accepted into the regiment? I know five years sounds like a long time but it would give me a chance of happiness that I don't really get from the affairs of the estate and I never got as a younger man. Grandpa Isaac and Jack Ryan were both passionate about this estate, but I'm different. It would be wonderful if I could get a break from duty. Maybe it would rid me of all my feelings of regrets about my life, if I got the opportunity to enlist." Louis had a sad pleading look in his eyes.

Rosita looked at him and it reminded her of the day he left Ireland when he was a child, going off to boarding school for the first time. She felt sorry for him then and she felt sorry for him now.

"Yes, brother, I'm sure that it would do me no harm to have to exercise my brain again. But, if I do agree to your daft plans, will you guarantee to come back with a nice bride with heirs available to take over the estate? Because I won't stay in charge forever." Rosita shook her head as she wondered which of them was madder than the other.

"I might even allow that to happen. As you know there are numerous ladies in London who would love to marry a handsome dashing army officer!" Louis said, with a grin on his face.

"Alright, brother. I'll lift the burden off His Lordship's shoulders and carry it until you return triumphant with a wife and heirs to this estate of ours," she said, smiling indulgently at her younger brother.

Once it was agreed, they both decided to move ahead immediately with a plan. They first ordered lunch to be brought to the office and then, each with notepaper and a pencil, began to write down what was required to be done to secure the future of the estate when it was Rosita's turn to take up the burden.

By six o'clock that evening arrangements were agreed between them that would alter both their futures. Afterwards, they spent the following hours reminiscing over the past, before Rosita returned to the Dower House, to discuss it further with Doreen.

As she walked back home, she knew that she had made the right decision and that her life really did need to focus on more than just Benjamin and Doreen.

The following day, as the two ladies sat having lunch in the Dower House, the door burst open and a very sorrowful-looking Benjamin rushed into the room.

"Why didn't you tell me, Mother?" he asked with a hurt look on his face.

"Tell you what, love?" Doreen said.

"About Uncle Louis. He's leaving and going into the army. I love all the time I spend with him and he even says he'll miss me!"

Doreen put an arm around him and embraced him, patting his back. Then Rosita went over and turned him to face her.

"You were in bed last night before I told your mother, and we didn't see you before you left for school this morning. Of course you'll miss him, Benjamin, but I know that he will write to you every week and you'll learn more about the military that way than most lads learn in a lifetime. He's only doing it for a few years and during that time you should be making friends with lads, and later even lassies of your own age. You'll shortly be leaving school and then you can earn proper wages while learning all about the estate from Jody. Louis will be back in five years, he's promised us that. Be glad for him, love. It was always his dream to go to military college but only now is he getting his chance. So, cheer up and let him see how grown up you are and he'll be home on leave very often. We can even go to visit him in London when he's on leave there. Now, Benjamin, let us all go down to the Regency Room in the Haven Inn and you can have whatever you want to eat, just as a treat to cheer you up."

Rosita was relieved to finally see a smile on his face. Oh, the ability of youth to bounce back, she thought, not for the first time.

The following months passed quickly as Rosita spent her time reconnecting with the estate workers. As a consequence, she saw less of Alice. As autumn passed, Alice came to the estate to talk with Rosita.

As they sat in the library Rosita noticed that Alice was looking anxious. "Is everything alright, Alice?"

"Rosita, with the passing of Jack and Eliza and the birth of Cormac, my beloved new grandson, I put Finn Cahill to the back of my mind. Bridie looked so relaxed and contented since Cormac was born. The problem is, I'm told by a reliable source that her brother has tried to see her many times since she left her job in Cork and I believe that she gives him money. Thankfully, he has never come back to Midleton since the night of the concert when you sent him on his way. Now, I think she might be trying to keep the problem away from us at Midleton, after she eventually found out what he did on the night of the concert for Margarita. It still worries me that he's a threat and I wonder if there is anything I should be doing now?"

"I'm surprised that he's not been around the past few years, but if Bridie is slipping him money, that could be the reason why. But I agree that it needs thinking about. Remember what I said about paying him to leave the country? Maybe now is the time to act."

"I don't know. The problem is that we still don't have any reason so we can't call the police. They would likely say that it's a family matter," said Alice, exasperated. "But if we give him what he wants, he could just keep the money and continue to be a nuisance. As you know, he's a really nasty piece of work and I've never heard a nice word said about him in West Cork. He sent his mother to an early grave and she still let him stay in the house until the day she died. Why are there always problems that I have to solve?"

Rosita laughed. "It's because you're such a good organiser."

When Alice left, Rosita spoke to Doreen and they both pondered on the problem but agreed that he would probably have to cause trouble before she could act.

"You can't go to the authorities and report him before he actually commits a crime," Doreen agreed.

Meanwhile, things were going well for Bridie and Gregory. Everyone in the house was besotted with young Cormac. Their first child, born after many years of trying, was now walking and beginning to string sentences and always loved holding the hands of his adoring family who would take him for walks around the farm. Bridie was contented, spending her time helping Alice in the farmhouse and looking after the child. Alice laughed often, telling Bridie that they were able to save on labour as Bridie worked every bit as hard on the farm as she had done at her sewing.

She just laughed when Alice suggested she rest sometime.

"I'm grand now that Cormac is thriving and walking. Sure, soon I won't have to lift him anymore and I'll get plenty of rest," she said.

Alice had grown to love her so much since she married Gregory. She reminded Alice of herself as a young girl. Bridie always wanted to be busy and spent most evenings sewing and stitching while listening as Alice continued to teach her how to improve her designing of clothes. Bridie was now able to create patterns for all types of women's clothes and Alice was really proud of her.

A few days later, word came from Mrs. Langford, the owner of the shop in Cork, that Finn Cahill was on the prowl again, telling anyone who would listen that his rich sister didn't help him anymore. The modiste from the shop sent a message to Midleton that he had been into the shop drunk and obnoxious, asking if she ever came into her shop now. "*I told him that I was reporting him to the police. I told him that he knew that she hadn't worked at the shop for a long time. I warned him never to return again as I will have already filed a complaint against him. That seemed to make him even angrier*," she wrote in the letter that Bridie read to Alice only, as Richard was away in London and she was fearful of what Gregory threatened to do to her brother if he ever bothered the family.

Bridie's hands were shaking as she put the note down on the table.

Alice stretched over to hold her hand.

"Don't worry yourself, love," said Alice, trying to reassure Bridie. "When Gregory gets in from the fields, we'll have to discuss it with him. Do you remember, a few years ago, Rosita and I had been saying that maybe money and a ticket to somewhere like England or even Canada might get him away from Cork. Maybe that might do the trick. Let us all put our heads together and try to deal with this."

Yet Bridie couldn't stay still for the rest of the day and by the time Gregory got in from the fields she was in quite a state.

"None of you know how bad he is," Bridie said with tears falling down her cheeks. "I've been sending him sums of money over the past few years but I was ashamed to tell you. Now he's getting more demanding and asking for more and more. I've seen over the years how he beat me up and threatened that if I told anyone he'd kill me and then start beating up our mother. When he was young, he had a fall from a roof and my mother always said that was what turned him into a dangerous bully. I'm so sorry that I have brought this trouble here with me. I never meant for that to happen."

Alice put an arm around her, to offer comfort. "We'll fix it between us and make it all good. We'll think of something that will work, won't we, Gregory?"

Alice had noticed that Gregory was unusually quiet and had said nothing.

By the time he finally spoke, he was incandescent. "He's a bloody madman and, short of him being locked up for life, that fellow will always be trouble. He has to be stopped one way or another even if I have to kill him with my bare hands!"

"You will do no such thing, Gregory Staunton!" Alice said. "You will not besmirch our name by stooping to his low standards. That's why we were suggesting that if we give him money and a ticket to England or even Canada it might be a way out."

"I wouldn't put it past that fellow to run off with the money and sell the ticket and come back for more. You don't know the half of him. Most people who know him in West Cork avoid him because he loses his temper over nothing."

"Well, has anyone else any better ideas? Bridie needs protecting and getting rid of him seems to be the only way out. But, first, would everyone please calm down for a minute?" Alice said in an effort to put a bit of common sense into the conversation.

Bridie was crying in the corner and, as she sobbed, again saying how sorry she was for the misfortune she had brought to their door.

Finally, peace reigned in the kitchen as quietness descended on the room, so that everyone could think.

Gregory was the first to speak.

"Alight," he said. "Could anyone tell me how do you deal with a man who brandishes a gun when he's angry?"

"Well, if that's likely to happen, we'd better bring in the police. They obviously know about him already and may give us better advice," said Alice, wishing that Richard was in the room with them. "As it's a rest day tomorrow, being Sunday, why don't we sleep on it and try to come up with a plan after church in the morning?"

They all agreed, and Gregory put his arm around Bridie to comfort her as they walked up to their bedroom.

On Sunday morning, soon after dawn, as an early sun beamed in through the large windows of the farmhouse, everyone except Cormac was woken suddenly as a thunderous banging was heard on the front door.

A voice could be heard roaring outside. "*Where's that stupid sister of mine? She's set the police onto me and I'm not going to prison for her!*"

Bridie was the first to reach the door and, as she pulled back the bolt, the door burst open and her raging drunk brother Finn grabbed her by the hair and dragged her out over the threshold.

Gregory was still tying his trousers as he raced down the stairs. "*You bloody madman, Finn Cahill! Leave my wife go or I'll make sure you get more than jail!*"

Finn began to cackle. "You must be as stupid as her if you think you can get the better of me. I have a gun and I'll always win." He laughed like a deranged man.

By now Alice had got one of the farmhands out of bed and sent him to fetch the police, before she ran to the front door. She tried to stay calm because nobody else seemed to be.

"What do you want?" she asked.

"I don't have to answer to a woman. I'll get what I want from that rich son of yours."

As Gregory went to grab his wife, her brother swung his arm around her waist while he removed a revolver from his pocket with his free hand.

Gregory and Alice stood back in shock.

"I want two hundred pounds from you immediately, otherwise I'm going to hurt her. So, get me the money and I'll take the boat from Cork and you won't see me again."

By now Gregory was blind by rage. "*Where the hell would we get two hundred pounds, you madman? Let my wife go and clear out of here because we've just sent for the police!*" Gregory made an attempt to grab Bridie, but Finn threw her to one side and she fell heavily to the ground.

As Gregory stepped sideways to lift her up, a shot rang out and it seemed to echo into the sky. Everyone was frozen to the spot.

Blood seeped out from Gregory's shirt and all Alice heard was her son saying over and over, "You're safe, Bridie, you're safe," before he slumped beside her to the ground in an unconscious state.

As Bridie screamed for help, Alice removed her apron and tried to stem the flow of blood that was seeping from her son's body.

The next thing Alice was conscious of that morning was opening her eyes in her own bedroom with Rosita anxiously watching her.

"Where's my son, my Gregory, where is he?" were Alice's first words.

"He's in the hospital, love. They've taken him up to Cork and Bridie is with him. He's alive, Alice, so go back to sleep for another while and then we'll take you to see him."

It was two days of her life that Alice could never remember and by the time she went to see her son, her husband Richard was home and by her side. They were informed by the doctor that although their son was lucky to be alive, he would spend his future without the use of his legs, as the bullet had hit his spinal cord.

Gregory's legs were paralysed and it took many days for Alice and Richard to accept the fact that their farmer son would never walk again. Throughout that week their daughter Emily tried to support them but she too was in shock and the world looked to be a dark place for them all.

Finn Cahill had been caught at the train station by the local police, and put in Cork jail to await trial. However, he was soon deemed to be a danger to the rest of the prisoners and even to the staff and he was sent by the authorities, on the advice of a physician, to the Criminal Mental Lunatic Asylum in Dublin. When Bridie heard the news, she informed everyone that she never wanted his name mentioned in the house again and that she didn't care whether he lived or died.

The rest of that month continued to be a fog for the residents of the Staunton farm and everyone else in the Beconsford Estate and the town.

Over the next few months, the clouds of darkness over the farmhouse never lifted. Gregory was brought home and the family had unearthed the Bath chair that Gregory's grandfather had used back in West Cork, during the Famine. But Gregory was having none of it. He told them to take the contraption away and that he'd stay in his bed.

As the month ended and another began, Gregory was still refusing all efforts to get him to accept his condition. Over in the Dower House, Rosita was feeling guilty that so much of her time in the past while had been taken up with running the estate and she hadn't had enough contact with Alice. If she had been more aware, perhaps she could have helped more, but now it was too late.

At the start of the third month after the shooting, Alice approached Rosita, wondering if she could think of anything to help her son come out of his despair. The news from the farm was that Gregory had all but turned his face to the wall. This made Rosita suggest to Bridie and Alice that it was perhaps time for a bit of tough love and she agreed to take on that task herself.

Rosita arrived in the farmhouse early the following morning and was greeted by Alice and Bridie, who were expecting her.

"He's still in the bedroom. He's eaten his breakfast but he's refusing to let us help wash him and that's another worry for us," Bridie whispered.

"Leave me with him and let me see what I can do. Could you bring in a tea tray for us as this might take a while?" Rosita asked, patting Bridie on the hand, as they both walked to the old parlour which was now converted into a downstairs bedroom for Gregory.

Bridie entered the room first and told him that Rosita had come to visit him.

As he grunted a greeting, Rosita sat down close to the bed.

"I'll bring tea in a while for our visitor, love. Just listen to what she has to say, please," Bridie said, as she tidied the bed covers.

"I've come to see how you're progressing, Gregory."

"What progress did you expect to see?" he asked bitterly.

"Well, feeling sorry for yourself lying in bed certainly isn't progress. Gregory, everyone is tiptoeing around you, like they're walking on eggshells over the past few months. It's because they love you and don't want you getting upset. Yet you have to remember that while you might not have your legs, you still have a good mind and you're doing yourself no good lying in this room ignoring the things that you can do. I realise that you're still very angry at what happened, but you need to start thinking about your future and that's the reason I'm here."

Gregory began to look thunderous. "What future in God's name do I have? I'm a farmer and I have no legs to walk on. Plus, that stupid Bath chair belonging to my grandfather is embarrassing for me to be wheeled around in and I'm not going to get into it. I'm gone, Rosita, I'm no use to anyone. The way I feel, I'd rather he finished me off with his gun!"

"Gregory Staunton, do you think it's fair on your family to think they'd be better off without you? I'll pretend you never said that, but I agree with you about that Bath chair. It is a bit rusty-looking. I might have a solution for that, but let's just talk about work first. You had been helping Louis with the books in the estate for some years when I took it over. Then you increased the hours you spent on the books because I'm useless at that sort of thing. So why haven't you at least even considered returning to that job? I do believe that you still have two arms and a brain in your head!"

Looking at Gregory's glowering face, Rosita realised that her self-appointed task was going to be even more difficult than she had expected.

"I loved that work, but it was only a small part of my week. I'm a farmer so how can I do my job when I can't even wash myself properly? A job is the last thing on my mind at the moment."

"Well, it's the first thing on my mind. I took over the running of the estate when Louis left to join the army. Now, not alone do I not have the support of a part-time bookkeeper, I have to do it all myself and I'm sick of it. I can't go on like this. You know that I always hated doing the books and I've come here today to offer you that bookkeeping job fulltime. The extra money you will earn, being full-time, would help pay for another lad to work here on the farm. You are family, Gregory, and

I need someone I can trust. What would please me most is for you to consider taking up this job offer."

As she saw him about to interrupt, she put her hand up.

"Let me finish. The Bath chair is only a minor problem. I will order the best available for you. As you are an employee of the estate, I will purchase that. In addition, I have a strong carriage driver and his helper, who can come to collect you every morning and take you to the estate office and in the evening after work they can bring you back home to your family. Plus, if you need to rest at any time during the day, there is a chaise longue in the office. What I'm saying is, you will be well looked after and it would give you some dignity back. But it's up to you. Choose to sit looking at the walls of your house or start to earn enough money for you to pay for a farm helper. You know that Bridie and Alice are worn out at the moment and poor little Cormac is becoming afraid of his daddy. That little boy wants nothing more from you than your time. You could read to him or just watch him play with his toys. Gregory, I can only give you a week to make up your mind. I have to get someone else by then, as I'm so far behind with the accounts."

Just then, the door opened and Bridie arrived with the tea. She set the tray down on the table only a hand's reach from Gregory. Rosita offered to pour.

Before she left, Bridie told them that she was in the kitchen if they wanted anything else.

Rosita was glad of the interruption, as it gave herself and Gregory time to think. As they sat quietly drinking the tea, Gregory looked in deep thought, before speaking rapidly, much to Rosita's surprise.

"I don't have to wait a week. I'm taking up your offer of a job. I had completely forgotten about all the people around me and all I thought about was what I didn't want. I know I won't get my legs back, but you're right. That fool Finn Cahill will win if I don't make some kind of a future for myself."

Gregory finished speaking, seeing tears in Rosita's eyes.

As Rosita let out a deep sigh, she put her hand on Gregory's.

"It won't be easy for anyone but, between us all, we'll work it out. In the meantime, thankfully, I have a bookkeeper that I can rely on."

She rose and called Alice and Bridie into the room.

"This gentleman here is starting work in the estate office, fulltime, from whenever he's ready," Rosita said.

Bridie almost knocked her down as she ran to kiss her beloved husband.

Later, Gregory joined them at the kitchen table for the first time since the shooting, He sat in the old Bath chair and it was the first smile they had seen from him since the day Finn Cahill turned all of their lives upside down.

Chapter Nine

Over the following year, life returned to a semblance of normality. Gregory worked diligently in the estate office and apart from bouts of tiredness in the middle of the day, he was a great asset to Rosita and a good confidant. Benjamin was beginning to grow up fast and he had started his work on the estate. Both Rosita and Doreen never saw a bigger smile on his face as on the first morning that he didn't have to ever go to school again.

With Benjamin out most of the day working, the women both found they had time on their hands, so Rosita started to socialise more. In particular she spent time in Cork with her nurse friend, Jennifer, the daughter of Doctor McNally who years earlier had supported and encouraged Rosita to follow her dream of studying nursing in England.

It was a warm summer's day when she arrived at the McNallys' home in Cork city. She was greeted by the now aging and widowed Doctor McNally. Their house was positioned on the top of the hill in Montenotte overlooking the River Lee which flowed gently past below. Rosita loved the view from that house and, when tea was served, they both sat at the window enjoying the scenery before catching up with the medical world in Cork city.

Doctor McNally, glad to be retired, entertained her as usual with his medical anecdotes while they waited for Jennifer to return from her work.

"You know, foolishly I thought that when the Famine ended in Ireland the health of the people in the county would immediately improve. But I was wrong. Many of those who survived that time seem to still pick up all manner of illnesses. I believe that their bodies never recovered enough to fight infections. I'm pleased that my daughter is taking the health of the poorer people seriously, because they are the ones that still suffer early deaths."

"Where is Jennifer working at the moment? I know she was in the Victoria Hospital when I was last here but she indicated that she was changing direction."

"You are right. She is now working as a visiting nurse with the poor and, while I'm proud of her dedication, what worries me is that she visits the prisons also. She tends to all the sick prisoners, once they have been diagnosed by the doctor. Many of them have contagious diseases and I believe that consumption is rife, especially in Spike Island off Queenstown. Although it is nowhere as bad as it was in the past when people died in their droves there during and after the Famine. But she'll tell you more when she arrives home soon and, when she does, I'll go and have a nap and let you girls sort out all the medical problems of the county for the rest of the afternoon." He laughed, knowing that those two women had an opinion on everything.

Jennifer returned home while they were still chatting and after they had caught up on family gossip, Rosita broached the subject of the state of the prison population.

"I know that the Cork City Jail is where most prisoners are kept but, from what your father told me, you're doing a lot of work now on Spike Island and it's very primitive there. Yet it's interesting, because I'm regularly in Queenstown and, even though the island is close enough to Midleton, I rarely hear anyone talking about that jail."

"That's because most people don't want to know anything about prisoners and very few know of the problems there. To be fair to the authorities, they have tried hard to improve things in recent times, but I think the main problem is that it should never have been a prison in the first place. The living accommodation is far too overcrowded. I believe that since they stopped sending prisoners to Australia in large numbers, the jails in this country have become breeding grounds for disease. Interestingly enough, I find that many of the prisoners are decent men. When one of them dies, they make and apply varnish to a new coffin for each man in order to give the dead a decent burial. I actually enjoy talking to them. Some of the misdemeanours they are in prison for border on the nonsensical. A bit of thieving from farms and shops can see you sent there. Often these men are just trying to either survive or feed family members. But enough doom and gloom. I want to know all about the life of a rich nurse who actually doesn't have to work for a living and is still a single woman!" Jennifer laughed, as she gave an affectionate pat to her old friend.

Later, as Rosita returned to Midleton in her carriage, she pondered on what she had heard from Jennifer. Was she becoming cossetted and losing touch with the wider world? She began to realise that since the birth of Benjamin, all those years ago, she had changed a lot. She'd known she had a secret and wanted to protect that fact plus keep her son safe. While she was doing that, she may have lost touch with the reality of the lives of ordinary people. Now that he was growing up, she knew that she might lose control of her boy altogether when he entered the adult world, and that made her sad. All she could do was pray that working on the estate would be his future. Yet, even if it wasn't, she realised that she had no control over what he did with his life. She had to keep reassuring herself that everything she had done in the past was for the best and she just had to hope and pray that life would turn out well for him.

"What's wrong with you tonight? You have a face on you like a slapped backside, so spit it out," Doreen said, smiling all the while as she looked at Rosita with eyebrows raised. "You've been distracted since coming back from Cork, when you should have had a grand day out with your friend. Explain yourself, Rosita Beconsford, and leave nothing out!"

"You are right, Doreen. I have to agree that I've been preoccupied since I got back from the city," Rosita agreed.

Over the hours that followed Rosita bared her soul to Doreen.

"Are you rethinking your decision to let people think that I'm Benjamin's mother?" said Doreen, horrified at the problems that would cause.

"No, definitely not! That can never change. How do you think Benjamin could cope with the fact that his mother rejected him at birth? He's a very happy, but sensitive boy. That's why he gets on so well with my brother Louis. I'm just realising that, with him growing up, he's not necessarily going to want me involved in his future and that scares me. I think that perhaps I should start doing things for other people and not just sit around doing very little, now that the estate is practically running itself, with Gregory on board, and the effort involved for me is not now too onerous."

"Well, if you are thinking of doing good for others, I'd love to help. I never enjoyed nursing that much and my role as a mother is nearly over just like yours. My advice is to take time to think it all out and don't try to do too much too soon. Give it some thought and talk it out with other people. Like your friend Doctor McNally and his daughter. As a matter of fact, I'm just thinking of something now as we speak. I remember you telling me that Margarita started a school choir in the neighbourhood when she was just a young girl and how much joy that gave to the children and their families in Midleton. I've often wondered why a lot of choirs seem to only have male singers. I realise that neither of us are great singers, but we can hold a note. Why don't you and I think about the idea of starting a lady's choir for the local women? You always said that to sing in a choir you don't need a voice like Margarita's." Doreen waited for a reply from Rosita, who looked as if she was seriously contemplating the idea.

"Well, Doreen, I wasn't expecting that from you, but maybe it has merit and we could have fun also. A choir would perhaps be a way of finding out how people are living and who needs most help in the town, without it looking too much like charity and nosiness on our part. If we found somewhere to practise in Midleton, we could include some refreshments and a chat at the end of the evening. You're the nosey one, Doreen. I'm sure you'd get lots of information from people over a cup of tea!"

"Well, I'll take that as a compliment and, while we're at it, why don't we give ourselves a name? Something like the Ladybirds might sum us up? Birds aren't always tuneful but they can always sing for their supper!" Doreen said, getting excited at the idea of something different happening in her life.

"Let us think it over and come up with some sort of plan and, even if it all falls through, we'll have had fun trying. At least it might get us mingling with people while trying to organise it."

Doreen and Rosita, with the help of Alice whom they had to force out of her sadness because of Gregory's health, applied themselves to their mission. Doreen and Alice knocked on houses in the village and were surprised to find that many of the wives they met had been in the choir as children and some of them had even learned to play an instrument. The smiles on the women's faces were a sight to behold as they immediately agreed to be recruited for the Ladybirds. Alice had already got Bridie on board to help make uniforms so that they would all look professional with everyone wearing the same clothes, and to ensure that none of the poorer ladies would feel inferior. Mary Ann Farrelly, who had become a schoolteacher having worked for Margarita's family as a young girl, had in the past learned piano, in order to teach music in the school. Although now retired, she was delighted to be asked to be the pianist for the choir.

When the choir became a reality, the excitement around the village rose. They got permission to use a room in the elegant town hall with its symmetrical curved windows on two floors and its clock tower towering over the building. The women were grateful when a piano was also put at their disposal.

On the afternoon of the first day of practice, the kitchen in Beconsford House, with the help of all the maids, was busy, as they made assorted sandwiches and tea cakes and lemonade as refreshments to finish off the evening after practice.

After that first evening's practice, Rosita observed the group and made a decision to leave early each evening, having enjoyed only a cup of tea, as she believed that it would make most of the ladies more relaxed if the lady of the manor wasn't around. She knew that they'd talk more openly to each other without her present.

That part of the evening, when they sat around after practice and chatted, while enjoying the refreshments, became a highlight of the evening. By the end of the first month, more and more of the women began to join in on the chat.

Noreen Cronin announced to the group that her husband had told her she should be at home with the children and not out gallivanting, but she had informed him that if he wasn't prepared to stay in, she would get a relative over as she wasn't going to miss out.

"It's the best thing that has happened to me in years. I've enjoyed every minute of it and I've even made a few more friends from the other side of town," Noreen said, as many of the women nodded their approval.

Another said that when her daughter was young, she had been in the school choir that performed in Blackrock Castle. Now she was overjoyed at being involved, since she was a widow.

Alice even decided to contribute to the conversation. "You may not know that I helped Margarita and Eliza with that event in Blackrock Castle where the children sang. I acknowledge that I was very sceptical about the whole thing at the time. I thought that the kids would be difficult or overawed by their experience but they proved me wrong. Back then they were all a credit to their families and the town. That's why I was thrilled when Rosita and Doreen suggested the choir for the mothers and the grandmothers. After all, the men go to the Haven Inn to relax so why can't the women have a night out?"

"Well, Alice, I think that some of the men are threatened by wives having any control of their own lives. Hopefully, they'll get used to it," Noreen said, not too sure that she was right.

Another voice immediately piped up. "Well, girls, I might have a solution for that. When any woman has problems with minding young children, my daughter has grown-up children and they could all help out."

"There were always going to be challenges," Alice said, "but that's a great idea. I know that the Beconsford fund would certainly pay a few shillings more for babysitting to ensure that there were no problems for the families involved. Maybe it will make the few cranky men a bit happier. If any of you miss a few evenings because of issues at home, that's not a problem either. Whenever you are able, come along and enjoy the evening." Alice spoke confidently, knowing already the difference it had made to their lives and her own. After all, the last thing they wanted was to have the choir cause problems for the townspeople. "I want you to know also why it's been important to me. I'm deeply grateful to you all because you have helped me to live again, since the shooting of my son. My husband Richard is delighted about it, knowing the joy that people get from singing."

Alice felt relief after she spoke, as it was the first time she had publicly acknowledged the pain she had endured and her need to begin to move forward again.

When Doreen, as she usually did, recounted these conversations later, while having coffee in the Dower House, Rosita was delighted to find that Alice was not now obsessing over Gregory as she had done ever since the accident.

Also, young Benjamin was a great asset to the group as he fetched and carried for them, so much so that they called him their stage manager, much to Doreen's delight. Maybe it is really helping even my own family, she thought.

An unexpected thing that brought a real richness to the choir was when some of the women in the town who didn't like singing, but who had learned to play the violin when they were young during the children's choir years, approached Rosita with a request to join. There were four of them and, with Mary Ann's help, they proved their worth. The inclusion of their music seemed to add a richness to the choir and they were warmly welcomed into the group.

One night in late November, Rosita made an announcement to the choir.

"I think we'll be ready to perform our first concert in time for Christmas but we'll have to work even harder in the meantime to have enough songs ready for a recital."

They all immediately agreed that they'd practise at home on their own as well as in the hall.

It was ten days before Christmas when Rosita stood in front of a packed audience in the seasonally decorated town hall, as the choir waited nervously behind her. She had agreed to be the spokeswoman for the group and was delighted that quietness descended when she began to speak.

"I hope that in a few minutes I'm less nervous singing than I am standing in front of you people now. None of us are high-level singers but I hope you will find that we blend well together because we all enjoy what we are doing. I am so grateful for your support tonight. The money you paid will all be spent on different types of musical instruments for the children in the area who want to learn to play. Crucially, we will be spending money also on proper tuition, just like our Margarita got from Mr. Johnson when she was young. Unfortunately, Margarita cannot be with us tonight but she sent her good wishes from New York and reminded me of what a positive difference a choir and music made to the children in Midleton back in the late 1830's. Margarita has already donated money to the fund and I am also hoping to persuade moneyed people in the town to help us. I now think I've said enough and I will just introduce our musical director and pianist Mary Ann Farrelly, plus the four ladies who will accompany her on their violins. I hope you all enjoy the evening!"

Rosita rejoined the group behind her.

They had decided to sing only songs that were popular and well known to everyone. They began with Steven Foster's "Jeanie with the Light Brown Hair" and followed it with "Hard Times Come Again No More". Before long the audience were tapping their feet to the music and joining in the chorus. Rosita was relieved by the time the interval approached and they broke for refreshments that were made, as always, by the staff in the Big House.

During the break, the members of the choir admitted that they were delighted with the response so far.

After the interval, the violinists and Mary Ann at the piano surprised the audience by playing haunting pieces suited to violins that even got applause from the choir.

When "Hark the Herald Angels Sing" rang out to end the concert, everyone applauded loudly, much to the relief of Rosita, Doreen and

Alice, who were grinning like young children as they left the stage and the audience finally stopped clapping.

Chapter Ten

Over the months that followed, the Ladybirds got invitations to sing in the Commercial Rooms in Cork and at various venues in the county. Generous donations followed, to buy instruments that included many trumpets which appealed enormously to the boys in the town and the fund paid for a tutor to come from Cork each week to train them. Alice joked that those playing the trumpets were liable to be thrown out of their homes if they practised too much!

As summer approached, the final concert was kept as a surprise from the majority of the choir, until after their final practice night in the hall. As they were enjoying their tea and an assortment of sandwiches and cakes, Rosita was pleased to reflect that many of the delicacies prepared each week were being brought home to give to their families as a treat. As they all prepared to go to their homes, Rosita made the announcement.

"I want you to know that the last eight months have been the most relaxing I have experienced in many years. The joy that we all have got from this venture is immense. The entertainment you have given to so many people is a valuable lesson for me in the way music can be a way of bringing balm to one's soul. It goes beyond the pleasure you give to others, because I for one have gained so much from the experience. I hope that you will all return to sing again in the autumn." She paused and looked around at them. "But, for now, I realise that you are eager to know where the Ladybirds are performing their final concert of the season."

As she told the excited women what was in store for them, they began kissing and hugging each other as they jumped around with excitement.

The following week all the women washed and cleaned their uniforms and each fixed a fresh flower of their choice with clips that sparkled and placed them in their hair to bring some glamour to their appearance. Finally, the moment arrived when they were escorted by Rosita through the hallway of Beconsford House. They looked in awe at the paintings on the walls and the wide impressive staircase leading to the upper floors. When they entered the ballroom, they smiled with delight as they walked to the top and faced the guests.

Rosita walked forward and introduced the illustrious guests of honour who had come to hear the women sing.

"Firstly, I would like to welcome you all and to thank the major donors to the fund who have generously agreed to continue to support the musical aspirations of this town. The ladies here are delighted to meet my beloved Margarita, whose inspiration helped start this choir. She is here with her husband Laurence and their son Theodore, who have taken the trip from America, especially to hear the choir sing!" Rosita beamed at Margarita. "Some of the rest of the guests, most of whom you will meet later, before this night ends will entertain us all. Margarita, Laurence, Theodore and Alice's husband Richard have all agreed to sing just for you ladies tonight, as a way of saying thank you for the work and effort you have put in since last autumn. Finally, thanks are due to my soldier brother Louis who kindly took leave from the army to come home to celebrate with us all. Tonight, he is our most gracious host." As both audience and choir clapped enthusiastically Rosita smiled, then raised her hands to silence the applause.

Then she announced: "It is our tribute to my beloved Margarita that we will sing a song we all know she loves – 'Kathleen Mavourneen'."

She rejoined the choir, hoping that the rest of the women were not as nervous as she was.

The choir began to sing slowly, softly and sweetly as the music from the pianist and the violinists seemed to reach towards the sky.

Rosita felt her heart soar and she was reminded of all the music played in the past in this room, yet this was the first time she had the experience of performing.

Then, with requests for an encore, they sang their signature tune "Silent Night", even though it was the height of summer.

When the concert came to an end, the waiting staff began to file into the room with food that had taken many days to prepare. Venison, beef, fillets of chicken and seasonal vegetables grown on the estate, were served as the best wine flowed, until Rosita insisted that the guests had now to sing for their supper!

What followed was a slightly raucous traditional Irish night of music that continued into the early hours of the morning when people had to be persuaded that it was time to go home to their beds. As it drew to an end, both Rosita and Doreen had tears of joy in their eyes. When it was finally time for the choir members from the town to leave, they were each presented with a small hamper of wholesome food to take home to their families.

As they took their leave, the choir members had a surprise for Rosita, Doreen and Alice. Much to their surprise they received handmade presents. Embroidered handkerchiefs, woven table mats and carved animals were among the gifts that were all crafted by their family members. They also made a special presentation of a fountain pen in a plush box to Benjamin, as their stage manager. He grew bright red with embarrassment, yet he too was delighted with his unexpected gift.

As she finally retired to her room in the early hours of the morning, Rosita felt the same excitement and happiness as she had when she attended the opera in Verona, more than twenty years earlier. Later as she lay in bed, unable to sleep, she watched the bright moon cast shadows on her bedroom floor and reflected on the evening and yet again wondered if all that group of family and friends in the ballroom would ever again come together for such an occasion. For that reason, she truly cherished this wonderful memory on a night when, in terms of money, the rich and the poor all sat at the same table, as equals.

Chapter Eleven

As the summer progressed, Rosita enjoyed many trips to Cork to meet her friends, the McNallys and the Perrotts. On a bright sunny morning without a cloud in the sky, with just a light cooling breeze in the air, she left the estate in the carriage to travel this time to Queenstown to see her friend Nurse Jennifer, who had sent her a message a few days earlier asking to meet her there. They had been seeing each other regularly over the past few years but this was the first time it was in Queenstown, close to Spike Island, where Jennifer was working that day. Recently, Rosita had been shocked to hear some of the stories of the men who were incarcerated in the jail.

Having greeted each other, Jennifer quickly got down to explaining why she had asked to meet her. But before she did, they settled themselves in the spacious lounge of the hotel that had in 1855 hosted a grand ball for Queen Victoria. The views from the room that faced the harbour beyond, where the River Lee meets the Atlantic Ocean, were spectacular and Rosita wondered why she didn't visit this town more often. They chatted happily while they enjoyed their refreshments, before Jennifer began to explain why she had asked for the meeting with Rosita.

"Rosita, I have a reason for bringing you here today. There's a young man in the prison on Spike Island called Thomas Whelan. Six months ago, he took some oats that he believed the farmer, for whom he had done a long day's work, had not needed. The oats were left in a barn that he was told to clear out. He was only getting a few coppers for the job. When he finished, he put the small bag of oats into his sack to take home. When the land agent came to inspect the work, he accused him of stealing. When Thomas objected to the accusations of the agent, there was a verbal altercation and the agent got nasty and decided to call the police. When the policeman arrived, the agent accused Thomas of robbery and said he wanted him prosecuted. Thomas told me that he'd heard of other notorious farm agents who deliberately left things around to tempt a casual worker and, in order not to pay for the day's work, try to catch them with the stuff and then take it back from them and refuse to pay their day's wages. They usually just threatened them with the police, whom they rarely called. It was just a nasty way of getting extra money for themselves. For some reason, and I believe it was because Thomas stood up for himself, this agent called in the law. It was a horrible way to treat anyone. Thankfully, he got only six months but now his time is up and I'm looking to try get him set up with a respectable farmer and was wondering if you could help me?"

Jennifer looked hopefully at Rosita.

After only a few moments' thought, Rosita answered.

"Don't look any further, Jennifer. I think I might have something that could suit him. Is he a strong man?"

"Yes, Rosita, he is and he has a good temperament and can read and write. He never got into any trouble while in jail. I met him only because he was helping an older man who was nearing his end and he was able to write letters for the man to send to his relatives. I'd stake my life on him, Rosita, and it's not often I'd say that in my job."

Jennifer was delighted that she had some good news to impart when she returned to the island later that day, and that raised Rosita's spirits too. They parted in great good humour, Jennifer telling Rosita that she would be in touch with her very shortly.

Less than a week later, Alice was in her parlour when Bridie brought a young man into the room. Alice was surprised to find that he only looked about thirty and was a handsome strong fellow with a warm smile.

"Alice, this is Thomas Whelan," she said.

Alice had been expecting him.

"Nurse McNally told me that you might have a position for me. I don't know if she told you that I've been in prison?" he said hesitantly.

"Yes, I know all about you," Alice said. "We need someone to help around the farm but, more importantly, to help my son Gregory, who is crippled since a shooting some years age. He's being brought to work each morning by the carriage drive and an assistant. He's the bookkeeper at the Beconsford Estate. All my family and especially his wife Bridie here, would prefer if he was a little bit more independent. We want him to have some life outside work and if he had someone strong enough to push him around in his Bath chair, we hope he might eventually have the courage to go into the town and even have a pint in the Haven Inn. If you are interested in a job here, you'd be working around the farm and helping to support my son. He knows we are meeting you today and we'd like you to meet him later."

Bridie was nodding approvingly.

"If my son is happy, the job is yours," Alice said, feeling sorry for this man with such an anxious look in his eyes. "No matter what, Thomas, we'll give you a month's trial anyway to help out with the farm, if you're happy to do that? We have a grand comfortable back bedroom in the house for you to sleep in and, as we don't stand on ceremony in this house, we all eat dinner together in the evening."

By the time she finished speaking, she noticed that Thomas was getting red in the cheeks and there were tears in his eyes.

"I can't thank you enough, Mrs. Alice, for this. You won't regret it, even if you don't want me after the month, I'm still grateful for the chance."

"Well, that's settled, lad. If you can wait until the carriage with Gregory comes back from the estate office, you'll get to meet him and you can also join us for a meal."

Later, when they all sat down to eat, there was an awkward silence until Thomas announced, "This is the first time in a long time that I've sat down to eat a substantial meal in a civilised household. Back home in the past the poverty was terrible after our parents passed away. I had to help raise my three younger brothers and it was only last year that all three of them found themselves work in England and America. I was twenty-eight years of age by then but I found myself rudderless without having people to care for. Because I love living in Ireland, I decided to go out and seek employment and I think you all know what happened to me then. If the family feels that I'm not what you all require, I will still thank you for what you've done by giving me a meal and a month working the farm."

There was silence for a moment, before everyone started to talk at once with Richard assuring him that they needed help in the farm.

Gregory gave him a reassuring smile, before he spoke. "We'll see how you and I rub along, but I like you already for your honesty about your past and I think we have a good chance that we'll be friends as well. Sure, I'm not too much older than you."

Alice, Richard and Bridie gave relieved nods to each other.

Before the week was out, Thomas Whelan had shown his worth and himself and Gregory had hit it off so well that they had already been out in the town and had even stopped for a pint. Alice breathed many sighs of relief as she saw sparks of the old Gregory returning.

Alice went over to the estate to tell them the good news. As she and Rosita sat relaxing while they enjoyed their tea and refreshments, they both agreed that life was finally getting good for them both and decided that they both should stop worrying so much about their families and live a more contented life and just hope that the future would be good to them all.

Chapter Twelve

1888

During the years that followed, the ladies in Midleton did not get everything they had wished for. Life had taken many twists and turns for Rosita and Doreen in the years since Benjamin was young and they had control over him. He had grown into a fine young man who had stayed in the estate, helping with everything and anything that needed doing. He had grown stronger and more handsome as he entered manhood and he had girlfriends that never came to much because he said he was not the marrying type. They believed that he had got this idea from the letters he still got from Louis, who after finishing his five-year army commission failed to return to Ireland. He had indicated to Rosita that he was living his young life at an older age and would eventually take a wife and have children. Rosita was happy to allow him his freedom because she was enjoying overseeing the estate and had a busy social life. The Ladybirds were still performing even though some of those that had started had retired and sadly a couple had passed away.

Sorrow had not passed Alice and Bridie by. Her beloved son Gregory, whose life had improved since Thomas had become his friend, had died seven years after he had been shot by Finn Cahill. He had enjoyed some happy years with the help of Thomas and Bridie, and young Cormac had seen the return of the old Gregory during those years.

A great surprise was to come when, two years after Gregory had passed away, Bridie and Thomas were married in a quiet ceremony in Midleton that was attended by all the family. They now ran the farmhouse and thankfully young Cormac had grown to love his stepfather and was a happy lad who gave Richard and Alice great comfort as they handed over the reins of the farm to Bridie and Thomas.

There was a new worry for Rosita and Doreen, who had to face the fact that their boy, who had worshiped his Uncle Louis, had grown into a man with his own mind and he was now telling them that he was firmly set on joining the British army.

Doreen had known that Benjamin was brooding since it was made clear to him that Louis Beconsford was unlikely ever to return to Ireland. Louis had told Rosita that he loved his life in London, training other officers in the military college but, thankfully, in all the years of his commission he had never gone abroad with his regiment. He had written home to say that he had become disillusioned with the ideals of the British army. He trained and sent all these men out to fight, some who returned either mentally or physically broken or indeed not at all. The idea that he had admired all things military in the past now appeared to upset him. The notion that he'd had in his earlier years, when he viewed the army as having glorious victories over bad people, was gone. Now this did not sit well with him anymore as he had begun to question the whole morality of sending men to fight, in order to win territory. That certaintly did not now accord with his conscience. When his commission was fully up, he happily turned his back on it for good. However, even though Benjamin knew all about Louis' uncertainties, he seemed to talk of little else except how he wanted to join the army.

"Haven't you heard what your Uncle Louis said?" Rosita almost shouted at him one morning at breakfast, while Doreen just put her head in her hands.

"I'm sorry, Auntie Rosita, but I waited here for years longer than I intended, thinking Uncle Louis would come home. Now I know that's not going to happen and I've worked hard in the estate helping you all I could but isn't it about time that I did what I want to do, for once?"

Rosita kept shaking her head as Doreen cried.

"Will you try to go for officer training? Louis could pull a few strings if that's what you really want," Rosita said, hoping and praying that he wouldn't try to enlist as a private.

"Of course I'm never going to be an officer. If I ever rise in the ranks, it will be on merit and not because I lived in a posh person's home," Benjamin said crossly. "I already have all the information I need and I hope to have both your blessings because I'm off up in the train tomorrow to apply to enlist in Victoria Barracks in Cork."

Both women were stunned at the speed at which this was now happening but realised that they had no more control over his life. He was an adult and wanted to follow his own path.

The next two weeks were a blur in the Dower House. He had been readily accepted into the Royal Munster Fusiliers and would shortly begin his training in Tralee in County Kerry, after which he said that he hoped to leave Ireland with his regiment.

On the day he left home for army training, Doreen had put on a special lunch for him. Benjamin had invited a strapping young lad whom he had met on the day he had enrolled to join them.

"This is my young friend David O'Shea."

The ladies both smiled when they saw this strong, broad-shouldered young lad who didn't look old enough to be in the army enter their home.

After they had enjoyed a good meal and the lads had drunk some beer, Benjamin and David left to get the train back to Cork, both looking handsome in their uniforms.

At the station, Benjamin had whispered to his mother that David was actually underage but the army believed him when he said he was older. Rosita and Doreen were both outraged, but Benjamin and David understood that such lads needed to earn money in order to help their parents rear the rest of their siblings.

"Don't worry about him, Mam, I'll keep an eye on him until he finds his feet," Benjamin assured them.

As they both hugged him, they knew that they had reared a good man and they couldn't alter the course he was now taking.

Six months later, the day they both dreaded was finally upon them. Benjamin arrived, again with young David, to say his farewells. Everyone came around to wish him luck and he promised that he would write to them wherever in the world he was sent. They insisted on going down to the train station and they stood waving until the train disappeared into the distance.

Over the years that followed, life in Midleton was punctuated by wonderful letters received from Benjamin wherever he was in the world. He had started out in Aldershot in England and later he nearly stopped their hearts when he told them that he was off to India. Rosita in particular was shocked at this announcement, as it brought back memories of where Benjamin's father had gone on his fateful journey. She offered silent prayers that he would return. His first stint abroad took close to a year but excitement filled the air when finally they heard that he was returning to Midleton on leave for three months.

"We're going to have to pull out the stops to ensure that he has a great time when he's at home and I for one am doing nothing except take care of him and feed him up. You never know what the food in India was like – I hope he hasn't lost weight," Doreen said, anxiously.

Yet she need not have worried. He arrived looking stronger and more handsome than ever, with his newly acquired suntanned appearance.

"I bet all the girls fell in love with you," was the first thing Doreen said after his arrival.

"You needn't worry, Mam, I'm like Uncle Louis. I'm going to have a good time before I become responsible for other people, but you will be the first to know if I ever meet a young wholesome Irish girl," Benjamin said, laughing.

By the time his leave was up and himself and David had enjoyed going to dances in Cork and having fun, Benjamin announced that David had met a girl that he knew from Dillon's Cross in Cork and he was going to be writing to her.

"I joked with him that I bet he'll be married before he is twenty-one and he answered that he hoped so! Thankfully, I'm way past that age and still have my freedom."

Benjamin laughed, as Doreen said that she hoped that he would settle down one day and give her a few grandchildren to care for. But he just kissed her on the cheek and said that his mother and auntie looked after him far too well and he couldn't see anyone replacing them soon.

On this occasion there was gaiety as the boys went back to their base in Aldershot in England, as decisions were being made about their next overseas tour of duty.

Two years later, the regiment travelled to Burma and it was when Benjamin arrived back from that duty that he learned the surprising news that, finally, Louis Beconsford was to marry the honourable Honora Carmichael in London. Rosita was disappointed to hear that the marriage was to take place in England, but at least it saved everyone in Midleton a lot of hard work. Herself and Doreen, plus Violet's family just had to make arrangements to go to London and they all looked forward to the break.

When the day of Louis' wedding finally arrived, it was a fine hot summer morning in London. The nuptials took place at St. Paul's Cathedral and Doreen was so proud to see Benjamin looking smart and handsome in his tailcoat and standing tall beside the groom in the church. Louis had insisted that the ceremony should be held only when Benjamin was on leave and Doreen and Rosita were both delighted with that decision. Louis' twin Violet was resplendent as matron of honour and her two boys were pageboys and her little girl was taxed with throwing flower petals in front of the bride, as she walked up the church. Sadly, Alice had some health problems and didn't attend the wedding. Her husband Richard attended and was in fine voice as he sang a hymn, backed by the church choirboys.

To Rosita's delight, Margarita, Laurence and Theodore all made it to the ceremony. Later the extended Beconsford family, with Doreen and Benjamin, all relaxed together and enjoyed a wonderful day, watching the boats sail on the River Thames from the windows of the Savoy Hotel where the wedding reception was held.

Later that evening Benjamin and Louis spent a long time chatting, before Rosita interrupted them.

"Should you not be with your wife, brother?" she asked smilingly as she put a protective arm around Louis.

"Time enough for that, sister!"

"I'm so happy that you have finally got yourself a wife, especially one who is young enough to bear children," Rosita said. "I'm looking forward to new life around the place."

Louis turned serious as he responded. "Honora is never going to live in Ireland, Rosita, I think that you should know that."

Rosita's jaw dropped as she digested the news. Secretly, she had thought that Honora was a bit of a spoiled madam but had put that to one side, as she was so happy for Louis.

"So does that mean that I'm stuck with this job for the rest of my life?" she asked, somewhat shocked by his announcement.

"Well, I have been trying to talk Benjamin out of the army to take over as the estate manager in Midleton but he says that he's going back to India shortly and he'll consider it seriously only after he returns from there, so I'm keeping my fingers crossed," Louis said, smiling at Benjamin.

"Well, that's a relief. I know Doreen would like him to leave the army tomorrow, but at least he won't be out of our lives forever. Thank you for considering us, Benjamin, unlike my beloved brother here who seems to have taken well to the lazy life as a London socialite!"

As the dancing and singing continued late into the night, Rosita and Margarita spent the whole time catching up while Doreen tried her best to be with Benjamin who seemed to have at least three bridesmaids hanging on his every word, hoping he would dance with them.

As Benjamin left the hotel the following day to return to his regiment in Hampshire, Rosita and Doreen hugged him until he became embarrassed. As he walked away, they both warned him to stay safe and come home to Midleton quickly. He readily agreed and as they watched him turn onto The Strand, at the top of the street, he turned around, waved and blew kisses to them, before disappearing around the corner. It was a sad moment for the two women left behind.

When Doreen and Rosita returned to Midleton, they were somewhat deflated and this wasn't helped by the fact that Alice decided that she and Richard would go to New York for an extended stay with Margarita.

"I think that I need a total change as I have too many memories of Gregory here and our daughter Emily has her own life with her husband and two children," she said. "In New York, we can go to all the music events, especially to watch Theodore, who seems to be taking the opera world by storm. After all, we have retired and Bridie and Thomas are doing a grand job with the farm."

"Don't worry," Rosita assured her. "I'd do the same thing myself but I seem to have something happening all the time that keeps me here, but one day I'll do exactly what you're doing, so good luck to you both. You deserve some joy to return to your life and there's no better way than a musical holiday to do that."

That time was turbulent for both Doreen and Rosita. After another stint in India, Benjamin came home on leave. He had already spoken to Louis in London and informed him that he wanted to continue with the Munster Fusiliers as he was now a sergeant with more responsibility.

"I'm loving the life," he explained to his mother and aunt in Midleton. "My officer believes that I have the ability to reach the rank of sergeant major in just another few years. Unlike Louis, I love the energy I get from being in a leadership role and I'm fascinated with the countries I have visited."

Rosita watched Doreen age in front of her eyes when she heard that news, when all she had hoped for was for him to settle down in Midleton.

Instead of voicing her disappointment, Doreen put a smile on her face. "Where are you going next then, son?" she asked.

"In two months, we're sailing to South Africa, but I don't want the word to spread outside this house, as it's just being planned for my regiment by the top brass at the moment."

"Well, at least we have you for a while, so I suppose we'd better make the most of it," Doreen said, shaking her head.

Rosita knew that she had been pinning her hopes on him becoming the manager of the estate but Rosita knew better. He was born for the military. Maybe it was his father's genes coming to the fore, she thought, as she resigned herself to spending more years overseeing the affairs of the estate.

Chapter Thirteen

1900

Doreen and Rosita had to wait for what seemed like months before they received the much-awaited letter from Benjamin. They both sat down for breakfast in anticipation, as Doreen began reading.

'My dear Mam and Auntie Rosita,

I hope you are both keeping in good spirits and not missing Alice too much. I was interested to hear the news that they have taken off to spend time in America. I admire their adventurous spirit and also envy them as I would love to go there someday. You two ladies should also be getting out to see such far-off places now that you don't have to worry about your little Benjamin anymore!

I'm still loving army life and seeing so many places! I've been in the same camp now for some time but you'll be glad to hear that I'm enjoying my time. We don't have too much happening at present so it's nice to have some entertainment now and then. In March there was a concert in Kimberly and in April there was a reception for a visiting church group. At both the events, thankfully, I was involved because the band of the Royal Munster Fusiliers performed. I was very proud of them and it was great entertainment for all those lucky enough to be there. I was thinking of you both and I know that you would have enjoyed yourselves if you were here.

I kept some souvenirs from those events and I will bring them home to you when my next tour of duty ends. We are not too sure how long our stay will be, but I will continue to write to you and give you any news that I have. David O'Shea is loving it here also and I believe that if he gets home in the next few years, he will marry his Sheila, who is now working in St. Patrick's school in St. Luke's in Cork city. He writes to her each day, but don't expect me to start doing the same for you two! I am far too busy with my work, plus I can't tell you much about our army manoeuvres.

I'll keep writing regularly and because I don't say it often enough, I'll say it now: I miss you both and I love you two so very much.

All my love,

Benjamin."

What subsequently happened to Benjamin during the Boer war was never fully explained to Doreen or Rosita. The news that no mother should ever have to hear in her lifetime arrived at their home in Midleton. The awful dreaded telegram stating that Seargeant Benjamin Trent was wounded in battle and subsequently passed away in a field hospital before he could be transported back to England. The telegram was followed swiftly by the arrival at the Dower House of an army officer from Victoria Barracks. He brought the condolences of the regiment to Doreen and told her that Benjamin had been a fine officer and she should be proud of him. He then presented Doreen with medals that would have been given to Benjamin as a result of his bravery. Doreen grasped them in her hands as if it would help her feel less pain. Rosita was just numb with shock. All they could do was cling to each other.

With Alice in America, they now felt rudderless. Although Violet, Bridie and Alice's daughter Emily were all supportive, nothing and nobody could truly understand the pain and heartache both women were going through. Rosita found that keeping busy and being exhausted at the end of each day helped her sleep but nothing really helped Doreen, as she withdrew into herself and spent most days sitting on a rocking chair, clasping his medals in her hands across her chest, holding them close to her heart, and not seeming to recognise the endless number of people who came to pay their respects.

A memorial service was arranged and was held in the estate chapel. No final goodbyes and no proper burial. Just an empty space at a table and hearts that burst with the sorrow that the life of a young man in his thirties had cruelly ended.

A month later a letter arrived from David O'Shea.

My dear Mrs. Trent,

I'm not too good at the writing but, as his best friend in the army, I had to write to you. I want you to remember that Benjamin died an honourable death, saving men like me who were part of his troop. I loved him so much and the awful thing is that I have now been raised to a sergeant and I don't want it because my best friend had to die for me to get this. I want to tell you that I will make him proud of me. In every battle, I will fight for him.

I don't know how to put into words what you must be feeling but I think that these things I found in his locker will bring you and his beloved Auntie Rosita some comfort. He had kept them from concerts and had said that you'd love them. I still feel the pain of losing him and can only imagine the grief you are feeling. I will visit you both when I next return to Cork.

He was my best friend. I'm having prayers said in St. Patrick's church in Cork, although I know you are not Catholics.

I can only say that he loved being a soldier and was a good man. I hope that brings you some comfort.

David

As Rosita sat next to Doreen, she looked at the contents of the parcel. Doreen was again grasping the medals which by now were on a chain around her neck. Rosita looked through the concert programmes and then held them tightly, hoping that by touching them it would bring her closer to the child to whom she had given birth. Tears yet again streamed down her cheeks and, although she was near breaking point, she knew also that she had to try to stay strong for them both.

Over the months that followed, Doreen's health began to decline rapidly. The doctors could not put a name on it. She had almost stopped eating and barely took a sip of water to drink. Rosita tried her best to get nourishment into her, but she seemed to have withdrawn into a melancholy out of which no one could lift her. It was as if Benjamin had been her whole life and without him she was broken.

A few weeks later as Rosita was eating breakfast, an extremely agitated Helen O'Callaghan, the live-in housekeeper who had joined them only recently, due to Doreen's illness, burst open the dining room door. All she could say, with tears streaming down her face was, "She's gone. Doreen is gone. She just never woke up this morning. When I went in to pull the curtains open, she wasn't moving!"

Rosita immediately ran to the bedroom and within seconds she had confirmed the worst.

"Helen, could you please call the carriage driver and get him to go for the doctor and then would you go around to Bridie and ask her to come over," Rosita said in desperation.

Helen immediately sprang into action.

"I'm going to stay in the room with Doreen until they arrive," Rosita said, not really knowing what she was saying.

As Helen ran out the door, Rosita went back into the bedroom and, pulling a chair to the bedside, she looked at Doreen. When she sat down, a fit of rage and anger came over her. *Why, why have you done this to me, Doreen Trent? I was hurting too, you know. I'm sick of being the strong one who always sorts everyone's problems. Nobody except you ever knew how difficult it was for me to live with my past and now you've gone and left me behind alone!*

As Rosita began banging her hand on the side of the bed, almost willing Doreen to open her eyes, she cried out loud, "*Why, did you do this to me? I'm just worn out and I'm getting old and now my son and my best friend are both gone!*" Tears of rage and anguish coursed down her cheeks. Yet, like every other time in her life, she knew that on this occasion she just had to deal with it. She had to, once again in her life, remember the wise words of her grandfather Issac: "*You can only do your best given the circumstances that you find yourself in.*" Yet at that moment she wasn't sure if she had any more fight left in her.

When the doctor arrived, he found Rosita with her head bowed and her hand placed on Doreen's heart. He touched Rosita's shoulder before he bent forward to examine the still body of Doreen.

"I'm sorry, Lady Beconsford, but there is nothing you could have done. Her suffering over the last year was in her soul. If it's possible to die of a broken heart, Doreen did. Bridie is outside and perhaps she and Helen could do whatever is necessary now, to assist you."

As he looked at Rosita, Doctor Lynch, the local elderly doctor, knew that she hadn't heard a word that he had said.

Bridie saw him out and he gave her all the information that was needed at this dark time.

The funeral that followed was a fitting tribute to an adopted daughter of Midleton. People of all ages lined the road from the church door to the cemetery, all united in prayer, as her coffin made its way to her place of rest. Rosita yet again found herself placing a single red rose on a coffin as it was lowered into the ground in a grave beneath a stone that already had an inscription honouring the death of Sergeant Benjamin Trent. Rosita knew that she would have a long road ahead to heal from this.

Chapter Fourteen

When difficult times came, Rosita did what she always did. Immersed herself in work, allowing herself little time to think. She had always found this helped her more with her feelings of melancholy than sitting around brooding and being angry about how life seemed so unfair. It was more than six months after Doreen had passed away when Bridie told her that all the previous members of the Ladybirds choir wanted to get together to hold a memorial concert in Doreen's honour. Rosita felt that it was appropriate, if too soon for her to participate. She hesitated but then said yes.

After Benjamin's death, the Ladybirds had stopped performing, for the year of mourning. Then, after the death of Doreen, the Ladybirds made the decision to disband, as their founder members were no longer there to encourage them.

Bridie was happy to repay all Rosita's past support for her and her late husband Gregory, as she set about the task of ensuring that Midleton's townspeople would organise a fitting farewell concert in memory of Doreen.

On the night that the event took place in the town hall, Rosita sat in the front row knowing that the ladies would not let Doreen down. As she looked around at the vast improvements made to the interior of the hall, it brought back so many happy memories of herself and Doreen practising with the Ladybirds.

The chairman of the council interrupted her thoughts as he introduced her to a gentleman.

"I'd like you to make the acquaintance of Mr Aidan Dermody, Lady Beconsford. He's down from Dublin this weekend and asked to attend the concert, as he has a considerable interest in the arts. I'll seat him next to you and after the speeches I will join you both."

Aidan was a tall, broad-shouldered man with silver hair and a gentle smile. His piercing blue eyes looked directly at her and Rosita was intrigued. She immediately wanted to find out more about this stranger.

"I'm wondering what a distinguished man of the arts would be doing in a small town listening to our little choir perform?" she said.

He looked compassionately at her before he replied. "Before I explain, please let me first commiserate with you on your recent loss. I am truly sorry to hear that your best friend and companion has passed away." He took her outstretched hand and gave it a gentle squeeze. "I'm in Cork city on business and in the past, back in Dublin and abroad, when the opportunity arose I had the pleasure of both listening to and meeting Margarita Beconsford. As I had time on my hands, I wanted to explore the town she always spoke about during her performances. Only then did I hear there was a concert on tonight. So, the other reason why I'm here is quite simple. I love listening to music, either sung or played. I've not got a great voice myself, so I indulge my love by listening to my betters! Is that enough reason for my being here, Lady Beconsford?" There was amusement now in his eyes.

"I thank you for your commiserations. It has been a very difficult time for me and I'm hoping tonight will bring at least some calmness to my soul. I too love listening to music as it seems to ease my pain, if only for that moment. On a less sombre note, welcome to Midleton and this event. But, would you please call me Rosita? Like my stepmother

Margarita, I am less than comfortable with people in Ireland using my title, except perhaps when it gets me a better room in a hotel or a ticket to an event that is impossible to procure otherwise!"

He smiled with an amused raise of his eyebrows.

Just then, the chairman began to welcome everyone as the concert was due to start.

Then a hush came over the auditorium.

The recital was just one hour in length and included a performance of "Amazing Grace" which Rosita thought was fittingly uplifting and appropriate to honour the life and death of her friend. As they announced that the last hymn they would sing was "Nearer my God to Thee", Rosita's heart began to pound. The choir had practised that hymn to be sung at a church service but, tragically, Benjamin had died before the performance and it had been cancelled. They had asked Rosita's permission to sing the hymn tonight and she had agreed that it would be appropriate.

As the choir, violinists and pianist put their hearts into singing that hymn, Rosita had to close her eyes to stop the tears from flowing. As she did, Aidan Dermody quietly placed a fresh white handkerchief on her knee and a grateful Rosita grasped it and wiped the tears from her eyes.

As the words *'Nearer my God to thee, nearer to thee'* faded away, the appreciative audience stayed quiet. Then the chairman asked if everyone would say a short silent prayer in memory of Doreen. This quiet time gave Rosita a moment to compose herself. She was so thankful to this wonderful group of women who had given everything to their performance tonight. She was very proud of them and she told them so when everyone stayed back for refreshments.

Later, while sipping some tea, she found herself again talking to Aidan.

"Thank you for the loan of your handkerchief but I will have to wash it before returning it to you, Mr Dermody. The chairman of the council has just told me that you would love to visit our estate. Perhaps you would like to call to my home, if you are free tomorrow morning? I could show you our Big House and return your handkerchief to you then?"

"I'd be delighted," he said, smiling. "But only if you would call me Aidan."

"Very well, Aidan," she said, smiling. "I'm overseeing the estate for my brother Louis who lives in London but I don't live in the Big House anymore – I reside in the Dower House. You can come to my home first and we can then walk up to the main house."

He agreed to join her the following morning for tea.

At eleven o'clock the next day, Helen knocked at the parlour door before entering with Aidan.

"I'll bring some tea and coffee for you and your guest, my lady."

Rosita thanked her before asking Aidan to sit down. Paradoxically, this morning he seemed less sure of himself than he had the previous evening. Rosita often found this with guests who entered the vastness of the estate and she needed to put them at their ease before they entered the opulence of the Big House.

"I usually prefer to entertain my guests here in the Dower House, which is small and cosier," she said.

"It is, indeed."

"Aidan, as you already know some aspects of my life, would you think it intrusive if I asked you to tell me something about yourself?"

Aidan relaxed into his seat. "Not at all. I work as a lawyer in Dublin. I got a degree in University College Dublin which I believe you know is the Catholic university. Later I worked in a lawyers' practice in Dublin until I decided to go it alone. I work primarily for large Irish companies and institutions and one of those is actually the Catholic Church."

Rosita laughed out loud when she heard that. "Will you be excommunicated for entering our estate, Aidan?"

"No, only if I went to a service in your church!" he said, smiling. "My work is quite interesting because of the variety of court cases and issues I deal with. Yet my main enjoyment comes at the end of each day when I retire to my club for dinner and later go to either musical soirees or to hear poets and writers discuss the affairs of the world. It makes me feel fulfilled."

"Wonderful! Do you have a family, Aidan?" Rosita wondered if she was being rude asking such a question.

There was a silence before he replied. "Over thirty years ago I lost the only love of my life. We were newly married and she was struck down by a fever that everyone thought she could fight, but she lost that battle. Sadly, she was with child at the time and her death ended my future as both a husband and a father."

"I'm so sorry! You must have been devastated."

"I was and it took a long time for me to recover. Music helped heal my soul and for that I have always been grateful."

Rosita began to think she was treading into waters that were too deep.

Just then Helen arrived with the tea tray and, after they had consumed their scones and tea, she suggested that she show him around the estate.

She first took him to see the Secret Garden and told him all the stories about its past, before walking him to the riverside and the forest beyond.

As they moved in the direction of the house, she related some of its history.

Aidan was captivated by the interior, and especially its picture gallery at the top of the wide staircase. She told him some stories of her ancestors and then led him to the ballroom. There, he spent time walking around and told her that in his imagination he could see beautifully dressed people waltzing around that room, with an orchestra playing. Rosita smiled as she told him that, sadly, very few large events happened there anymore.

As they finished their tour, he announced that he had to return to Cork for a scheduled meeting there later.

"And I've still not returned your handkerchief," Rosita said.

"Well, perhaps that means we need to see each other again," he said, smiling. "I have loved the tour and your hospitality, Rosita. I'm wondering if it would be very forward of me if I asked to correspond with you? Perhaps with information about musical events in Dublin that might interest you?"

"I'd love that, Aidan," she answered, surprised at how quickly the morning had gone. She sensed that this chance meeting might lead to a new friendship that she badly needed in her life at this time.

Chapter Fifteen

A year later, Rosita was at last healing after the deaths of Benjamin and Doreen. This she knew was helped by the emergence of her increasingly warm friendship with Aidan. He had come down to the estate on a few occasions and stayed overnight. She loved to offer him the hospitality of the Big House, and she was always looking forward to receiving his weekly letters.

One morning, she received a letter saying that he had work in Limerick the following week and he would like to call to see her before returning to Dublin. She was very happy with that news. It's funny, she thought, being alone perhaps gives you too much time to think and get irritated with inconsequential things. Since she was now meeting and corresponding with Aidan, she had someone with whom she could share her irritations and who would never judge her. In fact, he would often give her prescient advice that she usually agreed was correct. He was so full of knowledge and enjoyed so many diverse interests that when she was in his company time seemed to fly.

She smiled as she took pen to paper and invited him to spend a night or two in the Big House. When he had stayed there at the start of the new year, he had endeared himself to the staff by bringing them all little belated Christmas gifts and they looked forward to preparing a room for the man they called "that nice gentleman from Dublin".

When Aidan arrived in the early evening, Rosita had already arranged for dinner to be served to them in the comfortable parlour of the Dower House, with just a small table set with elegant candlesticks to match the fine cutlery.

He greeted her with a warm hug and then accepted a glass of his favourite burgundy wine.

But, when she asked how his day had gone, he just shook his head before replying.

"I've had more successful encounters than that with the people I had to meet today, but I'd prefer to eat dinner before telling you."

Since meeting Aidan, Rosita had again warmed to the idea of fine dining. This she had shunned over the years when she and Doreen would mostly eat dinner served on a tray, while they sat in front of a fire having chats with Benjamin. Tonight, when she and Aidan finished the fillets of best beef and dessert, they moved close to the fire to enjoy coffee and chocolate mints.

"So, what were you doing that you didn't resolve satisfactorily?" she asked. She loved the way he engaged her with stories of lawyers, judges and clients, knowing that she would not repeat their conversations to others.

"Well, I had one hell of a day. Did you know that there has been some trouble in Limerick between the Jewish community and a Catholic priest?"

"Well, I read about some problems in the *Cork Examiner* but I thought that the difficulties were only between the Jewish people themselves?"

"Well, that's a small part of it but what has enraged everyone, including the Catholic Church hierarchy, is that a short while ago a Redemptorist priest, Father Creagh, incited violence from the pulpit, calling for a boycott of the Jewish community. Since the 1860's, Jewish tradespeople, mainly from Lithuania and Russia have been fleeing persecution in their own countries and have settled in Limerick. They even have a synagogue although their numbers are small. Unfortunately, over the years there were small spats among their own community. The trading methods of a few of them were not appreciated by others – nor by some locals. This would have blown over but unfortunately Father Creagh, who is nothing but a mad zealot, worked out in his twisted mind that the Jews should be persecuted. I was in Limerick today with members of the Catholic hierarchy. We tried to emphasise to Father Creagh that religious persecution has no place in Ireland, but he is so bigoted that he wouldn't consider backing down. Since his sermon, some of the Jewish families have already been forced to leave because nobody is trading with them."

Rosita was horrified. "So, what is going to happen to him? Surely he must be stopped. I can remember hearing Margarita's grandfather Robert saying that nobody's class, creed or colour should determine if someone is a good or a bad person. If they have a good heart, that's what counts. Surely the hierarchy must get rid of him?"

"Well, Rosita, I wish that life was that simple. The Church would have to excommunicate him but they're reluctant to do that. He's a young priest in his early thirties and they hope he will apologise but, from what I saw of him, that's not going to happen. He described the Jews who came to Limerick as '*trying to fasten themselves on us like leeches and draw our blood*'. The Church has decided to move him, I believe to Belfast – but mark my words, that man will need a psychiatrist to understand and fix whatever twisted thinking is going on in his brain."

"So, what's now happening to the community left in Limerick?" Rosita asked.

"Well, I gained some knowledge of that from some of their leaders. Sadly, as I said, they have problems within their own community as well. Apart from the trading issue, it seems they are having spats regarding synagogue pew and grave charges. It appears that neither God nor man can sort out their internal problems either. It's a mess generally and now, since the Catholic boycott, many of these people have decided to leave and will end up looking around Europe or in America for a new home where they hope that they will be respected as they deserve. But that's enough talk of problems that neither you nor I can solve. How about you tell me all the news from your family around the world and I'll bring you up to date with the news from Dublin?"

When Rosita went to bed that night, she yet again reflected that her privileged life had cossetted her from many difficulties such as those caught up in the problems of the Jewish people in Limerick. She resolved to speak to her friends, the Perrotts, in Cork and see if any such trouble was happening there, while realising that she could likely be able to do very little to help such people. At least, she thought, I am grateful to have Aidan to keep me abreast of such happenings in Ireland. Paradoxically, there are some parallels with me, as many Irish patriots would see me as an unacceptable British landowner whom they hate.

During the year that followed, Aidan and Rosita corresponded regularly. The effect on Rosita was that she began to feel that life was passing her by. There she was, stuck in Midleton, whereas Aidan's life in Dublin seemed filled with both interest and joy. She longed for some of that as it had been in short supply since Benjamin and Doreen had passed away. The final straw was when she received a letter from him highlighting both the cultural events that those in Dublin had practically on their doorsteps and those he was about to enjoy in Europe.

My dear Rosita,

Over the past few weeks, we have had some wonderful singers and musicians entertaining us at the Bohemians musical society evenings, after which discussions and glasses of whiskey are usually the order of the night.

Shortly, I will again begin my travels by spending a few days in Paris to attend the Opera there and later enjoy the sun in Nice and Monte Carlo. I will think of you when I eventually reach Italy where I look forward to listening to my two favourite singers, Fiorello Giraud in "Pagliacci" and Francesco Signorini in "Cavalleria Rusticana". I will send you some postcards during my travels and we will meet hopefully in the autumn when we can again enjoy some good music together.

I know that by attending opera performances plus listening to the myriads of Italian singers will, as always, give me enough energy before heading back to my work in Dublin later in the autumn.

Your good friend,

Aidan

As Rosita put the letter down, an unusual feeling of deep envy rushed through her. I'm getting old, she thought, and yet in my head I'm still young and I should be enjoying my life more. Aidan, she knew, was just three years younger than she and he had created a life for himself having suffered as much tragedy as she had in his early life.

Over the days that followed, she came to a decision. She was not going to live her last years out as an embittered spinster within the walls of a large estate that now began to feel more and more like a prison.

Chapter Sixteen

Throughout the years that followed, Rosita kept her sanity by yet again keeping busy. What she now wanted above all else was to get on with her own life and that included having a conversation with her brother in London. Louis by now had two sons. The younger one, Nigel, was a quiet and kind young boy, just like his father, but his older brother Giles was rude, a bully and the apple of his mother's eye. At a young age, Giles had all the haughtiness of his entitled mother and Rosita knew who it was who reigned in their household and it certainly was not Louis. The thought of Giles becoming the next heir to the Beconsford Estate turned her stomach, but she was not going to voice her opinions because she had made other decisions about her own future.

In Ireland the efforts of the Land League and the continuous endeavours of the Irish people to get more autonomy was beginning to pay off for them. Now landlords had to show much more respect towards their tenants. This fact wasn't a great issue for her as she had good relations with most of their farmers, but she saw the way Irish nationalists were on the rise. Although she loved Ireland, Rosita realised that she was not in love with the estate any more. Too many of her family had passed on.

One day, she told Violet that she could not stay in a room with Louis' wife without feeling like giving her a smack. Violet had laughed and agreed.

"Thank goodness that I have such a lovely home and family," she said. "Let Louis' young son do his worst in the future, but I can assure you that it will not give me any sleepless nights!"

Rosita smiled and nodded in agreement.

It was the following summer, when Aidan had yet again gone on his vacation, before Rosita was ready to bring to fruition her plans for the future. First of all, she decided to return to the house in Hertfordshire. She had held on to the lease and still diligently paid the rent, as she always loved to have the security of it to return to from time to time. It had over the past almost thirty years been used by her own family and friends when visiting London, and by short-term guests of the Marquess of Salisbury at Rosita's insistence, as the family had been so good to hers in the past. Now she needed to go to London to see Louis and tell him that she was making plans for her own life. However, she had still not formulated exactly where her future lay.

It was early summer in 1908 when Rosita made her way to London and her first port of call was to meet with Louis where she assured him that the estate was in good hands. Jody was continuing to be a very competent as well as experienced estate manager and Bridie's second husband Thomas proved to be an excellent man with the accounts and also a good eye to have watching how things were inside the Big House.

As she made her way by car to Hatfield, she found a certain peace in her soul as she had so many good memories of Benjamin as a child and the fun and enjoyment they used to have there. The feeling was bitter-sweet but she knew that she had to look forward to what life could offer her from now on. She always enjoyed seeing the façade of her house, with its small red bricks and latticed window panes and the decorative white timber on its eaves which looked like white lace.

The front lawn was still tended each day by the gardeners and it all looked as picturesque as it must have done a century ago. She decided to spend the summer months there while deciding how to plan her future.

Rosita began to enjoy socialising with the family within the walls of their beautiful home, something that she had rarely done when Benjamin was young. Robert Talbot, the Marquess of Salisbury, was such a lovely man and close to her own age. He was good company, when he could get away from his work in political life.

She was also again enjoying painting in the garden. On a lovely sunny July morning, as she was absorbed in sketching, she had an unexpected visit from Mabel Gray, a friend who had worked under her in the hospital, back in the eighteen seventies. She was surprised and delighted to see her.

"How are you, Mabel?" she said warmly as she led her into the front room and invited her to sit. "It must be more than thirty years since we last met! This is a surprise."

"I've often thought of looking you up," said Mabel, "but I expected that you'd be back living in Ireland. It was just yesterday that your name came up and Matron told me that she had heard that you were back in Hertfordshire." She took a long pause before continuing. "I hope you'll excuse the intrusion but unfortunately I am here on a mission of mercy. I've had an unusual request from someone who is a patient at the infirmary where I now work in North London. I'm hoping that you can help me. I have a lovely young woman in my ward. Her name is

Stella Irvine. Sadly, she has not too long to live and it was only two days ago that she was told that she's not going to survive. Shortly afterwards, she mentioned your name and her eyes lit up when I told her that I had known you in the past. Now, I don't know anything else but she pressed me to try and contact you and, if I found you, to beg you to come and visit her. She was a singer but has now fallen on hard times since her illness. I believe that she has a son but, strangely, when she was told that she had only a short time to live, it was you she wanted to meet. I don't know how she knows you but it seems very important to her. I agreed to try. Luckily, Matron had been told that you were staying here at Hatfield House. The infirmary in North London is not that far from here. Stella has been hospitalised with us for the last two weeks. Sadly, for a singer, her lungs have become so bad that she is breathless most of the time. It seems like a miracle that I tracked you down so quickly – I was sure you were back in Ireland or some other exotic country. What do you think, Rosita? Would you be able to come and see her?"

Rosita didn't hesitate. "Well, I don't know the lady but I am intrigued. It seems very sad that she has a son. I hope she has family around her."

"Nobody has been in touch so far but I do believe that she's been trying to keep it quiet from her friends."

"Mabel, of course I will go to see her. Someone like her deserves to have her wish granted if she hasn't long for this world. She may have known my stepmother Margarita who was a great singer and used to sing in London quite often in the past."

Mabel sighed with relief. "How soon before you could come to the hospital?" she asked, looking anxiously at Rosita.

"I can get a car to take me up tomorrow. I had better make it the afternoon because I don't want the wrath of the ward sister to come down on me if I come out of visiting hours." She smiled as she remembered the many tyrant nurses who thought their only duty was to keep patients in a sterilised environment, and away from their families who might contaminate the ward.

"That's wonderful, Rosita! I'm delighted that we can do something for someone who has a wish but no future ahead for her."

After Mabel left, Rosita shook her head, wondering what this woman wanted. Perhaps if she was a singer, she might have actually known Margarita.

The following morning Rosita dressed carefully but not expensively for her visit to the infirmary. She had in the past often encountered jealousies from nurses who saw her outside the hospital setting wearing elegant clothes.

When the carriage arrived, she was waiting and on the journey had to stop herself from fretting as she wondered why this woman wanted to see her so urgently.

On arrival at the infirmary, the matron greeted her warmly. She was welcomed into a parlour where they were served tea and biscuits.

The matron gave her some details of the patient. "I believe you know that her name is Stella Irvine, Lady Beconsford, and that she was a singer. She first took sick at the end of last year and now, sadly, she had to be hospitalised and is nearing her end. She is quite distressed. This is why we acceded to her request to speak to you."

"Thank you for allowing Mabel to contact me. I just hope that I can be of some assistance to her. Is she ready for this meeting?"

"Well, she's coming to this room to meet you. She is due shortly and will be brought in a Bath chair by Nurse Mabel. She asked for some privacy and, of course, I agreed. She is a lovely lady and I'm sure that some years ago she was a true beauty."

Matron stopped speaking as the door opened and Mabel appeared, pushing a much younger lady than Rosita expected into the room. The woman looked thin and frail, but her lush auburn hair still gave a hint of her past beauty. She smiled wanly at Rosita.

Mabel and Rosita exchanged warm smiles, then Rosita went to Stella and, stooping down, took her hand, observing what looked like relief in her eyes.

Rosita waited until both Mabel and the matron left, before moving the Bath chair closer to her own seat. Rosita sat down, then smiled and reached out to touch Stella's cold hand.

"Please tell me how I can be of assistance," she said. "I would like to help you if there is anything I can do. Take your time." She smiled, not really knowing what else to say.

Stella lifted her head before speaking, looking as if each word was going to be difficult for her. "I don't know where to start but I suppose at the beginning is always best. As a child, I was brought up for ten years in an orphanage in East London where my mother had put me when I was five. She was a lovely woman but she had consumption and had to leave me there. I wasn't ill-treated or anything – I think because I was always smiling and singing. When I was about ten, an elderly man and his wife, Mr. and Mrs. Ring, heard me singing at the Sunday church service and offered to take me to live with them. They were childless and I was delighted because they were really kind. When Mrs. Ring died, I took over the housekeeping, but when I was only fifteen Mr. Ring began to lose his memory and a nephew of his took him to live with them. He gave me just a week to get out of the house. He was nasty, so he was!" At this, Stella began to cough.

Rosita hurried to pour some water from a jug on the Matron's desk and held the glass to Stella's lips to sip and told her that she had all day and not to rush.

Stella closed her eyes and rested for a while before continuing. "I always knew that I wanted to be a singer, so what I did was stand near the theatres in London and sing outside them and people would give me money. I made enough to pay for lodgings in the East End where they were cheap. After about a year, just before I turned seventeen, I was taken on by a group of strolling players, to tour with them around the country. I spent the next few years with them, mostly just in the chorus. That group were like family but they kept saying that I would have to leave them, that my voice was too good to waste on their group. It was their belief in me that got me a start in Hastings, when the seaside shows became popular. I got asked to sing in their chorus and that was my big break. After that I got asked to do more shows and when Christmas came I was picked for pantomime in London, which was a really big break. It was then that I began to make good money."

Stella took another break to catch her breath and sip some water, before continuing with her story.

"I also got some private bookings to sing in army messes around London and the south. I quickly learned how to make the soldiers behave themselves and listen to me sing. These concerts made a lot more money for me. I was saving loads because I wanted to be able to live in comfort when I was too old to sing and dance. You know, living in an orphanage makes you very worried about having a roof over your head. I never wanted to end up living in the East End which was very rough."

Again, she stopped, and Rosita encouraged her to drink some more water and take as much time as she wanted, though she anxiously wondered where Stella's story was heading.

"It was when I was twenty-five that it suddenly happened. I fell in love. I was singing in an army barracks and a handsome man standing inches taller than most in the room held my gaze. After I finished, I smiled at him and he walked up and asked me if I would like a drink. He was ever so polite. He spoke beautifully, like the officers, and I was smitten straight away. I was delighted when he asked me to meet him. As I was working in London then, over the next couple of months we got to meet regularly, but only when he was on leave. I had my own room near the theatre and he'd escort me home. He told me all about himself. Once I knew he was due to go abroad with his troop I had no hesitation about letting him sleep with me for the two nights before he sailed. I was loved and in love."

Rosita was thinking how the same thing had happened to her all those years ago but, as she saw the love in Stella's eyes, she quickly put aside thoughts of the despicable lieutenant whom she had once loved.

As Stella stopped to rest again and take another drink, tears appeared in her eyes. "That was the last time I ever saw him. Because I wasn't his wife, it was hard for someone like me to get information out of the army. But I did find out that he died from the injuries he received in combat. I was distraught and unwell for many months after I got the news and I had to live on my savings. What I only then realised was that I was nearly four months pregnant with no husband."

Rosita gasped. How well she understood this poor young woman's dilemma!

"I realised that I couldn't continue to work. Yet, here's the funny thing. I was elated." A big smile brightened her face as she remembered.

"I realised that I really wanted his child and promised myself that I would keep the child safe for the rest of my life. My happiest day was when I held my little boy Charles in my arms. He has been the best thing that ever happened to me. And now I'm going to die and all I can think of is how he can cope when I'm gone. My whole life for the past seven years has been to make my boy happy and have him educated."

Rosita felt overwhelmed with compassion as she waited for the young woman to continue her story.

"I went back to work after he was born and got a young girl from the orphanage, where I had been, to come and live with us. I was earning great money again, working wherever I was asked to sing. When it was time for him to go to school, the other artists were amazed to see me sending him to a private school. When he was seven last year, I decided to put him into boarding school. I was so happy that he immediately loved it. He's a proper swank but with no airs and graces because I never stop telling him how lucky he is. You see, his father was a kind of a gentleman, but not exactly. I knew his mother's name and when I got sick earlier in the year and I couldn't earn any more money, I looked for her, but they found a record that she had died. Just a year after her own son. She was an Irish lady but she had lived in England for many years. She died back in Ireland."

Ireland! That was where the story was heading. Suddenly Rosita's heart was in her throat.

Stella continued. "Charles' father's name was Benjamin Trent."

Rosita gasped aloud but Stella didn't notice, absorbed in her story.

"I've been at my wits' end since I heard of my fate and I hadn't the energy to think what to do but when I told the nurses in the hospital that his mother was a nurse and that her best friend was named Rosita, who lived in a castle in Ireland, Nurse Mabel took an interest. At the time

Benjamin told me that his aunt was a ladyship. I'd said I didn't believe him but he insisted that it was true. When I asked Nurse Mabel to try to find out about you, she said that she'd ask around to see if anyone knew of your whereabouts."

Rosita's heart was pounding and she felt herself shake.

Stella now also looked shaken as she put her hand on top of Rosita's. "I didn't mean to upset you but I thought you could maybe help in some way to get a good family to adopt him because I know that Benjamin's mother has no relatives that he knew of. You can probably understand that the very last thing that I want for Charles is for him to be orphaned and in a home like me. You know, I told him always about his lovely father and he'll have good memories of him. Also, I was going to ask you if, as a friend of his granny, you could talk to Charles for me? I haven't the heart to break the news about me to him myself and I certainly don't want the school principal or the matron here to tell him. Maybe I'm a coward but telling him would be too much for us both. That I do know."

As Stella took some more sips of water, Rosita's stomach felt rigid with shock and she couldn't think straight. She touched Stella's hand, hoping her own wasn't shaking too much.

"Stella, I will do everything possible to help your son. I loved his father too. His mother and I both raised him."

Joy and hope flooded Stella's face. "You loved him? You raised him?"

"Yes, my dear, I did. Now, if you could wait for a few minutes while I go to the ladies' restroom, I will come back and we can talk some more about your wishes."

Stella nodded. Tears flowed down her face but now they were tears of joy and relief.

Rosita left the room. She asked a nurse to direct her to the restroom and also asked her to tell Nurse Mabel to go and sit with Stella until she returned to the room.

She closed the door of the closet and sat on the seat, dropped her head into her hands and couldn't stop the tears flowing. It's like history repeating itself, she thought, but the difference is that Benjamin was sure to have married Stella if he had returned from the war. Now I have a young grandson and I don't know what to do. *Think, woman, think*, she kept repeating to herself. It should be the most wonderful thing for any woman to hear and yet here I am, with all of my life experiences and I don't know what to do.

What she did know was that she had to compose herself immediately and get back to a lady who was near death. She dried her tears and patted some powder on her face before returning.

When she re-entered the room, Mabel nodded to Rosita and then left them alone again. Rosita knew the first question she needed to ask. She sat opposite Stella and this time gently took hold of both her cold hands, before speaking.

"Stella, I'm sorry for keeping you. Could you tell me where Charles is attending school at the moment?"

"It's in Devon. It's a good boarding school but not like Eton college or those ones that you'd know about. When he was very young, I had a housekeeper, Janice, who lived in our house and so was with him when I was away. Then, during the summers, the three of us would tour around different places like Hastings, Brighton and even Blackpool or wherever I was in the shows. Later he went for a few years to a private tutor near our home. You see, I realised he was very bright and I wanted him to have the best education I could afford, so that he could get a proper job when he grew up. He's just in his second year at the school." Her eyes yet again filled up with tears. "I have always paid his fees on time but I haven't worked since late autumn, so I don't have enough saved to pay for next year's fees. The money he will get when our little house is sold won't be much because I owe the bank for the loan I took out to buy it."

For the first time in an hour Rosita began to feel more in control, relieved that she could offer something practical. "Stella, his mother and I brought Benjamin up and, as neither of us ever married, one of my greatest heartaches was when he died in battle. I wish he had lived and you could have married, but life doesn't always play out the way we want it to. I have ample personal funds and I can assure you today that your son's education will continue until he wants it to finish, whether at university or whatever else makes him happy."

The light that shone from Stella's tearful eyes seemed to brighten the whole room.

"So, is he at school now?" Rosita asked. "And do you want me to go and visit him? Or I can arrange for him to come here if that is what you want?"

"I'd dearly love to see him. I was about to ask Matron to contact the school, then I heard that you were actually in England so I asked to see you first. Would you be able to tell him that my health isn't good? You know, he's learned a lot about his granny's lovely friend. If you could do that for me, I'd be very grateful. I couldn't bear to tell him that I won't be around to see him become a man. The sadness we would then share would be just too painful for me to take to my grave."

It was another hour before Rosita left.

Back home, she immediately used the telephone to contact the school headmaster. Arrangements were made for her to drive to Devon on the following day and bring Charles back to London to see his mother.

Rosita hired a car to travel to Devon and arrived exhausted after the journey. She stayed overnight in a hotel in order to be rested for the ordeal ahead of her. The following morning, she went to the school and was introduced to a handsome young boy who had jet-black hair, just like his father, but it was the Beconsford eyes looking at her with such trust that confirmed to her that he was her grandson. He stared at her with the same sad look as her brother Louis had when he was young. She promised herself there and then that she would take better care of him than she had of his father. She told him, as gently as possible and not quite the full story, about his mother.

Later, when they drove away from the school in a car hired by Rosita to take them to London, she held his hand and told him everything she could about his papa.

Two days later, Rosita found herself praying outside the ward door as the ashen-faced young boy came out of the room with his head bent. Now, looking at his tear-stained face, she saw the eyes of her father Victor Beconsford looking up at her. All Rosita could do was to put two comforting arms around the boy and assure him that everything was being done for his mother.

Rosita spent the weeks that followed sharing stories with Stella and Charles of all the happy memories she had of her beloved Benjamin.

"Was he really born in Devon?" Charles asked, excitement in his voice.

"He was indeed. In a village called Croyde on the edge of Saunton Sands in a beautiful house on top of a cliff edge that looked down at the seashore below."

"Although I love London, since I went to school in Devon I really love it there – the fresh air and the smell of the sea salt from my dormitory is lovely. London, where we lived when I was younger could sometimes be a bit smelly." He wrinkled his nose and smiled lovingly at his mother.

Rosita thought what a mannerly boy he was and so articulate for his age. She also thought that if Doreen had known about him it might have given her a purpose to stay alive, but that was not to be.

"But I want to know more about Ireland and your castle that my mother keeps telling me about. Is it really as big as mama says and has it a dungeon?"

Rosita laughed. "No, it doesn't have a dungeon and it's not a castle but it's called the Big House in Ireland and to the people it does seem like a castle! It has grand gardens and forests and a river flows through the estate. It even has a secret garden. For now I'm going to stay close to you in England for a while, but I will take you to see it soon, I promise you that."

As Stella's time on this earth began to tick away, Rosita could see that her son seemed to think that she was recovering and believed that she could get better, but the smile on her flushed face was more to do with her happiness at her son's delight at meeting his new Auntie Rosita.

On a bright sunny morning in late summer, with the sound of birdsong outside the quiet private side ward where she had spent her last few days on earth, Stella Irvine passed away, with her son and Rosita by her side.

Charles had spent the last few weeks of her life living in the house in Hatfield with Rosita. She didn't fully understand her feelings yet, because her thoughts were filled with the sadness that Charles would be orphaned at such a young age.

On the day before she passed away, Stella had asked Rosita if she would agree to be named as her next of kin and guardian to her son. Rosita assured her that it would be a privilege. She was being asked to guide her own grandson into adulthood, but the notion was tarnished with great sadness because Stella would not be there to see him grow up. The same thing had happened to Rosita herself back in 1838 when her mother Fleur died while giving birth to her. But she had never missed her mother as she never knew her and she was showered with love from every other member of her family. This little boy had nobody and, sadly, she couldn't tell him that he had an uncle and auntie and lots of cousins in Ireland and England.

Stella's burial took place in her native London after a fitting service with a choir comprising all her friends, while others from the theatre companies joined the hospital staff in the church. During the service, Rosita kept a protective arm around the small boy by her side, and later in the church grounds she handed him the single red rose that he placed on the coffin of his mother as she was laid to rest for the last time.

As they left the graveside, Rosita, still holding tightly to Charles, assured him that she would love him and take care of him until he was a young man and wanted to make his own decisions about his life.

A month later, Rosita and Charles drove back to his school, to start his third year there. She promised him that he would be taken over to visit Ireland for Christmas. Although he hugged her tight before he entered the school door, she saw that within a minute he was running around with a group of his friends, which pleased her enormously. Ah, the exuberance of youth, she thought. They seem to cope far better with tragedy than adults do.

Chapter Seventeen

As Rosita sat in the comfort of her parlour with a sliver of late autumn sun brightening up the room, she reflected on how much she had enjoyed spending the years she lived in this vast expanse of the Hatfield House estate. She was also full of gratitude, constantly aware that someone must have been looking down on her to guide her to England at the very time she needed to be there. She shuddered to think what might have happened if she had not been contactable when Stella was dying, but she put those thoughts away as everything had turned out well. Young Charles had happily settled back at school, if the little letters and hand drawings that she received from him and cherished, were anything to go by.

Before she returned to Ireland, she would relinquish the lease of her home in Hatfield and she knew she would have to begin to make more decisions regarding what she wanted to do with the rest of her life, especially now that her grandson was part of that future.

On her return to Midleton, she found a couple of letters from Aidan, who was back again in Dublin after another trip abroad. But now there was no envy inside her. Charles being part of her life made up for everything. He was a delight and she couldn't wait to see him at Christmas.

When Stella died, Rosita had informed Aidan and her extended family about becoming a guardian to Charles and everyone had expressed their delight as they all looked forward to meeting him.

As she sat by the window of the Dower House parlour, looking down at the river meandering below, she penned a long letter to Aidan, with the great news that finally, after a lot of red tape in England, she had been officially appointed as Charles' legal guardian. She told him how happy that had made her. She posted it to him on the following day and he sent her a reply within the week. He too was delighted for her and was looking forward to coming to Midleton for the Christmas festivities.

That Christmas turned out to be more joyful than any other Rosita had experienced in the recent past. As a member of the family, Charles was spoiled by all the staff in the Big House. Every member of the household and family gave him a special present, knowing that it was hard for such a young lad to spend the first Christmas without his mother.

Aidan came down to visit over the holiday and one surprise was that young Charles had been having riding lessons at his school and Aidan had in the past enjoyed being around horses. Rosita was so happy to see the young boy on his pony, being led out each morning by Aidan, their ripening friendship helped by a shared love of horses. At the start of the new year, Rosita and Charles returned to Dublin with Aidan, and she was pleased to see how well they enjoyed each other's company, although Rosita complained, but with a smile on her face, that they spoke too much about horses and that her only interest in horses was how fast they could pull a carriage! Before returning to Devon, they all spent a day in Dublin Zoo, much to the delight of the young boy.

At last, Rosita took Charles back to England where she knew he would be among friends until the summer holidays. She missed him greatly but it gave her an opportunity to concentrate on the plans that were still running around her head. She knew that she had to take things one at a time for the immediate future, because Charles had now become her priority but, early in the summer, she would return to London to have the final conversation about the estate with Louis, before she went to Devon to take Charles home to Ireland for his summer holidays.

Chapter Eighteen

Dear Aidan,

How delighted I am to hear that soon we might be able to communicate more often with each other due to the arrival of the telephone! I am so looking forward to listening to your voice from faraway in Dublin. What a novelty that will be for us both!

I have also got some more news. Some months ago, Dan O'Leary, the young grandson of Brendan O'Leary (who owned the carriage we used for deliveries during the famine years) bought a motor car and he is hiring it and himself out. I have booked him to take Charles and me around the south and east of Ireland next August, before he returns to school. I will make it a full month of holidays and hope we can spend some time in Dublin with you before I return with Charles to Devon. I really hope that you will be in Dublin at that time and that you can join us for trips in the car to places like Kingstown and Howth. I've often eaten in the Royal Marine Hotel and the Grand Hotel in Malahide and would love to share a meal there with you, while watching the yachts and boats sailing in the harbour.

These are exciting times, aren't they? I never thought I'd live long enough to hear a voice from miles away or to drive in a vehicle that moved twenty miles in one hour! We certainly live in interesting times.

I'm so looking forward to hearing from you.

My best wishes, Rosita

As spring approached, Rosita arranged to stay for some weeks at the luxurious Savoy Hotel in London, as she didn't want to encounter Louis' disagreeable wife Honora in their home.

When she and Louis met in Rosita's favourite restaurant overlooking the River Thames, Rosita opened the conversation.

"Louis, you've known for a long time that I was wanting to move on with my life away from the estate. That changed somewhat when I got guardianship of Charles. However, I have finally made up my mind. I am not going to oversee the estate after Charles has spent the coming summer in Midleton. I'm going to keep staff in the Dower House until such time as I set down roots elsewhere but I won't be managing the estate after July next."

Although she had expected some form of negative response from her brother, Louis just smiled and congratulated her.

"Finally, sister, you are going to get the life you want to lead. I've been expecting this day to come for years and I'm happy for you. I'm never going back either and, as the estate is being so well managed at present, I have no worries for the future. I've produced the heirs you asked for, Rosita!"

Louis went on to say that he didn't blame her for her decision and told her how grateful he had been to get the life he wanted and she should do the same now.

"I enjoyed most of my years in Midleton," Rosita responded, "but it's only over the past years that I realised I had become the dutiful child, while you lived your dream in the army. But as I always say, brother, it's never too late to follow your dreams, and that's what I'm doing now, especially with young Charles and Aidan in my life. As Charles spends much of the year in school and loves being there, I will have the freedom to pursue whatever I wish." She rose to her feet. "So, I thank you for your blessing, brother," she said mockingly as she gave him a bow.

"That must have been the first time you have ever asked someone's permission to do what you always intended to do, regardless of what people advised!" Louis said, joining into the frivolity of the moment.

Having enjoyed her time in London, meeting both her own and Margarita's extended family and friends and the good people in Hatfield House, Rosita returned, renewed and rejuvenated from the break.

Rosita's summer plans became even more exciting when Aidan called to the Dower House some weeks before she went to collect Charles in Devon. Having greeted each other and as always enjoyed a civilised sit-down meal, Aidan looked at her, hesitation in his voice.

"Rosita, I'm going to ask you something and, if I've stepped over a line, let me know."

"I will, Aidan. Now you have me both interested and intrigued," Rosita said, wondering what was coming next.

"Well, just hear me out and then you can tell me what you think. I know that you're going back to London in September, having dropped Charles back to his school. As you know, I always try to get my holidays abroad when the weather is cooler in September. Would there be any chance that I could meet up with you in London and that you could join me on my trip to Europe? I have just one commitment at the end of September. I have to attend some meetings at a Bishops Conference in the Vatican in Rome, but I am free to do whatever you would like during the rest of that month. Have I overstepped the mark by asking you?" Aidan now looked quite anxious.

As he looked at Rosita, she suddenly burst into a fit of laughter that she found hard to stop. Full of mirth, she answered. "Aidan Dermody, are you seriously asking a titled Protestant lady to accompany you to the Eternal City? I'm trying hard to understand how you'll explain that to any of the Catholic bishops! But I will answer your question. Yes, of course, I would love to go on an adventure with you and, no, you have not offended me. We are, after all, just friends, aren't we?"

"You know, Rosita, that's one of the reasons I liked you from the day we met. You're not pompous and you tell things as they are. Of course we're just friends, aren't we?" he said, joining in with her laughter but blushing at the same time.

When they finally settled down, they spent the rest of that day planning and arguing about all the places they liked and didn't like, before Aidan had to return to Cork where he would be sleeping in the Bishop's residence, before attending scheduled meetings the following morning.

Both of them now having phones meant that their holiday plans could be advanced more easily and, whenever they just wanted to chat, they used the telephone. However, Aidan had warned Rosita that the telephone people could listen in on their conversations, so nothing serious or private could ever be discussed over the phone.

Rosita had so many plans for the summer that it seemed like no time before she went over to England to bring Charles back for a much-awaited holiday. He spent the month of July, just like his father Benjamin had, roaming around the estate and eagerly getting involved in enjoying the freedom it gave him. Rosita brought him regularly to the Regency Room in the Haven Inn and, like all the children in the past, he loved the tiered plates filled with sandwiches and dainty cakes, followed by ice cream, usually topped off with hot melted chocolate.

Having spent July in Midleton, Rosita set out with Charles to show him the beauty of her beloved Ireland. As promised, they spent the month of August on a journey to see Rosita's favourite seaside towns and many that she had never seen before. They had toured many of the beaches on the south coast before they stood on the golden sandy beach in Tramore, County Waterford, where Rosita explained to Charles that Margarita's father had survived the shipwrecking of the *Seahorse* in 1816 on the very spot on which they were standing. She explained to him that in later years each time any of the family went through that seaside village, they met the son Jacob and later the grandson Cornelius of the Murray family who had nurtured Jack Ryan back to health after that devastating night when hundreds perished as three ships hit the rocks. Cornelius still lived in the cottage where Jack had resided after the ship went down.

Having enjoyed the hospitality of the Murray family in their cottage, Rosita and Charles continued on their way.

They explored the towns of Waterford and Wexford and spent three days in glorious sunshine on Brittas Bay in County Wicklow. Charles loved what looked like miles of golden sand along the beachfront with its sand dunes behind, where he could run freely up and down. At the end of each day, they relaxed with Dan O'Leary the driver, who seemed also to be enjoying himself, all eating ice cream and drinking bottles of fizzy orange, before going to the local hotel to eat and sleep.

As they neared the end of their travels, they drove over the bridge looking down at the River Aughrim below. Then they could see Aidan waving in the distance as he stood outside the picturesque Woodenbridge Hotel. When they stepped out of the car, Aidan put his arms around both of them and escorted them inside the hotel. Later, while enjoying dinner, Charles told Aidan all about the lovely ice cream and fizzy drinks he had enjoyed on the way up from Cork and a smiling Aidan wagged his finger at Rosita.

"You are spoiling this young man. He'll expect me to do the same for him now that we're in Dublin but I will instead make sure that he eats all his vegetables and his meat at dinner." He laughed at the dejected face of Charles and ruffled his hair. "Don't worry, young man. I'm not an ogre but I want you to be healthy when you return to school and not be getting sick from eating too much rubbish given to you by your indulgent auntie."

By now Charles realised they were joking and as he looked at them he told them he was very lucky to have such a good Auntie Rosita and Uncle Aidan, as he now called him.

The following day they drove through the wide expanse of the Wicklow Mountains, with the heady smell of peat from the turf being cut and stacked. Their first glimpse of the Sugarloaf Mountain indicated that they were very close to the destination which Aidan was especially looking forward to. For him, it was an unexpected opportunity to see a house and gardens that he had in the past only heard about from others. Rosita had got an invitation from the Wingfield family to join them in Powerscourt Estate for a tour of the gardens, followed by tea on the lawn.

Unfortunately the family were away on that day but the housekeeper gave them a warm welcome and the head gardener took them to see the gardens. What surprised Rosita was Charles' fascination with the building itself. He was excited to hear from the housekeeper that King George the Fifth had been a guest in the house almost a hundred years earlier.

Both Rosita and Adrian were overawed by the grandeur of the gardens and, as it was explained to them that the family were endeavouring to replicate the gardens at the Palace of Versailles, they looked at each other and said together: "We're going to go there next month!"

The following morning, as they left the village of Enniskerry, they drove up the hill with its narrow road which had large trees on either side. The trees formed a canopy of green over the car. Charles was delighted as he always described those kinds of roads as tunnels. Rosita delighted in them also, but mostly loved the small cracks of sunlight that formed a bright scattered pattern on the roadway. Soon they were in the delightful mountains of Dublin and they had taken this route because Charles insisted that they find the old lead mines in Kilternan. The mine had exhausted its lead by the 1860's and was now a smelting facility for ore. When Charles saw the chimney, on the top of the hill, which seemed to reach into the sky, he was very excited.

"A boy at school told me that it is the longest chimney in the whole of England or Ireland, because it goes way down into the ground for miles."

Rosita thought it was impressive but felt that Charles might be exaggerating somewhat.

"Well, Charles," Aidan said, "I've known about the mine but didn't know all that exciting information about it." He could see how delighted Charles was to be able to go back to school to tell his friend that he had seen it.

Finally, the holiday came near to its end as they arrived in Dublin. Aidan had already secured a booking for them at the Shelbourne Hotel. Charles loved his time there, enjoying the opulence of the dining room and going across the road to the park with its ponds and ducks and the summer flowerbeds, rich with colour.

They also made their promised trip to Kingstown where Rosita again enjoyed seeing the boats coming and going from Wales. She often watched the waves lapping the shore, feeling that it was like a lesson in watching the rhythm of one's life. The soft sound of gentle waves lapping onto the shore was like the times when peace reigned in our hearts. Yet it could turn without much warning and send its crashing foam onto the shore, just as we are sometimes forced to live in turmoil. Today the sea was at peace with the world, as was she. It was a unique experience for Rosita to have her grandson and a good man by her side and it raised her spirits.

She pointed out the Hill of Howth across Dublin Bay to Charles, but she explained that they wouldn't have time to go there on this occasion.

"Always keep something for the next time," she said to him. "That was always my motto."

"You're always saying that, Auntie Rosita, when I want to do extra things each day," he astutely observed.

Aidan just looked on with amusement.

As they left Dublin for England, Dan O'Leary, who said it was the best holiday he ever had, returned to Midleton and Aidan went back to work.

As Rosita and Charles stepped out of the car at the school in Devon, the boy put both his arms around Rosita before saying, "Auntie Rosita, you're as kind as my mama was. I'm going to miss you." Then he immediately seemed to be embarrassed at this demonstration of love. Rosita smiled as she saw him turn swiftly and look around, fearing that some of the other boys had seen his gesture of affection.

Rosita clasped his hand in both of hers and said, "And I love you as much as your mama did." As they held each other's gaze, Rosita knew that they had crossed a line and reached a mutual love that would bind them more strongly together. As the young boy put his arms around her waist again, she knew that she didn't have to worry anymore: they loved each other unconditionally.

When Rosita arrived back in London after her long journey, which involved a two-hour delay, she took a car from the train station to the Savoy Hotel.

As she stepped out, she was greeted by the porter.

"We will take your bags to your room because I've been warned by the maitre d' to get you to the restaurant before dining closes. Your guests are already there, Lady Beconsford."

"Thank you. I will just powder my nose in the ladies' room before joining my guests."

When Rosita walked through the ornate rotunda that led to the River Restaurant, she was grateful to see the two gentlemen were sitting at a window table that had wonderful night-time views of the Thames as it flowed gently in the distance. I love this place, she thought, with its exceptional restaurant that had already hosted many distinguished guests, including King Edward the Seventh who was by now a regular diner.

Tonight, Rosita had eyes only for the two men who stood up to greet her.

She first embraced her beloved younger brother Louis. "Yourself and Aidan look to have made each other's acquaintance so I don't have to introduce you," she said.

As she turned to Aidan, he extended his hand and clasped hers. "We're both delighted that you got here safely, as we were getting worried."

"It was the train. Two hours delay due to a tree blocking the line, or so we were told. But I'm here now and I'd like to eat before catching up on my brother's news, as I see him so rarely of late." She patted her brother on his hand which looked rather thin and was cold to the touch. He doesn't look too well, she thought. He'd looked much better in the spring. "I hope they're all looking after you in London, Louis. You look as if you need a bit of feeding up."

"I'm fine, sister, just over a slight chill and feeling well again. No need to ask how you are. You're looking better than ever and far too young-looking for a woman of your age!"

He laughed as she playfully slapped him on the arm before sitting down to enjoy a much-needed meal.

They spent a very pleasant evening together and discussed many topics from the politics of Ireland and England to legal anecdotes from Aidan, who had a way of telling a story that would keep a whole room entertained. At that moment, she felt proud to be his friend and saw the look of respect that Louis accorded him.

He fits into any company and I'm lucky to have found him, she thought. He has brought so much joy to my recent past that I hope it continues.

She sat back and listened to her two favourite men enjoying themselves.

When Louis left, Rosita promised to call him again before she returned to Ireland in October.

Aidan and Rosita then spent time in the bar enjoying a drink and admiring the electric lights in the room.

"Wouldn't it be lovely to have the luxury of electrical lighting in our homes in Ireland?" Rosita mused. "I wonder if it will happen before my time on this earth is over. It's one of the things I love most about this hotel. To be able to flick a switch on a wall and have lights come on must surely be one of life's greatest luxuries."

Later, Aidan accompanied her to the lifts that saved walking up the stairways.

Before she entered her bedroom, he kissed her on the cheek and looked into her eyes, saying, "After tomorrow we'll be starting our trip to freedom. I hope that you're looking forward to it as much as I am."

She nodded, with a smile on her face.

Chapter Nineteen

After a relaxed and calm crossing from Dover to Calais, Rosita and Aidan finally arrived in the centre of Paris in Place Verdone where they were staying at the Ritz Hotel. They had booked adjoining rooms and, having freshened up, they met at the restaurant for dinner. To those observing, they looked like a happily married couple, the irony of which was not lost on Rosita.

As they ate their way through a five-course banquet, Rosita said, “Did you know, Aidan, that the owners are the Swiss hotelier Cesar Ritz and the French chef Auguste Escoffier, who were in a previous life the manager and chef at the Savoy in London? Unfortunately, towards the end of the 1890’s they were dismissed. It appears that Cesar Ritz was involved in the disappearance of over three-thousand four-hundred pounds’ worth of wine and spirits! Apparently, before he was dismissed, the Savoy customers had always been telling them both that they should open a hotel in Paris and that is exactly what they did!”

“Well, Rosita, as a mere peasant Irishman I am not usually privy to such elite salacious gossip, but I love to hear that rich people are as likely as poor people to steal, although the rich rarely get jailed for it! They usually have so many friends in high places that they can use privilege to save themselves. I trust, Rosita, that you are not considering running off with the silver cutlery tonight?” He put a hand across the table to hold hers, turning serious as he squeezed it gently. “Rosita, you needn’t answer my question about the cutlery, but please hear me out while I put another question to you. We have known each other for some years but, whether it was after the first day we met, or after all the years I know you, I have found you to be the most engaging woman I have met since my wife was alive. Yet, I fully understand that there is no way on God's earth that a titled Protestant lady and a Catholic lawyer, whose work is mainly with the Catholic Church, could possibly marry. But I want to ask you just one question. We're on our holidays, we're free of all society's shackles and we are consenting adults. Would it be possible for us to be more than friends?"

She gazed back at him and took his hand in both of hers before replying. "Aidan Dermody, I thought you'd never ask. I've waited for this moment a long time. I was almost at the point of asking myself!" A big smile broke across her face.

Aidan was almost shaking as he put his head down and closed his eyes. When he raised his head again, he said, "I've just said a prayer of thanks to the gods of love and have also given my heart time to stop pounding. You've just made an old man very happy, Rosita."

"Well, that makes me ancient, as I'm older than you," she said, still smiling.

Later that night when Aidan and Rosita held each other close enough to hear their hearts beating together for the first time, no words were needed as they sealed their love. Later, both slept the sleep of the just, with no feeling of any guilt whatsoever, just the knowledge that each of them felt young again and this was not something either expected to feel as they both moved into their older years.

The rest of that month for Rosita was almost a blur of happiness. They adored their time in Paris and Versailles and wandered around the gardens where they agreed that the Wingfield family in Powerscourt were doing a very good job of creating a replica but they each agreed that the smaller gardens in Powerscourt had more charm. Nonetheless, they both agreed that the palace and gardens at Versailles were magnificent.

As the month of September neared its end, it felt all too soon for them when they finally arrived in Rome. While there, Rosita stayed in the Hotel Hessler Villa Medici while Aidan went into Vatican City, to reside where his meetings were being held.

Before they parted, Aidan told Rosita to have fun and he would return to her in three days.

"What are you going to say if anyone asks with whom you were on holidays?" Rosita asked with an amused smile on her face.

"I've been with my best friend, of course. After all, that's what we are, isn't it? And even if they know you are female, let them speculate. Are we more? Or are we just good friends? We need not say which. Let them make their own judgement and whatever they may think certainly does not worry me. Some will say we are more, while most will say we're too old for that sort of thing!" He laughed and he kissed her firmly on the lips before departing.

When he was gone, Rosita began to reflect on their wonderful journey from Paris through Versailles and down to Milan where they had watched opera at La Scala, before continuing to Florence to see the cathedral, the magnificent Uffizi Gallery and the numerous churches where music seemed to seep from the walls. They listened to great Italian opera and especially enjoyed the church music in St. Mark's English Church, close to the River Arno in Florence. Her endless memories from that trip would be always very special as they were the first with Aidan at her side.

It was well into October before Rosita returned to Ireland. She had met with Louis again in London and thought that he was even thinner than in early September.

When she finally got back to Midleton the autumn leaves had already spread their gold and crispy leaves on the paths of the estate. Her first port of call was as always the Secret Garden, to see what new flowers were now blooming and to enjoy the scent of the numerous herbs which varied depending on the season. When she walked inside, she sat in her favourite sun spot and proceeded to open a letter that had arrived from Margarita, who she by now realised was never likely to return to Ireland. Since the death of her beloved husband Laurence some months earlier, she now lived with her son Theodore and his family in their large house in the centre of Manhattan. Rosita smiled as she opened the letter, as she had already received a cable with the good news from America.

My dearest Rosita,

I realise that you know by now of the birth of my twin grandchildren, who are a double joy to me. I had begun to think that Theodore and Angela would never marry and I had to almost engineer his engagement to her two years ago. The twins are called Bob, after my grandfather Robert, and Isabella called after Angela's mother. The thing that saddens me most is that my Laurence didn't live long enough to see his grandchildren. I really feel privileged to have lived long enough for this moment to arrive. I now know that I will leave this earth happy, having finally looked into two more sets of eyes that will keep the memory of my Laurence alive for future generations. I would love you to see them, but I doubt that they will make the long trip to Ireland with the babies for a long time. I'm glad to see that Angela is quite a home bird since her marriage and she says that singing was always only a pastime for her and she is far more content to run a home than travel around the country doing work that is unpredictable even at the best of times.

I still meet Maeve Maguire every week and she brings me all the gossip about the family of our dear departed friend Sylvia. Two of Sylvia's grandchildren are now at university and her grandson says he wants to be a sea captain like his late grandpa Alan Bates. My goodness, how time flies! It doesn't feel that it must be sixty years since we spent the famine years in America.

Alice and Richard send their love and they are now enjoying pottering around in their garden and being waited on hand and foot by the housekeeper that Maeve Maguire secured for them from Ballyeoin in West Cork. It's lovely having Irish friends and family living close by. I would love to see you, Louis and Violet and their families more often but I did enjoy my years in the Dower House and I can't complain about any aspects of my life, as most of it has been truly wonderful.

I'll finish now, as all I seem to do these days is reminisce about the past. Thankfully I keep thinking only of the good things that happened and don't often dwell on the terror brought upon the nation of Ireland during the Famine.

Please tell all my relatives how much I miss them and make sure some of them come over to visit. Of course, the one person I would love to see is you but I think I finish every letter making that point!

All my love,

Margarita

As Rosita held the letter on her lap and continued to sit among the scented roses and herbs in this special place, she knew that she was finally ready to let it all go. She was over seventy years of age and, although most people felt lucky to still be alive at that age, that was not her way of thinking. I feel as lively in my mind as I did at twenty, she kept telling herself, although the effort of getting out of the bed in the morning was definitely affected by creaking bones!

Later that day she went to the farmhouse where Bridie and her husband Thomas still lived with Cormac, Alice's grandson. Cormac had turned out to be such a decent lad and a hard worker. He helped his stepfather keep the farm running seamlessly, but Bridie was always telling him that he should get himself a wife. He would then smilingly argue that he had plenty of time for that in the future. She told Bridie that she would return in the morning to have a chat with her.

The following morning, as she knocked on the door, she noticed the carefully tended summer roses, sunflowers and hydrangeas at each side of the doorway. They looked as well tended and as much a delight to see as when she was a young girl visiting the farmhouse, when Alice lived there as a young girl.

When Bridie opened the door, Rosita hugged her before she was invited into the always warm kitchen.

"I have the kettle on the boil. Now tell me what brings you across so early in the day." Bridie's eyebrows were raised in expectation.

"I knew you'd be quick to spot that I had something to discuss with you," Rosita said, suddenly realising how much she missed her beloved Alice and her friend Doreen.

Bridie saw her pensive look and, after she set some scones on the table, placed a hand on Rosita's shoulder. "You're missing your family, aren't you? But, you know, you're very lucky to have Doreen's grandson in your life and that nice man friend of yours in Dublin. I think that they've both given you a spring in your step. You know, we all need some purpose in our lives and you lost yours when Benjamin and Doreen died and then on top of that Alice ups and goes off to America. Benjamin's death was a tragedy and it knocked the stuffing out of a lot more people than yourself and Doreen. It seemed to shake your brother Louis to the core – he had grown to love Benjamin like a son. You know, at that time Louis told me that he felt some responsibility for Benjamin joining the army."

Rosita's stomach turned over at that. "Everyone shared our grief back then, Bridie. I felt as close to Benjamin as if he were my own son."

"I know you did, love," Bridie said. "I could see it in your eyes from the day the bad news arrived. Doreen and Benjamin are now reunited and I know that they will always be in your heart, but I'm glad you've moved on and it was the greatest gift for you to have young Charles come into your life." Bridie was remembering her husband Gregory as she patted Rosita again.

"Perhaps we can get on to brighter things," Rosita said, hoping to change the mood. Poor Bridie had lost so many people herself in unusual circumstances during her lifetime. "As you've been talking about moving on, well, I've made a big decision in that regard. I'm making a clean break from this estate and Cork and moving to live permanently in Dublin."

Bridie was shocked. "Why would you want to do that, love? You have a beautiful home here, haven't you?"

"I want to make a complete break from everything, Bridie. Although I'm not responsible for the estate anymore, because Louis lives in London and his wife and young sons won't live in Ireland, everyone in the estate still turns to me in a crisis and I'm getting too old for such responsibility. I want some more fun. I started over this summer and I loved every minute of it!"

"Well, I'm glad to hear that. What kind of fun have you in mind?"

"First of all, Charles is now happy in his high school in Devon. He's a very bright boy, you know, and I'm hoping that he'll eventually go to university, but I'll allow him live whatever life he wants when he reaches adulthood. I'm just happy to be in his life. You know, Bridie, I have lost many important people during my life and when Benjamin and Doreen both died, I was feeling angry with all of them for leaving me and burdening me with so much responsibility here in the estate. You know that Louis should be in his rightful home here in Midleton, but he's ruled with a rod of iron by that uppity wife of his. I can barely sit in the same room as her – and now that young brat of a son of theirs, Giles, who never learned to have manners, is going to be the next Lord Beconsford. I don't know how Louis puts up with it, but he always was a peacemaker and he is never going to change. So I want out of here before the time comes when Giles Beconsford is old enough to be sent over to Ireland by his mother to check up on how I run this estate. I've made a decision that before I move from here permanently, I'm off to have that fun in America and I am not booking a return passage until I feel like returning. I want to spend time with my beloved Margarita, as Theodore is often away and his wife Angela has her hands full with her twins. After that, who knows where I'll end up! I want also to catch up with all my friends, who are still alive, in New York. After that I'll come back. There again, maybe I'll never come back!" Rosita then realised that Bridie was looking anxious. "I'm only joking. I am going to end my days in the land of my birth. That's how much I love Ireland."

As Bridie breathed a sigh of relief, they relaxed and enjoyed the rest of the visit chatting and keeping up with all the news and gossip from both East and West Cork until Rosita finally left, satisfied that she had stopped procrastinating and had finally made some big decisions.

Chapter Twenty

Another Christmas came and went and, as the weather began to improve, Rosita booked her passage from Queenstown to New York. The weekend before she was due to leave, Aidan came down to Cork and they attended a musical show in the Everyman Theatre in Cork city, dining in the Imperial Hotel.

After an enjoyable stay in the city, they returned to Midleton as Aidan had insisted on helping her get organised for the trip, saying that he was forever packing bags and knew how much she would need to take.

"Now that I know that you want to live close to me," he said, "I want you to enjoy your stay in America and don't worry about looking for a house in Dublin. I'll arrange for a good friend of mine, who has an excellent eye for properties, to look for some suitable places that you can view when you return."

When the departure day arrived, Rosita stepped gingerly onto the tender that would take her to the liner beyond, as Aidan held her hand and warned her to take care of herself. When she finally boarded the ship that had sailed from Liverpool before calling in at Queenstown on its journey to New York, she had a warm feeling of being loved by a good man. She knew that she was lucky to have found such a love in her autumn years. She was also pleased that on this occasion she could travel in comfort from her own home county of Cork for her trip to America. Yet, it still brought back memories of boarding a ship at Liverpool during the Famine and leaving her beloved papa behind. Yet she was grateful that all her childhood memories of the famine years in New York were good ones. During this trip she hoped to appreciate the fact that she had freed herself from all duties and obligations for the first time in her entire life. Young Charles was thriving and now was her time. She felt a new type of freedom. She had always been someone who had certainty about where her life was leading but, today, as she walked into her large cabin with views of the vast sea outside, she decided to let life now bring her whatever it offered and she would embrace whatever that was.

As the ship sailed out of the harbour, she watched from deck while the fort at Camden across the bay and the spire of the impressive St Colman's Cathedral faded into the distance.

It was a clear day as they entered the vast expanse of the Atlantic Ocean which would become their home until they would sail up the Hudson River in a just over a week. She returned to her cabin and read a book while waiting to go to dinner.

As she entered the vast dining room, with its chandeliers and sparkling white tablecloths and shining silver cutlery, she looked gratefully at the opulence that surrounded her as she was travelling in first-class luxury. She was immediately greeted as Lady Beconsford by the head waiter and was escorted to the captain's table.

The trip lived up to all her expectations, with every type of entertainment on both dry or wet days. She enjoyed the relaxation of playing bridge with a group of enthusiastic ladies and she promised herself to keep that form of entertainment going when she eventually moved to Dublin.

As she stood on the deck on a warm spring day, with a light sea breeze blowing, the ship sailed up the Hudson River past the Statue of Liberty, before it docked at Ellis Island. She loved the idea of a free nation and the concept evoked by that statue.

As soon as she left the portside buildings, having completed the formalities, she emerged into the sunshine of New York where a car was waiting for her arrival. Standing beside it was a smiling and waving Theodore Flaherty with his beautiful wife Angela at his side.

"Hello, young stepbrother! You're looking more handsome every time I see you. You are the image of your Irish grandfather Jack," she said, as she kissed the handsome man in front of her, before hugging his lovely wife.

"Mom can't wait to see you and she told me that I'm in trouble if I delay in driving you to our home," Theodore said, smiling, as he piled the luggage into the back of the car. "By the way, she is still treated by everyone like the star that she was and she will sing for anyone who is willing to listen, so don't expect to see a doddery old lady! It's only because of her mobility issues that she's unable to be out and about."

"I know! And she's so happy here! She never stops telling me stories about her family and neighbours, usually funny anecdotes about her friends that she calls old!" said Rosita, laughing, as she stepped into the car.

As they drove through Manhattan, Rosita could see the impressive eleven-storey Tower Building, and was in awe of the massive structure that seemed to stretch endlessly towards the sky.

"In Ireland, our house in Midleton is seen as a mansion," Rosita said, "but here it would be lost in the middle of this. I wonder if Ireland will ever have such buildings?" She shuddered at the thought of the skyline in her own country being overshadowed by such structures.

"That's what is described as progress here, Rosita," Theodore said. "Our population keeps growing and we need to house all the people coming from Europe and have places for them in which to work. I love its brashness yet I am even more grateful that I have an Irish heritage."

They entered a tree-lined road with large detached homes on either side, then turned into Theodore's driveway towards the end of the quiet cul-de-sac. Rosita was pleased to see that its driveway was lined with tall oak trees. Flower beds were evident at either side of the front of the house.

Margarita could be seen sitting in her chair, in the garden, with a blanket on her knees, waving at the oncoming car.

Rosita walked from the car, reaching with outstretched arms and embracing a delighted Margarita. Then a beaming Angela re-emerged from the house with a baby in each arm and Rosita was delighted to make the acquaintance of the two beautiful additions to the family.

Over the following week, chat, gossip and a steady stream of guests including Alice and Richard came to the house to greet Rosita. She also delighted in spending time with little Bob and Isabella, giving Angela a much-needed break.

During this time, she would always be in the company of Margarita, who loved spending time either in the garden or in the back parlour, where the sun shone through the large windows of her home. They looked directly out upon the manicured lawns with its extensive variation of flowers beds also to the rear of the house. While sitting together each day, a lifetime of memories was recalled by them both. Rosita only then realised that Margarita was actually an old lady and getting quite frail. That shocked her as Margarita had always been such a lively presence in her life.

At the end of the second week, excitement increased among family and friends of Margarita. Theodore had told Rosita that a benevolent concert had been organised in the Hotel Astor, as a tribute to Margarita's life in opera. The previous year, Margarita had enjoyed the Peace Society dinner, attended by President Taft, at the Astor Hotel and Theodore had promised her then that he would have a dinner in her honour there sometime in the future. Margarita had laughed and warned him that he had better hurry up or she might not still be around to enjoy it! True to his word, her son had made arrangements for the event, without his mother knowing too much about it, as soon as he heard that Rosita was visiting America.

Angela had arranged for the twins to be minded during the evening of the concert, in a suite at the Astor. Unbeknown to Margarita, Angela was going to duet with her husband on the night, to honour her mother-in-law.

When the day of the concert arrived, Rosita tried to take her stepmother in hand.

"Now, Margarita, you must allow me coiffeur your hair and dress you for this evening. After all, you are the guest of honour," she said.

"I'll dress and look appropriate for my age and, apart from my beloved necklace given to me on my ninth birthday, I will appear demure as befits my status," Margarita responded, laughing.

"Just trust me, Margarita. I'll make sure you look wonderful."

When the time to depart for the hotel arrived, a resplendent Margarita emerged, dressed in a shimmering light-grey silk dress with a rich red-velvet jacket. She looked every inch the star as she was helped from the chair and given her walking cane.

Rosita linked her arm to support her on their way to the waiting car.

"My goodness, will I be going in that grand car?" she asked, when she saw the latest Ford Model T stopped outside the house.

"According to your son, nothing is ever good enough for his beloved mother, so enjoy the journey because I certainly will," said Rosita as she and the driver settled Margarita into the back of the elegant motor car.

When they arrived at the Hotel Astor, Theodore was in the foyer, waiting to escort his mother to the front row of the ballroom where they would join Alice, Richard and their good friend Maeve Maguire.

As Margarita made her entrance, the audience stood to clap, much to her delight.

As, beaming, she took her seat, she turned to Rosita and placed a hand on hers. "Isn't this like the old days? Do you remember that wonderful night in the Verona Arena, with my Laurence singing? It was the most marvellous occasion and it definitely started my wanderlust, and now I'm wondering what I did to deserve this?" Margarita had a big smile on her face.

As the orchestra began to play, Margarita was transported back to all the places she had spent listening to such beauty and it still made her heart soar with delight. Music truly is the food of love, she thought as the audience clapped when her beloved son appeared on the stage, smiling at his mother and bowing to the huge audience.

"I'm going to sing you some songs, all favourites of my mother," he announced, "but first I want to tell you a story about how this song gave me a love of Ireland, the childhood home of my mother and the place of my birth. A few hundred years before my mother was born, the Penal Laws passed by the English rulers forbade intermarrying between Catholics and Protestants, and Catholics were penalised in all sorts of ways. The Catholics were stripped of all their religious freedoms. These laws also tried to banish all notion of Ireland out of the vocabulary and the poets and songwriters of that time had to hide their patriotism by calling Ireland such names as *Kathleen Mavourneen – 'Kathleen My Beloved'* – and *Róisín Dubh – 'Dark Rosaleen'*. The song 'Kathleen Mavourneen' tells of love and struggles for a different Ireland, and it was always a song my mother loved. Although these events happened long years before she was born, she taught me the history of her country and how music and poetry played its part. Margarita is Protestant and she married into the aristocracy. When her husband Victor died at a young age, she married my father, before coming to live in America. But Margarita always remained a strong and proud Irishwoman and she still is to this day. I will dedicate it to all the Irishwomen in New York, many of whom have been forced to leave their native land due to poverty. I tip my hat to all those brave women who made their way to the Land of the Free. I salute you all!"

As Margarita looked on with pride, her son began to sing.

"*Kathleen Mavourneen, the grey dawn is breaking,*
The horn of the hunter is heard on the hill
The lark from her light wing, the bright dew is shaking,
Oh Kathleen Mavourneen, why slumber you still?"

As the Irish in the audience shed a tear, Margarita felt immense pride in the wonderful son she had reared. As he sang, memories of another land rose within Irish hearts and, for Margarita, bittersweet memories of her beloved husband singing it to her during good and bad times throughout their lives.

When the applause died down, Theodore continued to sing and when he finally left the stage his performance was followed by the orchestra, choirs and other singers who had all asked to take part in this tribute to Margarita.

Rosita looked at Margarita and realised, sadly, that it was likely to be one of the last times she could enjoy such an evening.

As the evening drew to a close, Theodore appeared again on stage, holding the hand of his now retired soprano wife, Angela. She announced that she had a request from her husband to sing "Casta Diva", from the opera *Norma* especially for the grandmama of their newly born twins Bob and Isabella, who were at that moment upstairs in a hotel bedroom, probably being lulled to sleep by the sounds of the concert.

The audience burst into applause and she paused, smiling, before continuing to speak.

"My husband often retells a story that is true. On the night of the Big Wind that hit Ireland in 1939, Margarita sang this song. The story goes that its sound in the forest had a calming influence that helped save the life of her granny, Molly, who was trapped under a tree."

Margarita smiled though she felt that her part in the story was exaggerated. It was Old John the herb man who had thrown Molly forward and taken the brunt of the falling trees that saved her as, sadly, he himself lost his life. Yet it was nice to think that her American family were not forgetting the stories from the past in Ireland. That gladdened her heart.

Angela began to sing the exquisite aria and Margarita's heart lifted with each word, as she sang along in her own head.

The voice of Angela faded and the clapping brought Margarita back from remembering the past as her son announced that he would sing a final duet with his wife.

The strains of the orchestra commenced the "*Vogliatemi bene*", from the first act of Verdi's *Madama Butterfly*, which Theodore and Angela knew was Margarita's favourite new opera. As their voices soared so did her heart, to a point that she again felt transported back to her youth where a deep love of such profound music was nurtured in her by her mother Eliza and Mr. Johnson in Midleton. As she listened to the sad and plaintive music come to an end, she knew that with young composers like Verdi and Puccini this form of art was in safe hands and would live long beyond her time.

Rosita watched Margarita's face and saw a mixture of ecstasy and sadness. It was a sad moment of realisation for Rosita. As the audience showed their appreciation and the curtain closed for the final time, Rosita knew in her heart that it would shortly be Margarita's time also to leave the stage.

Rosita decided to spent a few more months in America and continue to enjoy the company of all her Irish friends and relatives. She spent a lot of time with Maeve Maguire, who had come to America during the Famine with the late Sylvia from Ballyeoin in West Cork. After the Famine, Sylvia had changed the face of Ballyeoin through her patronage. Maeve Maguire still looked both strong and sprightly after a lifetime teaching in New York. Her achievements in her long career were her greatest pride. She always said that she might not have married but she had hundreds of children to love during her lifetime.

One evening as Rosita was enjoying some sherry as a guest in Maeve's cosy home, Maeve confided in her that she always wanted to spend her final days back in Cork but, now that all her family were dead, including her young brother Ollie, she wasn't sure if it would be a wise move. As soon as Rosita heard that, an idea struck her and she held her breath as she made a suggestion to Maeve.

"You know that my friend Aidan has already looked at some elegant Georgian houses in Dublin and I've decided to purchase one in Fitzwilliam Street. I like his description of it and I'm going to make it my home, for however long more I have left. Aidan assures me that it is a beautifully maintained house and ready for occupation. Because of what you have just said, I wonder if you would consider becoming my companion, or whatever you'd like to be called, and live with me in Dublin? There would, of course, be a good remuneration for you. You would not be expected to housekeep, but perhaps you could oversee the small number of staff. Your job would mainly be spending time with me and keeping an eye on me, of course!" Rosita looked at Maeve, waiting for her reaction.

All an astounded Maeve did was jump up and throw her arms around Rosita, with a beaming smile on her face. "I can't believe this! I was going to ask you to allow me travel back with you and then see how things went from there. Now all I can say to you is *yes, yes, yes!* And thank you!"

The two ladies sat up for most of that night, excited about the future and planning their return to Ireland, as they both continued to drink quite a few celebratory glasses of sherry.

Two weeks before the ladies were due to return to Ireland, Margarita Beconsford-Flaherty died peacefully in her sleep, surrounded by her American and Irish family. They all agreed that she was contented in her final days, having Rosita and Alice by her side for the final weeks of her long life.

In a private service for family held in New Jersey, Margarita was laid to rest beside her beloved Laurence. Before she was lowered into the ground

Theodore read a poem, written by their good friend Maeve Maguire, as the rest of the family stood by his side.

"Weep not for me but for those I leave behind.
I will carry their burden to the end of time.
I will be strong for those who weep
Weep not for me, for I am free.
I'll hold your tears within my heart
I'll help to ease your pain.
As darkness falls upon your shoulders,
My spirit still remains.
My life was long, our love was strong
Please weep no more – my spirit lives on.
When we reunite, your hearts and mine,
We'll rest together till the end of time."

As tears fell, Rosita and the family members each placed a single red rose on top of the coffin, as she said a prayer also for all her own family who had passed. Her mama Fleur who had died giving birth to her, her father Victor and her grandparents Isaac and Deborah and of course her beloved son Benjamin and friend Doreen.

Two weeks later, as the liner sailed down the Hudson River, passing again beneath the Statue of Liberty, Rosita said another prayer of gratitude for the country that allowed people such as her companion Maeve and all the many Irish emigrants to prosper and achieve long healthy lives in that land.

Chapter Twenty-One

It was early in June when Rosita and Maeve's boat docked in Queenstown where Dan O'Leary was waiting with his car. When they arrived home in Midleton, they spent their first few days just resting and recuperating from their trip which had seen them hit a summer storm in mid-Atlantic that kept them lying in their beds for almost three days.

In August, Rosita and Aidan enjoyed a month spent showing Charles around France. It was a lovely experience for Rosita as she now looked at things through the eyes of her grandson. His main fascination was still with architecture, and he was particularly fascinated by the Eiffel Tower. He also loved the boat trips on the Seine, watching all the wonders of Paris from that vantage point.

Rosita and Maeve spend that autumn organising the move to Dublin, which they agreed to postpone until Charles had enjoyed Christmas in Midleton.

Most of the family spent Christmas that year in the Big House. Sadly, Louis didn't make it home for even a short stay, as his health was not at all good. He's worn out living with that shrew of a wife, Rosita thought, glad that they had just Bridie, Thomas and Cormac, plus her sister Violet's family, for Christmas dinner. Maeve fitted in really well, telling the children all about the schools and what children learned in New York.

Rosita later took Violet aside and spoke to her, before Violet and her family returned to their own home.

"You're looking very pensive, Rosita," Violet said, as they took a stroll through the Secret Gardan in the sharp crisp winter air.

Rosita agreed, before telling Violet her plans.

"As you know, shortly I'm leaving this estate for good. You don't have to worry because you will not be asked to step into my shoes to help out. Louis is happy with the estate management team that's in place. Violet, I just got sick and tired of all the responsibilities, but there is also more to it than that. During the past few years, I've felt that the Irish people are beginning to use their voices more, since the Land League gave them farming rights. More men like Daniel O'Connell, who in the past so eloquently advocated for Irish freedoms, are now emerging, men who are also eloquently expressing a hope for Irish freedom – and that is no surprise to me. It looks like they want their country back. I feel Irish myself, but they would all view me living in this large estate as just a pawn of the British. I actually don't feel at times that I'm safe here anymore. Yet I never want to leave my native land."

Violet interrupted her, with concern in her voice. "That's painting a gloomy picture about us all, Rosita, which I don't agree with. Our families have always cared for its workers and farmers. It's alright for you – you don't have children so you can up and leave and go anywhere, but our children and grandchildren are going to have to live their lives out in Cork." Violet was rather upset at the tone of the conversation they were having on a previously happy Christmas Day.

"Violet, I'm sorry, maybe I'm overthinking the whole thing but I have met so many intelligent and articulate Irish writers and artists both here and abroad, and especially on my trips to meet Aidan in Dublin, who are thinking along those lines. Aidan has a good ear to the ground and he says that seems to be the way of thinking. What I am trying to tell you is that I finalised the purchase of a house in Dublin a couple of months ago. Aidan secured it for me while I was in New York and, as you know, I've already told Louis that I'm returning the house and lands to its rightful owner. Our brother Louis and his two sons are its future. Unfortunately, my future is already upon me and I want to spend it in peace and tranquillity in Dublin where I hope to enjoy theatre and music. That is where I want to end my days, with Maeve and I hope Charles when he finally leaves Devon. I will, of course, keep bedrooms for my favourite sister and her family." Rosita was hoping to lighten the gloom that had appeared on her sister's face.

As she tucked her arm into her sister's and they returned to the house, she began to realise that the decision she had made was far-reaching but she knew in her heart that she wouldn't regret it.

Maeve Maguire certainly didn't seem to regret her decision to return to Ireland, as she was always smiling and happy, especially as she organised all of Rosita's belongings that they needed to take to their new Dublin home. Rosita found that leaving Cork took longer than she expected but by early spring the two ladies finally arrived at the front door of their new home in Fitzwilliam Street. It faced a small tree-lined park across the road in the square. All the houses surrounding the square were elegant Georgian homes. The house looked welcoming with its tall narrow three storeys topped with six neat chimney stacks, assuring them that this would be a warm and comfortable place to live. The semicircular curved glass above the elegant door was segmented like a folding fan and wide steps led up to the front door.

As Rosita turned the key, given to her by her solicitor in Cork, she felt a breath of calm air seep through her body and knew in her bones that she would find contentment within these four walls.

Aidan was waiting to greet them and he brought them straight through to the kitchen to meet their new housekeeper and daily maid.

A beaming Mrs. Jordan turned from the stove and bowed. A smiling Rosita held out a hand to her.

"I don't stand on ceremony and we are going to be together a lot. I'm delighted to meet you and this must be Mary White?"

Rosita turned to welcome the blushing pretty young girl and thanked them both for joining the household.

When the introductions were over, Aidan spoke. "I have asked for dinner to be served once you have both freshened up and seen your bedrooms – then you can sample Mrs. Jordan's culinary skills!"

Later, they sat down in the spacious dining room with its rich mahogany table which Aidan assured them could be enlarged with a centre panel to fit up to twelve people, if required. In the corner of the large space sat a highly polished Steinway piano. This was bought by Aidan as a welcoming present for the house. He's such a generous man, Rosita thought, looking with pride around her new dining room where she hoped to spend many nights in the company of friends new and old.

The meal that was served was just what they needed. Soup and hot fresh buttered bread, followed by lamb cutlets with vegetables every bit as good as anything that the kitchen served in Midleton. Rosita voiced her approval and thanked Aidan and the staff for the welcome they had received.

"Now I'll leave you ladies to look over your new home," Aidan said. "In the meantime, I am going to meet my men friends at the Bohemians musical society's weekly meeting. They are all agog at the idea that I am fraternising with female elites!"

Rosita already knew that the Bohemians was a club for gentlemen only.

"So, I can't go along with you? Is that what you are saying?" she said, laughing. "However, if I can't join in, I have a great idea. Tonight, please issue an invitation to four of your singing friends and ask them to join Maeve and me on Friday next for dinner, whereupon, having eaten, they can then entertain us with their musical talents."

Aidan was highly amused by her suggestion. "Therefore, what you are suggesting, my lady, is that if Muhammad can't go to the mountain, then the mountain must come to Muhammad?"

"Exactly, Aidan. I don't see why only the men can have all the fun while the women sit at home. I'm just looking for a solution to a problem I have with men only clubs!"

"Very well, I will pass on your invitation and you'd better ensure that the wine will flow for them, as they will expect no less," Aidan said, smiling as he bade them farewell.

Rosita's dinner party on the following Friday was such a success that all the Bohemians men were clamouring to get an invitation in the future. The following Friday was just the beginning of a weekly experience for Rosita and Maeve that helped them meet and mingle with a diverse group of gentlemen whose love of music was as great as Rosita and Aidan's. At the end of each evening of food, drink and entertainment, Rosita arranged for their by now regular driver Jackson to take her rather inebriated group of guests back safely to their own homes.

Chapter Twenty-Two

Over the following couple of years, Rosita never for a single moment regretted her decision to live in Dublin. She loved city life and the number of diverse things she could pursue. She enjoyed lunches in the Shelbourne Hotel, trips to the Abbey and Gate theatres and by now her famous musical soirees in Fitzwilliam Street on a Friday evening. Each day that she woke, she found herself saying a prayer of thanks for having met Aidan and for still being in such good health. She was lucky also with the two women who joined her staff, young Mary White and the cook Mrs. Jordan. Not alone did they work in the house but they kept Rosita and Maeve updated with all the amusing stories pertaining to their extended families and friends in Dublin. While Mrs. Jordon lived in, her family were scattered all around Dublin and she regularly visited them. Rosita often thought that the working-class people of Dublin seemed to have a much better time than many of the upper classes with their stiff upper lips. The working class women certainly seemed to laugh and joke about life more than those in more polite society.

Yet Rosita knew that behind much of the smiles and laughter of those who had the luxury of having jobs, there were many who lived in the tenements in the heart of the city who didn't have much to be cheerful about. Even those who were working found it hard to make ends meet if they had large families. This was evident in 1913 when numerous workers went on strike in the bakery and railway industries. They did this with the support of James Larkin who engineered the lockout. Though in the end the workers had to give in, on the brink of starvation, it showed her how those who are discontented with their lives can rise up and rebel against their employers if they are sufficiently united. Yet amid such turmoil, Rosita loved the energy of the city.

During that period, Charles made trips home during his summer holidays and at Christmas time. Maeve and the other ladies in the house were so kind to him and he was growing up to be a strong and handsome boy who endeared himself to everyone he met. Apart from feeding him well, Mary White often brought him down to Grafton Street with her, where they would sit in tea rooms and she'd tell him about all the characters that wandered the streets of Dublin. On those occasions he would also walk with her by Trinity College and he would later tell Rosita how much he loved the architecture of the buildings and in the streets surrounding its hallowed walls.

Rosita began also to introduce him to people such as Sir Howard Grubb who made telescopes in Rathmines and to various other possible employers who might be of help to Charles when deciding on his future career. But his only fascination seemed to be with the buildings that housed these businesses.

"I want to study the design of buildings when I leave school," Charles told Rosita, knowing it would be no surprise to her. "I hope you don't mind if I study in Dublin. I love the Georgian buildings here and I want to learn that business."

Rosita was delighted and she assured him that she would give him every support. With that in mind, later that same evening, having considered Charles' ambition, Rosita came to a decision to take Charles out of his school in Devon and let him finish his education in Dublin.

Shortly after making that decision, she was very relieved that he was at home in Ireland because by the time it took to relocate Charles to Dublin, she realised that Europe was getting restless. There had been rumblings of discontent since the start of the new century, but after the assassination of the heir to the Austro-Hungarian Empire, Archduke Franz Ferdinand, in 1914, the possibility of a war starting in Europe looked increasingly likely.

Her worries came to fruition when on the 4th of August, 1914, England declared war on Germany, following the Germans' refusal to remove troops from neutral Belgium.

Rosita's only happiness at that time was the fact that her grandson was still too young to even consider entering the military.

By the beginning of 1915, sons of Ireland, many whose families were known to her, began to join the army in droves. Recruitment was encouraged and men joined up from all walks of life, from those with positions in banking, insurance and business, to those who lived in poverty and saw the army as a way of feeding their families. Around the country recruitment known as 'Pals' regiments were being established. This encouraged groups of friends and colleagues to join together and many young men liked that notion. Many officer types, who had their schooling in such establishments as the exclusive Jesuit Belvedere College in Dublin, were encouraged to join this just war in defence of small nations like Belgium. Many of the young men thought it would be an exciting adventure and the war would probably be won by Christmas.

Aidan knew many of the men who were joining with their 'Pals'. One day, as the war continued, he came to Rosita, shaking his head as he gave her more information about those joining up.

"You were right about Ned Devitt, who works in the bank. It seems that at least some of his old school friends are also joining the army and are all in the same regiment. I believe that he was encouraged to join by William Martin Murphy, the president of his golf club in Milltown, who recruited many members for a 'Pals' regiment. I can't for the life of me comprehend their thinking, as they're all professional men, most with families. I can't help but feel that perhaps they're trying to relive their bachelor days and see this as an exciting game. Most of them have told their families that they expect that it will all be over within the year. Oh, the folly of it all! They don't know what they've let themselves in for!" Aidan was hugely exasperated at what he saw as their foolishness.

Although Charles was young, Rosita had been warning him for years that if he ever considered joining the army in the future, she would find it hard to forgive him.

"Your father died in a senseless war in Africa and his death killed your grandmother so I don't ever want to go through another trauma such as their deaths," she regularly cautioned him.

However, another problem arose in Ireland, as mutterings grew of turbulent times to come, closer to home. The war in Europe appeared to take the attention of the British authorities away from Ireland. These utterances of unrest were said behind closed doors but what was different this time was the fact that people of integrity, including idealists, writers and those within the arts and culture set were stating that Ireland should now seriously consider seeking independence.

It was the middle of spring 1916 when Aidan arrived at the house early one morning with some very worrying news.

"Something is being planned in Dublin and I think Maeve and you should stick very close to home for the time being. Thankfully Charles' school is nearby, but make sure he doesn't go wandering around Dublin on his own or with Mary for the time being," he warned Rosita. Within weeks his information proved to be correct.

At the commencement of the Easter weekend, shock waves suddenly shot through everyone in Ireland, as men who called themselves the Irish Republican Army marched through Dublin and announced a Proclamation of Independence from Britain on the steps of the General Post Office. They then took control of the GPO and other locations around the city. When shots began to be fired between the rebels and the British army, nobody felt safe in the city but Rosita ensured that both her family and staff were ensconced in her home in Fitzwilliam Street and that included Mary. Even then she still felt that their home was too close for comfort to Boland's Mills which the rebels also took control of during that long Easter weekend.

By the time law and order was semi-restored, she knew that irreparable damage had been done. Nonetheless, she was even less prepared for what was to follow.

Maeve came into the parlour having just learned a few unsavoury things.

"Rosita, I need to tell you before you get your newspaper. It's on everyone's lips in the United Arts Club." She had just come from having afternoon tea there with a friend. "You remember Monica Ryan who married Percival Lea Wilson? He was seconded by the police early on in the war to go to Europe with the Royal Dublin Fusiliers. As you know, he came home to his wife in Dublin early in 1916 and went back to his old job as some kind of a chief constable with the police. The talk is that he showed utter contempt for the men who caused the rising over the weekend. I have it on good authority that he was particularly nasty to Tom Clarke, one of the signatories to the Proclamation of Independence, making him strip naked when he was taken to the Rotunda, before he arrested him with the rest of the leaders. They are now all being held in Dublin Castle while their fate is being determined." Maeve felt anguished at this unexpected turn of events in her life in Dublin. She almost wished that she was back in New York, but knew that her future now lay in supporting Rosita.

The entire episode threw everyone in Ireland into a state of flux, as so many Irishmen were at this time fighting with the British in Europe and some brothers of those men were at the same time marching for independence in Ireland. Neighbours and even friends didn't know who to support. But less than five weeks later, the actions of the British authorities made people sit up and think about whom they would pledge their allegiance to in the future. Shock turned to horror as slowly and methodically the British authorities began to execute, by firing squad, fourteen of the men who were deemed to be ringleaders in the rebellion. Included in that number was their leader Pádraig Pearse, teacher and poet. 58-year-old Tom Clarke, who had been shamed on the streets of Dublin, was also executed as well as poet Joseph Plunkett who, just a few hours before his death, married his beloved Grace Gifford in Kilmainham Gaol. The last insult was the execution of the internationally acclaimed Labour leader James Connolly, who had been wounded in the rising and was executed while tied to a chair.

After the executions, the disgust of the world came down hard upon the shoulders of the British parliament and Rosita knew that Ireland was now a country that had seen enough and would likely refuse to bend over and be beaten any more by the British whom far more Irish now saw as the enemy that needed to be gone from their lives.

As Rosita thought things might settle down again, Mary arrived for work in a state of panic. Rosita had to sit her down on the sofa to calm her and get any sense out of her.

"What's wrong with you, child, has somebody died?" Rosita asked the anguished girl.

"No, your ladyship. It's my Jimmy. You know the lad I've been seeing for the last while. He came around to my house very late last night in a panic. He had been told that the police and the army were looking for him. I knew that he had been bringing things around Dublin in his horse and cart for his boss for a month. It turned out they were things used during the uprising and the police were told that my Jimmy was involved. He wasn't connected with the rebels at all but his boss put the blame on him and said that it was Jimmy that was involved, just to save his own skin. But that's not true. Jimmy was only doing as he was told by his boss. Last night my mam let him sleep under the kitchen table at our house, but warned me that she will only let him stay in the house until I get home from work this evening. I don't know what to do and that's a fact!" She started to cry.

By now Maeve had walked in but thankfully Mrs. Jordan had already gone to get provisions.

"What does he think he should do?" Rosita asked, trying to get some sense out of Mary.

"He thinks he needs to get out of the country but he says the police will be watching the ships leaving Dublin docks," Mary said, tears now streaming down her face.

"Alright, child. Go with Maeve and get yourself cleaned up and have a cup of tea. Let me think about it and I'll come and get you from the kitchen later. Don't say anything to Mrs. Jordon if she arrives back. Let me deal with her later."

Maeve ushered Mary out through the parlour door.

Rosita sat thinking for over an hour. She was upset that people like young Jimmy Walsh, whom she knew was a decent, hardworking lad, would be stigmatised and arrested when people higher up had been just using him.

Having deliberated, Rosita left the room and asked Mary to bring in some tea and join her in the parlour. A few minutes later Mary arrived, with Maeve carrying the tray on this occasion, saying that Mary would probably have let it fall.

When they sat down, Rosita began to tell Mary what she had in mind.

"Do you know what size clothes Jimmy wears?" Rosita asked.

Mary looked astonished but she answered, "I do, yes, I often buy stuff for me brothers and I know all the different sizes."

"Alright. I'm going to give you an amount of money. It's a rather large amount, so don't let it be stolen. Go to the shops and buy a suit and a shirt for Jimmy and also get a good quality pair of shoes in his size – and socks. Bring them back here and I'll give you further instructions. Don't leave until Mrs. Jordan arrives home with the provisions and when she does send her in to me. Be back as soon as you can and we'll see what we can do then."

A shocked and bewildered Mary left to go to the kitchen with the money already firmly fixed in a deep pocket of her uniform.

Later, Rosita explained to Mrs. Jordan that there was a misunderstanding about Mary's boyfriend's involvement in the troubles at Easter and that she was to keep quiet about it and anything that happened in this house over the following few days. Mrs. Jordan reassured her by saying that she knew Mary's Jimmy very well and he wouldn't harm a fly.

By four o'clock that evening Rosita had unearthed an overcoat and hat that, sadly, had belonged to Benjamin and that she had kept for years in a wardrobe. When Mary had returned with the purchases, she put the hat and overcoat into another bag and gave that bag also to Mary, with instructions of what she wanted her to do with them, before she ordered a cab to take the girl to within a block of her home. Rosita explained that she didn't want suspicions to be aroused if a cab drew up at Mary's home.

Mary did as Rosita said and, with her heart thumping in her chest, returned to her home, praying that nobody had followed her. Mary entered through the back door of the house and she put her finger to her mouth to quieten her family as she went upstairs to where Jimmy was by now in the boys' bedroom. When she entered, her heart went out to him as she saw him sitting on the side of the bed, looking dejected and forlorn.

"I just want you to listen to me. We have no time to chat but please do as I'm asking and everything will be fine. You must change into these clothes and go out the back door and walk towards Fitzwilliam Street quickly, but don't run. Stand tall and imagine that you really are upper-class. Hopefully nobody will recognise you and when you get to Fitzwilliam Street, knock at Lady Rosita's front door. I'm going to walk a good distance behind you to keep an eye out for you and we'll just pray that you get there safely. Do you understand what I want you to do?"

A now bewildered Jimmy just nodded his head.

Mary stepped out of the room while he changed and she was taken by surprise when a smiling, confident-looking Jimmy stepped out onto the landing.

The trip back was thankfully uneventful, apart from a policeman patrolling on the opposite side of Merrion Square.

A knock on the door of Rosita's home heralded the arrival of a rather handsome-looking Jimmy. Maeve ushered him into the parlour, where Rosita was waiting. She felt a pang in her heart as she saw the young man in front of her dressed in her beloved son's clothes and had to remind herself that Benjamin would have been grateful that they were put to good use.

"Jimmy, I'm not going to discuss anything about the police looking for you but I do want to help you. Can you tell me what you would like to happen and I'll see what can be done," Rosita said, trying to reassure him.

"I need to leave the country if I can. I know I'll end up in jail if I'm caught. You saw what they did to the men in Kilmainham Gaol. I wouldn't last any time in there."

"Alright. Mrs. Jordan is preparing a quiet room in the attic for you and later Mary will bring food to you and again tomorrow morning. I'll see what I can do for you by then. Just promise me one thing, Jimmy. That you'll keep in touch with Mary after you leave. She's put her neck on the line by helping you today and I know that she loves you."

"Lady Rosita, I love my Mary too and I'm hoping to marry her when we're older. You have my word on that," Jimmy answered with an honest look in his eyes that convinced Rosita of his intentions.

As soon as Jimmy had gone up to the attic with some food to eat, Rosita telephoned Aidan's housekeeper and then made a phone call to their usual driver Jackson asking for him to call on Mr. Dermody and bring him to Fitzwilliam Street when he was free.

At nine o'clock that evening Aidan arrived in the house with a look of concern on his face. Rosita sat him down in the parlour and handed him a glass of wine. When Rosita had made the decision to help Jimmy, she'd already had snippets of information from Aidan about men in Dublin being rounded up.

As Aidan put his wine glass down, he looked extremely worried. "Rosita, what I said a few days ago is true. It appears that hundreds of suspected rebels are being taken off the streets and transported directly to Wandsworth prison in London. I'm sure when people realise this is happening it will provoke even more acts of rebellion by the people of Ireland. I don't know how it is all going to end, but I worry about you, Rosita. Having a title may put you in danger and I'm very anxious about you. I'm trying to work out how to keep you safe."

Rosita put a hand up to quieten him. "Don't worry about me, Aidan, but there is something I need to tell you and I would like you to hear me out." She looked into his eyes, knowing that he was not going to be happy about what she had to say.

She began to explain the whole situation about Jimmy but as soon as she said that Jimmy was now in her house, Aidan shot up from the chair.

Rosita looked at him and felt her heart thumping as his face grew red with rage, something she had never before witnessed.

"Have you lost your mind, Rosita? What in God's name made you think it was a good idea to harbour a suspected Republican felon in your home? It's nothing less than sheer madness! If the police come knocking at your door you will be in serious trouble and what are you going to do next, may I ask?"

"Aidan Dermody, I do not believe that young Jimmy is a felon and I do not care what people think of me. I'm an old woman and I'll not be led by anyone when I make a decision. What the British have done since the rebellion is nothing short of barbarity and extremely short-sighted. They are antagonising the whole Irish population, many of whom were not supporting the rebels at all. But, leaving that aside, I am going to make sure that this boy gets a future far away from Ireland and not be stuck in a prison. You've just confirmed for me that the British are rounding up as many Republicans as they can and taking them out of the country to put them in jail. This young lad moved equipment in his cart for his boss and shouldn't be on any wanted list. I will help him and the only person I will have to answer to is my own conscience and that is fine with me. I'm now sorry I've involved you in knowing this, Aidan. So go home and continue to live your pampered life and only return when you've calmed down!"

Rosita stood up and opened the parlour door.

Aidan stood up and there was a look of shock on his face.

"I am leaving and I want you to respect my situation," he said. "I wish you to understand that for me this conversation never happened. I might be semi-retired but I have to work with both the Irish and the British and as a lawyer I cannot in all conscience take sides regarding what has happened in this country in recent months. I will bid you farewell for now."

With that he left the house and Rosita found herself sitting on the chair as she shook her head, trying to work through what in God's name had just happened.

After a sleepless night, Rosita knew she had to take action with regards to Jimmy. She made a phone call to Beconsford House and spoke to Jody, the estate manager. She followed that up with a call to have her car brought around in the afternoon. Then she went up to young Jimmy and sat in a chair facing him. He looked white-faced and sad.

"Are they going to come here and get me?" he asked.

"Don't worry, I have everything sorted. Later today you will leave with a case I have packed with some more clothes for you. A driver will take you to my home in Midleton in County Cork. I have already informed the driver that you've been unwell and want to rest on the journey. Don't tell the driver anything about yourself, just say that you're a friend of the Beconsford family. When you reach Midleton, the estate manager will have arranged for you to board the next boat leaving Queenstown for New York. I will give you an envelope with money and a letter of introduction to my stepbrother in America. He should be able to sort you out with accommodation. As I've already said and now emphasise: I have told the driver of the car that you've been ill and he's to let you rest on the long journey to Cork. Mrs. Jordon will pack a hamper of food for each of you. I'm now going to get Mary to come up to you and you can spend the next couple of hours planning your future with her, based on what I've just told you. I'm sorry, Jimmy, but you won't see your family before you go. When your boat has left Ireland, I will call on your mother and assure her that you will be in safe hands when you get to America."

By now Jimmy was shedding tears and Rosita left, hoping that Mary would give him some comfort and reassurance before he went away.

Rosita returned to the parlour and sat down to write a letter to Aidan and she wasn't in a forgiving mood. She was still furious and asked if his angry response to a friend who had made a difficult decision in troubled times was appropriate. She further wrote that she wondered if it was his own reputation in good society that he was most concerned about. She finished by suggesting he spend time reflecting before they would meet again.

The following day she decided to put the whole episode out of her mind when she and Maeve took themselves off to the United Arts Club in Lincoln Place for dinner, which gave them an opportunity to listen to interesting conversationalists such as Lady Augusta Gregory, to assess their views on the horrific events of the previous month. There were always inspiring people in the club and the Yeats family were high on that list. She gave thanks to the fact that there was at least one club in Dublin that invited both men and women to join.

A few weeks later, Rosita let out a sigh of relief when Jody the estate manager phoned her and told her that Jimmy was safely on his way to America. She shared the news with Mary and shortly after that they both went to talk to Jimmy's mother and give her the news. Rosita did not know what kind of reception she would receive but was grateful that Mrs. Walsh was smiling with delight at the news about her Jimmy.

"I'm ever so grateful to you, Lady Beconsford. I'll not tell anyone what you did for us. Our Jimmy is a good lad and I know he'll make us all proud of him in America where he'll have a chance of making something of himself. Thanks so much to your help, m'lady."

Her response made Rosita feel justified in her actions.

Now she just had to see what was keeping Aidan away from her for so long. Luckily, since the Easter Rising they hadn't yet returned to the Friday night dinners with the Bohemians.

As she and Maeve spoke over dinner, later that day, Rosita was somewhat reassured with Maeve's attitude regarding Jimmy.

"Don't take the blame about what you did for Jimmy, Rosita. You are and always were a good person. Just keep being yourself, doing good for others where you can," Maeve told her, while saying a prayer that Aidan and Rosita would patch up their differences.

It was more than a month later before Rosita finally received a letter from Aidan. She sat in the parlour to read it, wondering how badly this event had affected their normally unconditional love and acceptance of each other.

My dearest Rosita,

I took much time to digest your letter because it shocked me that you should think I would consider my own reputation, on that dark night of our relationship. My sense of shock was only to do with you and your reputation. I mentioned being a lawyer only because I realised that if you were in trouble I would want to be by your side but could not if I was seen to be colluding in your crime. The whole episode upset me greatly. I was shocked to later find out that many of the hundreds of the Irish rebels who were indiscriminately been taken off the streets of Dublin and transported to Wandsworth Prison in London were just like Jimmy and only peripherally involved in the rebellion.

I don't know where things are going to end but I worry mostly about you and my need to keep you safe. Yet, when I reflected, I realised that because of the times we are in I can't give you a guarantee of anything, except my love and friendship. I know that in the mad world in which we live at present there are bad or mad men that could jeopardise your safety due to your perceived British connections. So, for my sake and Charles, will you please take care of yourself?

I would love the opportunity to put my arms around you and hold you close but that is entirely your call.

I will finish by saying that I am truly sorry for my behaviour on that night,

I am yours

With love, Aidan

When Rosita read the letter, she smiled in relief, because, although she had decided many years ago that she would never regret any decisions she made, even if they proved wrong, on this occasion she'd had many a sleepless night until Jimmy was safely out of the country and nobody in Dublin had linked her name with his disappearance.

She immediately telephoned Aidan's office and left a message to request that he call around whenever he was free.

That evening, as they sat together in the upstairs parlour watching the moon shining over Fitzwilliam Square beyond, they had a long conversation in which they discussed the fact that maybe she was too independent in her thinking and Aidan, out of sheer goodness, wanted always just to protect her.

By the end of the evening, she had done her own apologising and knew that she did, on occasions, need her beloved Aidan to take care of her.

As it came time for him to return to his home, they again held each other closely and knew again the feeling of the unconditional love they felt for each other.

Chapter Twenty-Three

Over the next couple of years, Rosita tried to live her life in relative normality. On occasions she woke from a nightmare that really frightened her. In her dream the war in Europe was never-ending and Charles was smiling as he told her that he was joining the army. But in the dream the voice was that of her dead son Benjamin. But it was Charles who stood in front of her dressed in the Royal Munster Fusiliers uniform. She always woke immediately, with her heart pounding until she remembered that Charles was asleep in his bed upstairs, probably dreaming only of becoming a fully fledged architect in the future.

Finally, in 1918 the Great War ended. It was already called the "War to End All Wars". Twenty million people had died and more than half of the number were innocent civilians. Everyone agreed that nothing as wasteful of human life should ever happen again in Europe. Two hundred thousand Irishmen had joined the British army and fifty thousand of them perished. Thankfully, David O'Shea, Benjamin's friend, had survived. He had fought bravely in the Battle of Aubers Ridge, in May 1915, where three hundred men died on that day in just two hours. Lieutenant Colonel Victor Rickard, the commanding officer of the 2nd Battalion of the Royal Munster Fusiliers, died with his troops and later his wife commissioned an iconic painting of the soldiers on the eve of battle as they were given general absolution by their chaplain, Father Gleeson. Rosita saw that picture in a newspaper, cut it out and had it framed and it sat by her bedside. Although David survived, his lungs were damaged. He was one of the first group of soldiers to ever experience chemical warfare. Thankfully, he returned to Cork where he continued to reside with his wife Sheila and their ever-growing family. Aidan's friend Ned Devitt had returned unscathed.

Sadly, that war took the lives of so many very young men throughout Europe and Rosita wondered, not for the first time, what changes for good came out of it.

In early 1919, her own brother Louis died and she attended his memorial service and burial in London, in the place he requested, close to his wife, who had passed away a year earlier. Rosita's thoughts at that time were how his sons would deal with the estate in Midleton. The son and heir Giles had not improved as a human being since growing into manhood and she knew that the estate meant nothing to him except as a money-making business to keep him in style in England. Thankfully, she had never regretted leaving Midleton and she was regularly visited by Alice's grandson Cormac and his mother Bridie.

When she returned from London, the relative peace in Ireland slowly began to dissipate. After the British general election in December, 1919, the huge shift to electing Republicans, except in Ulster, allowed Irish nationalists to declare that they would not take up their seats in Westminster. Instead, on the 19th of January, they set up Dáil Eireann – the parliament of Ireland – and met for the first time on the 21st of January in the Mansion House in Dublin.

More worrying was the fact that on that day there was increased civil unrest when two RIC constables guarding a delivery of gelignite to a

Tipperary quarry were ambushed by eight Irish Volunteers. The two constables, Patrick O'Connell and James MacDonnell, were shot dead. This was to be the start of a continued thrust for a fully independent Ireland.

She had been pleased to see that Michael Collins, from County Cork, not yet twenty-nine years of age and a good friend of Aidan's, had become the Minister for Finance but the rest of the news around Cork was not good.

When Rosita returned home from a short holiday abroad, a letter awaited her from Bridie, and its contents did not give her much hope that peace would be established anytime soon.

My dear Rosita,

I hope you are by now recovering after the sad news of the death of your beloved brother Louis. I had hoped to see you soon but am not sure that you should be around Cork in the next while. Cormac is friendly with those such as Michael Collins and unrest around Cork is rising. Cormac believes that what is causing this level of agitation is that the Cork-based Republicans were not involved in the Easter Rising in 1916 and it rankles with them. Now they seem bent on getting rid of everything British by every means that they can.

Since the Irish faced the threat of conscription in early 1918, many parts of Munster have been under military law, a fact that turned most undecided Irishmen towards supporting the Irish Republicans. Since then, as you know, RIC men have been shot and murdered in rural areas and people have little sympathy for the dead men. With regards to you, Rosita, around Cork and particularly North and West Cork, it was rumoured that some vulnerable Protestant people have been murdered indiscriminately amid justifications that they are spies for Britain. I know that Michael in his new role as Director of Intelligence for the Irish Republican Army, has founded what he calls "The Squad", with the sole purpose of killing RIC intelligence officers. I know that Michael is a great man and he should be the head of a peaceful nation and not be in the middle of this mayhem. Some Republicans are taking things into their own hands and are marking out Protestant people, many of whom are in fear of their lives and are leaving their homes. Therefore, I would caution you, if you are thinking of coming to Cork, as you indicated to me some months ago, please change your mind and stay in Dublin for the time being.

Please stay safe, Rosita,
Love, Bridie

But Rosita did need to make a trip to the estate in Cork, to take what possessions of her own that were still in the Big House and the Dower house. She had no intention of allowing that brat Giles Beconsford, who barely recognised her presence and saw her as just an old lady, to lay claim to anything of sentimental value that she had left in her old home. However, she postponed the journey, as she too knew that it could be unsafe for her to travel to the County of Cork at that time.

Rosita realised that she was now living through a new dawning in Ireland, where those who were looking for an Independent Ireland were beavering away at trying to find a peaceful solution to the problem. There were pockets of unrest all over the country in 1920, but this came to a head when the British army sent a regiment called the Black and

Tans to keep order in Ireland. By now there was no Irish support for the British government, after they sent in these soldiers. It was believed that many of that group of soldiers were recruited from the overcrowded jails of England and the Irish people were furious when they were let loose on the streets of Ireland. The Black and Tans became the most hated regiment ever to set foot in any country. They were indiscriminate in their actions and what the British government did not expect was that many in that regiment had no moral code whatsoever. Bridie told Rosita about one of her friends who had a market garden in Cork. On market day they sold their produce in Queenstown. When they returned to the city, having sold their produce, the family had to hide most of their profits in the shoes and in the pockets of their young nine-year-old son to ensure they weren't robbed by the Black and Tans. When the train arrived at the Glanmire Road station, they would be met by Black and Tans and regularly searched. All the soldiers were doing was robbing their money and it was nothing to do with finding criminals. Yet the authorities seemed to turn a blind eye to this and usually refused to do anything about it. Rosita was shocked by this lack of law and order and knew it would only escalate, until the issue of full independence was resolved.

Rosita was now friends with many people who were trying to achieve independence. Her introductions to those such as Michael Collins and Eamon de Valera were made through Aidan, whose closeness to the Catholic Church authorities meant that their circle of friends was quite diverse.

One morning in June 1920, Maeve entered the parlour where Rosita was sitting and handed her the *Irish Times*.

"You won't believe what I just heard. You know your friend Monica, whose husband you were disgusted with for with the treatment of Tom

Clarke during the rebellion. I heard people behind closed doors at the time saying that Michael Collins was incensed by his behaviour. The reason we haven't seen Monica around in recent years is that her husband was posted to Gorey to head up the police force there, probably because of the outrage at his actions in Dublin. Have a look at that report." Maeve pointed to the article. "It seems that two masked gunmen killed him in front of everyone in the main street in Gorey yesterday. The whole country is shocked and now afraid of further reprisals from the British." Maeve looked anxiously at Rosita who was now sitting shaking her head and looking every inch her age.

"You know, Maeve, I'm almost glad I'm old. I'm realising more and more that I have no answers to a lot of questions, even about myself. Am I Irish? Or am I British? Because I don't know anymore. My friends and acquaintances come from both sides of the divide and it doesn't feel comfortable being in the middle. I feel Irish. My father and grandfather and many previous generations were all born in Midleton. Monica must feel much the same, she being Catholic and him from the Anglican community. What a mess! Yet life will go on and atrocities will continue to take place and there is nothing we can do to stop it. You know fighting and wars are just all about power and you know what the biggest tragedy is? Each side in any conflict has a deep-seated belief that they are right! But I don't condone reprisals such as happened to Monica's husband yesterday. I know Michael Collins. He is an intelligent man who believes that Ireland should be free. I greatly admire that man but it doesn't sit well with me if he instigated that attack. But that is just my opinion." She continued to shake her head in despair.

The only thing that brought her satisfaction at that time was that their young maid Mary had finally crossed the Atlantic Ocean to marry her Jimmy who was successfully working as a car driver in New York. At least I made a positive change in two young people's lives, she thought, amidst all the discontent around the country. Thankfully, Mary's friend Kitty Malone from Capel Street, who was every bit as bubbly as Mary, had joined the household and her home continued to be a harmonious place for everyone.

Chapter Twenty-Four

It was the middle of November in 1920 that Kitty came to her parlour requesting a day off on the following Sunday. Rosita assured her it was fine but Kitty insisted on explaining.

"I met a very nice lad at the dance last Saturday night and he asked to meet me for the dance again this Saturday. But he also asked me to go with him on Sunday to the football match between Dublin and Tipperary in Croke Park and I agreed to meet him, if I could get the day off."

"Of course you can have the time off. Just let Mrs. Jordan know straight away. But I didn't realise that you enjoy going to see football games!"

"My mother said the same thing when I told her," Kitty said, laughing. "I don't like watching rough games but I do like Lorcan, the lad I met. He was a real gentleman and he walked me straight home to my front door last Saturday night and he didn't take any liberties with me." Kitty blushed as she saw the amused smile on Rosita's face.

"Well, I'm glad of that and, as it's so important to you, I'll put a little extra in your pay packet on Friday and you can treat yourself after the match." Rosita smiled to see the pleasure on Kitty's face. She was always delighted at the effect that just a small gesture of kindness had on people who had little means and depended on wages to cover their weekly expenses, with little left over for extras.

As Kitty continued to beam with delight, she again thanked Rosita profusely, before she returned to the kitchen to tell Mrs. Jordon of her good fortune.

Kitty's family lived in the ground-floor flat of a very tall house in Capel Street, with six other families occupying the upper floors. The Malone family had four rooms to themselves and their two daughters, and often their mother Esther rented out one room to get extra cash when times were tough. But, since Kitty had started working, she had done up the room and they now had a permanent lodger who added much-needed rent to the family earnings.

On the Saturday night Kitty left for the dance in high spirits. She had a great night out with Lorcan and told him about the extra money in her wages.

"We can maybe get fish and chips on the way home from the match tomorrow!" she said.

It was half past ten that night when she arrived back home from the dance. Her mother was waiting, hoping the night had gone well.

"You're looking very perky, love. Was it a good night again tonight?" Ester asked as she smiled at her beloved daughter.

"It was brilliant, Mam, and he walked me home again. He didn't want to meet you now as he thought it was too late and he wouldn't wish to intrude on the family. He really is a nice fella and I can't wait to go with him to see the match in Croke Park. He said he'd like to meet you when he calls tomorrow."

"He's welcome!"

"But be nice to him, Mam!" Kitty warned, eyes shining, and her mother let out a roar of laughter.

"Well, he must be very special for you to agree to waste a day off on a Sunday watching a game of football!" Esther said.

"Well, he was talking so much about it that I had to pretend I loved sport in the hope I'd see him again. So don't tell him I don't when he calls to collect me."

"Don't worry. My lips are sealed."

"I can't wait for you to meet him!" Kitty said, with the excitement of youth in her voice.

"I'll be very nice to him, but don't go breaking this young lad's heart and then leaving him in a few weeks, like you did with that last lad who tried to court you."

"Sure, I've only just met Lorcan, but I think he could last longer," Kitty said cheekily, as she picked up a slice of buttered bread from the table, before announcing that she was off to bed and she'd see her mother in the morning.

The following day, Lorcan Burke, a young car mechanic from Dorset Street walked to Capel Street to meet Kitty. He had a spring in his step because he had been going to the match alone and was delighted that a good-looking young lass was going to be on his arm at the game.

After her mother chatted to him at the door, she nodded her approval to Kitty, who was dressed in the new coat she had bought in McBirney's on Aston Quay, having saved for ages before she could afford it.

The two linked arms as they crossed the road to Rutland Square. They noticed a lot of army activity as they continued on their way to Croke Park. As they came down the hill, with the grounds in view, they were surprised at the number of Royal Irish Constabulary and auxiliaries that were milling around the place. As they approached Jones

Road where Croke Park was situated, truckloads of Black and Tans were trundling past them.

"I don't know what that lot are doing around here today but I have nothing much of value for them to steal, if they search me," said Lorcan. "I have a friend from work who goes to the boxing club and he tells me that the fellow in charge there is called Major Dudley. He is one of the top brass of the Black and Tans. My friend tells me that he's a nutcase. He's been all over the world with the army and apparently he'll kill anything that gets in his way. He's a boxer and if he's in a temper you'd need to keep out of his way. I never saw him myself, though."

By now Kitty was tightly clutching his arm and, as they neared the park gates and the ticket sellers, she began to feel sick in her stomach on seeing the hundreds of people milling around and the strong army presence.

As Lorcan was about to pay for the tickets, she pulled him back.

"Lorcan, I'm sorry. I'm not used to these kinds of crowds and seeing all these soldiers. I am not going to spoil your day, but I'd rather go back into town and maybe I'll see you later around tea time and we can go for our fish and chips?" She looked at him appealingly, hoping he'd understand.

"Ah, come on, Kitty!" he said, taken aback. "There's nothing to be scared of. I'll take care of you!"

She put up a hand to stop him. "Go and enjoy your match, please! Have fun and I'll see you later. I'm happy to walk back. It's not far. I'm sorry if I've upset you and I really want to see you later."

"Are you sure then, Kitty? I'll come right up to your house after the match and maybe we can go to another dance after our tea?"

"That's sounds grand, Lorcan," said Kitty, much relieved. "Go off now and enjoy your day and I hope Dublin win!"

She watched him buy the ticket and hurry to the turnstiles as it was getting late and he wanted a good place to watch the match. Then, as she turned around, she saw a couple of street vendors selling hot pies and cups of tea and she decided to treat herself before making her way home.

The hot pie tasted delicious and she sat on a wall, savouring its taste and enjoying the tea in a tin mug which she had to return to the man in the stall when she finished drinking from it. She was enjoying herself just watching the people go by, happy not to be in the middle of the large crowd, until suddenly she heard the trundling of another set of army trucks coming down the hill. They crossed over the road, with soldiers jumping out and heading, guns lifted, in the direction of the grounds. Kitty found herself rooted to the spot as she saw the ticket men running away and being chased by what she knew were Black and Tans. Bedlam ensued as some of the soldiers ran to the entrance to the grounds, screaming at the men to open the gates and let them in. By now she could hear the roar of the crowd as the match had started. She was numb with fear but she couldn't move, until suddenly she heard the sound of gunfire whereupon she dropped her tin cup and, even though her legs felt like jelly, ran across the road to the footpath on the other side, where she promptly got sick. She was leaning against the wall, hearing the sound of gunfire from the park, when a kindly old gentleman came up behind her and told her to come with him and he'd make sure she got home safe. She had never felt so grateful in her life as she did now and she grabbed on to the man's coat and began to run with him up the hill. When they got to Russell Square, they stopped to catch their breath. The man told her that he had started to run after he saw a boy who was watching the match from a tree being hit by a bullet and slumping to the ground.

As the horrified pair walked back down towards Capel Street, the man kept calling the Black and Tans all the expletives in the world that he knew. "*The British will rue this day!*" he kept saying over and over again, until he left Kitty at her home, where her mother folded her in her arms as she promised the gentleman that she would go down to the church and light a candle for him at first light on Monday morning.

Lorcan had got himself a good vantage point in the grounds. The people beside him were talking about what had supposedly happened that morning – a big operation had been carried out by the Republicans – British spies had been shot in their beds at dawn and the authorities were incensed. Lorcan now understood why so many military men were around outside the grounds.

Then the match started and he was soon enjoying the excitement, with the goalkeeper making two great saves early in the game.

Suddenly he heard the sound of gunfire and turned to see a boy perched on a tree to see the game slump over. A wave of tension swept through the crowd. As people heard more shots, they began to dash towards the exits but, to their horror, they were prevented from leaving by the army, who insisted they stay inside in order to be searched. Men, women and children began to panic as more shots were fired. By now people were piling up on top of each other by the exits in their efforts to leave, believing that they were about to be killed.

At this point, Lorcan had moved towards the pitch, hoping it would be safer there. Then suddenly he heard shots and watched in horror as a player in a Tipperary jersey slumped to the ground in front of him. As a teammate rushed to help him, Lorcan saw another spate of bullets hit the ground just beyond them. Lorcan froze as shots now appeared to be coming from every direction and he could see more and more people stampeding for the exits and swarming over others who were lying on the ground. Then he heard crying nearby and saw a young boy, about twelve years old, lying down with his cap in his hands. Lorcan knelt beside him and asked if he was alone.

"Me dad's lost in the crowd! I was afraid and ran over here."

Lorcan knew where the dressing rooms were. He grabbed the arm of the boy, put an arm around him and told him they were going to run. He shielded the boy as best he could as they ran. When they arrived safely at the entrance to the dressing rooms, Lorcan pushed his way in with the boy. There seemed to be close to a hundred petrified people inside, with many children crying and wailing. Thank goodness we're safe in here, Lorcan thought as the young boy continued to cry by his side. There were injured people on the ground and a priest seemed to be giving the last rites. What felt like an eternity was followed by a sudden quietness as the gunfire ceased.

Then a soldier holding a gun burst into the dressing rooms and went straight up to the priest whom Lorcan realised was Monsignor Browne, a close friend of some of the Tipperary players, and stuck a gun into his face.

As shock set in again for everyone, the soldier lifted the gun above the head of the Monsignor and fired a bullet into the ceiling, calling out "*We have avenged our fallen comrades!*" Lorcan then knew that this was about the morning killings that the spectators had been talking about earlier.

The soldier then turned back to face the crowd, telling them all to put their hands up. He marched them all out onto the pitch where Lorcan could hear a senior army officer shouting a warning that no more guns were to be fired. As Lorcan stood close to the boy, trying to comfort him, he realised that they were some of the lucky ones. As he continued to stand with his arms held in the air, he said a prayer of thanks that his life and that of the people by his side had been spared.

The next few hours were an agony. They were held with arms still lifted above their heads as they were all searched. But no guns or weapons of any kind were found on anyone. When they were finally told to go home, darkness had fallen. As Lorcan crossed the field with the boy still clinging to his hand, they saw a sight that they should never have witnessed in a lifetime. The body of the slain Tipperary footballer was still lying on the playing pitch in a pool of blood.

Lorcan walked the boy to his home in nearby Drumcondra Road, where his grateful mother was cleaning blood from the boy's father who had got crushed in the crowd while trying to find his young son. Lorcan left the by now very happy and relieved family and made his way down to Capel Street to Kitty's home. It was now nearly nine in the evening and when he knocked at the door it was opened by Esther. She didn't invite him in but gently told him that Kitty was asleep but that she was in no fit state to talk to anyone.

"She heard the first shots being fired and was so terrified she needed help to get home."

"I'm so sorry, Mrs. Malone, I never expected this to happen."

As she put an arm around the shoulders of the exhausted young man, who seemed to have aged in just half a day, she looked him in the eye and said, "I think, Lorcan, it would be best if you went home for tonight and let Kitty see how she feels in the next few days."

Lorcan nodded his head as he turned away for fear his tears would be witnessed. He had liked Kitty but now it could be over even before it had begun. I hope we're not like ships that pass in the night, never to see each other again, he thought as, head bowed, he set out for the safety his own home. Ten minutes, he thought, that's how long the shooting took, just ten minutes and yet that ten minutes had changed the lives of so many people.

During that dark night, a curfew was placed over Dublin. Trains didn't run and people stayed off the streets.

The following morning, Kitty didn't turn up for work, and Rosita was worried as she knew about everything that had happened the previous day.

At ten o'clock there was a knock at the front door and a few moments later, Mrs. Jordon appeared in the parlour and introduced the lady by her side.

"This is Kitty's mother and she just wants a word with you."

"I'm sorry to disturb you, Lady Beconsford," the woman blurted out, "but my Kitty is still in bed this morning. Thankfully, she didn't go into the match yesterday, but she heard the first shots being fired outside the grounds and she is still in deep shock."

As the story of Kitty's ordeal came to an end, Rosita was horrified. She assured Mrs. Malone that Kitty must be given time to recover.

"I'm so sorry to hear that she got caught up in it all. Mrs. Malone, please tell her to stay at home and see how she feels by next week. I'll give you her wages for next Friday now and tell her to come in only when she feels ready. Shock can sometimes be worse than a physical illness, so warn her to take things easy for a while."

A deeply grateful Mrs. Malone was in tears as she expressed her thanks and left.

Over the following few days, it was established that fourteen people had been killed, including three children, and dozens wounded. It was the bloodiest Sunday ever seen in Ireland and was starkly written and rewritten about in all the newspapers.

It was late Wednesday night before Rosita heard the details of the mayhem that had taken place early on Sunday morning, some seven hours before Tipperary and Dublin kicked off in their infamous football match at Croke Park.

Aidan came to the house and told her what had happened. She was deeply distressed as the story unfolded.

"It's difficult yet to get the full facts, but last night I met with a lawyer friend who is close to the British authorities and this afternoon I sat with a man who was involved with the Republicans on Sunday and who asked me to recommend a sympathetic lawyer to him, who maybe had Republican leanings. The stories I heard from both sides shocked me. Apparently a planned execution of British spies, who were officially known as the Dublin District Special Branch (DDSB) and also as D Branch, was organised by Michael Collins. Early on Sunday morning a group of men from the Dublin brigade of the Irish Republican Army and 'The Squad' met near Sackville Street, from where they travelled via the docks by rowing boat to the south side of the river. At the corner of Westland Row, they met with more comrades. Most people in the city were still in their beds and the authorities were not patrolling at that time. The message given to all the men was the same. They were to eliminate all British spies, intelligence officers and agents of the British Crown, who were staying in the city. The man I spoke to today was attached to the first group who were sent to a house close by in Upper Mount Street. When the door was opened by a maid, they asked where Lieutenants Peter Ames and George Bennett were sleeping. Although Ames' room was locked, they entered through open folded doors at the rear. They took the two men to the back bedroom and one of the volunteers whispered, '*The Lord have mercy on your souls*', as he shot both men dead. It seems that those Republicans were lucky to make their getaway, because they were met with gunfire that hailed from across the street when they left the house. The man I talked to assured me that he did not fire any shots. Later, most of those involved in the Upper Mount Street attack got safely back to their homes. The intriguing part is that it appears that one of the men in the group was going home to get ready to play in the football game in Croke Park in the afternoon."

"Are you telling me that one of the Republicans who played in the football match later had earlier been involved in the murder of two men?" a shocked Rosita said, finding it all hard to take in. She was finding it very hard to grapple with the craziness of the entire day.

As Aidan resumed his story, she continued to shake her head in disbelief.

"At much the same time as these men were being shot, all around the city of Dublin knocks came on doors, in lodging houses, hotels and peoples' homes. At each house single and even double killings occurred. These men from the British secret police, who had been sent over by London, were shot and murdered in their beds. Fourteen British agents were shot dead and only seven of them escaped. It seems that it was a well-planned attack and the police and authorities in Dublin Castle were unprepared. They were seething with rage that such atrocities could have happened right under their noses and I believe that some of them were out for revenge. It appears also that some of the Republicans weren't properly prepared to carry out the killings as they were not seasoned assassins."

Aidan saw how upset Rosita looked and realised that she had heard enough for one day.

As he held her close, while telling her to stay safe, he knew that this story was going to play out for a long time more.

He was right. It was later discovered that the British forces had been thrown into a panic late on Sunday morning. They had shut down Dublin Castle, as families of those working for the British in Dublin banged on the locked doors, looking for somewhere to hide. Even the Lord Mayor of Dublin requested protection. As chaos reigned in the city, the police also took over the Mansion House, the seat of the unofficial Irish parliament. The heightened state of tension in the city on that day must surely have contributed to the chaotic events that unfolded later in Croke Park.

As a result of the British attack on the crowds and the players at the football match fourteen died, including three children. The police had fired 114 rounds of rifle ammunition, while 50 rounds were fired from an armoured car outside the Park. Another forty people were injured but a far greater number of people were mentally scarred on that dark day.

A little over a week later, Rosita heard on good authority through her contacts, that the story first told by the British that the attack in Croke Park was started by Republicans was false. A report written by Major EL Mills immediately after the events on Sunday night said there were no shots fired in the ground before the police opened fire. The responsibility for that fell mainly on the shoulders of Major George Vernon Dudley who was in charge of the Black and Tans. It seems that a plainclothes Black and Tan soldier, Ronald Knight, was so incensed by the early morning killings that when he entered Croke Park, he opened fire on a group of men.

Rosita learned also that a difficult meeting took place as early as Monday in London between Winston Churchill and Henry Wilson, chief of the Imperial General Staff. Churchill had been dismissive of the spies who were shot by the Republicans and that enraged Henry Wilson. Churchill had stated that they were sloppy and badly trained to allow themselves be ambushed so easily. Wilson already knew that neither Churchill nor Lloyd George, the Prime Minister, had any belief that spies were important in this type of warfare. A furious Henry Wilson appears to have retorted that Britain was not governing Ireland at all and that they were leaving it to the Black and Tans to do the governing and now look where that had got them.

Rosita knew by the end of that week that much of the world had by now lost all respect for Britain's handling of the Irish situation but she also felt that the Republicans had too much blood on their hands. It was an open secret in Tipperary that there was a constant cat-and-mouse game played between some football players in the region and the British army. The army even played petty games to provoke the locals, whom they thought were gunrunning. One of the Tipperary player's football boots were thrown out the window of the train in which the team were going to Dublin for the match and the player was unable to play. But Rosita had expected that a moral duty should have restrained the legitimate army of Britain from disgracing themselves by firing into a crowd of innocent bystanders at a match. Her own brother Louis would have been deeply shamed by their behaviour on that day.

She knew that it was only a matter of time before full independence became a reality for Ireland. The use of such force by the legitimate British army, that had been respected around the world due to its recent stance on fighting a war to safeguard small nations against the might of Germany, had now literally shot itself in the foot. By murdering fourteen people attending a football match, including the Tipperary player Michael Hogan, they had brought shame to their front door. Three of those murdered were just children: Jerome O'Leary, aged ten, Perry Robinson, aged eleven, and Billy Scott, aged fourteen. On that truly bloody Sunday in Dublin, the people knew that a line had been crossed.

Withdrawal from Ireland now seemed inevitable as the British were sick to the teeth of the trouble that Ireland was causing it, especially so soon after losing so many of their own young men in the war in Europe. Talks began to take place in Britain that were emphatically rejected by the Ulster Protestant community.

Rosita listened to the news of the final talks, where her friend Michael Collins was one of the leading figures, and was pleased when an agreement was reached to give a new Status of 'Free State' to twenty-six counties of Ireland with the six northern counties choosing to remain part of Britain and ruled by the parliament in London. She knew it was a compromise but that Michael Collins was intelligent enough to realise that would have to do for now. Yet she knew also that Eamon de Valera would not view it quite the same way. She was delighted at the outcome but with more hope than expectation that the new Ireland could live in peaceful times from now on.

Chapter Twenty-Five

As time passed Rosita wondered if it were ever possible to come to an agreement on any territory that was changing hands and expect it to be accepted in good faith by everyone involved. Within months of the London agreement, splits and cracks began to appear in the newly independent Ireland. What was by now being called a Civil War began at the end of June in 1922 and it caused turmoil in this fledging nation. Those who wanted a thirty-two-county Ireland were taking up arms against their own people. Brothers had differences even inside their families and tensions arose between the new government and the Republican army spurred on by Eamon de Valera, who disagreed with Michael Collins' compromise.

It was August 1922 before Rosita finally left Dublin, with Jackson driving, to make her long-awaited trip to Cork to remove her sentimental possessions from the Beconsford Estate. The estate was now being run by Neill Patterson, a son-in-law of the now elderly Jody, but the Big House was all but closed up as Giles Beconsford had decided that he didn't want to spend money on staff wages and was apparently considering renting the house to a rich County Cork gentleman. When she visited the house, she took most of the possessions that held memories for her to Bridie's farm in Midleton.

She later enjoyed lunch with Bridie and Cormac, intending to later go to Cork city to see her friends there.

After they'd eaten, Bridie was the first to leave the table. "I'm off to town to get some knitting wool that I ordered, so enjoy yourself in Cork and I'm looking forward to meeting you in the Imperial Hotel in a few days. I can't wait for my night in that grand hotel!" Bridie was laughing as she went out.

Rosita was about to leave the table when Cormac put a hand on her arm and asked her to hang on for a while, as he wanted to talk to her.

"Aunt Rosita, I'm worried for your safety while you're in Cork."

Rosita stopped him by patting his hand. "Don't worry about me, Cormac. I'm an old lady and I don't worry about my own safety. You're sounding like Aidan who is always at me to be careful – but I don't take any notice of him either." She smiled reassuringly at him.

"But you don't seem to understand what horrendous acts of savagery are being carried out, especially in West Cork. Aunt Rosita, I'm just going to give you one example to make you understand why I'm worried. You're the daughter of a British Lord and a Protestant and that seems to be enough for some nationalist elements in the county. Did Aidan talk to you about Dunmanway? I wrote to him to try and discourage you from coming down at this time."

"He tried to tell me but I wouldn't let him – I wasn't going to let anything stop me moving around my own country and especially my own county of Cork!"

"Well, I'm telling you now because I heard it from someone in the know, who lives in Dunmanway. It happened when we had a truce, after the War of Independence. At the end of last April, before the recent civil war broke out, there were about a dozen men murdered. Over a couple of days Republicans killed six men they believed were British informers or loyalists. But they didn't stop there. They also murdered four of those people's relatives. Those men had one thing in common: they were all Protestants. I don't want anything happening to you. I know you're a good person and I also realise that I can't make you do anything that you don't want. I know how independent you are. I can only put the facts to you."

"Cormac, I appreciate that you care so much, but I've lived through a World War, an Easter Rising, a War of Independence, an Irish Free State, and now a civil war. I'm not a fool, Cormac, and I won't walk into trouble deliberately. I have Catholic, Protestant, Irish Nationalist and British friends and I'll continue to enjoy the company of them all as long as I have the energy to leave my home. Until then, I will not change. Now, Cormac, I believe that my driver Jackson will arrive shortly to take me to the city, so I'll have to leave you. But thanks for caring." She rose to her feet and ruffled the hair of the grown man by her side. He shook his head in resignation.

In Cork city, she spent a wonderful night at the home of her great friends, the Perrotts, where their choice of guests was always a delight. She made the acquaintance of Walter and Clare Dwyer with whom her own family had done business in the past. They were accompanied by their son William who was a charming storyteller who regaled the guests with gossip about the upper-class Merchant Princes, as they were known in Cork. As ever, the Perrott family had invited good musicians and Rosita spent the evening relaxing to the expert piano-playing of Aloys

Fleischmann who accompanied other guests who could hold a tune. The evening reminded her of the dinner parties held by her grandfather Isaac in the Big House when she was young. This evening with old and new friends was a lovely reminder of her own family's past.

The following night she spent with her friend, Jennifer McNally, who was now housebound with arthritis. That was another journey of reminiscences and by the following day she was ready for a relaxing evening at the Imperial Hotel where herself and Bridie would dine and sleep.

Rosita left Jennifer's house early the following evening to meet up with Bridie. As Jackson drew up on the South Mall in front of the Imperial Hotel, the sun was beginning to set, casting shadows on the road as she stepped from the car. She thanked him and said she would be ready to leave around noon on the following day. She turned around and smiled as she looked at the façade of the historic hotel. She loved the various windows facing the street and remembered looking through them as a child, when she would watch the expensive carriages stop and allow their elegant ladies and top-hatted gentleman alight to enjoy the delights of the hotel.

On the steps she was greeted by the porter who recognised her and swiftly stepped forward to take her luggage from Jackson.

"I'll deposit your luggage in your bedroom immediately, my lady," he said, as he whisked the luggage from beside the car.

Having thanked the porter and waved at Jackson, she entered the hotel. As she walked towards the staircase, she smiled with delight as a face that she saw infrequently smiled broadly back at her.

"Are you leaving because I've arrived, Mr. Collins?" she asked, as the man whom she greatly admired walked towards her.

"How are you, Miss Beconsford?" he said, holding his hand out to greet her.

"Michael, it's a lovely surprise to meet you here! I'm sure you don't spend much time in Cork since you are running the affairs of the Irish State?"

"You know I haven't lost my feelings for the place of my birth and I believe you too still love returning to our dear county."

"I'm meeting Bridie Saunders to catch up on the goings-on around the county so, if you would care to join us for a drink, we'd be delighted." Rosita smiled at the handsome man by her side.

"I'm sorry but my work commitments will keep me in my bedroom for much of the evening," Michael said apologetically. "I have to prepare letters for dispatch notes to Dublin, in particular to the Finance Department, and I have a six o'clock start tomorrow morning. I'm off to West Cork tomorrow. But, please send my regards to Cormac. He's a good lad and Bridie's family should be proud of him. By the way, I met the rising portrait artist Caroline Donfield with her daughter Meibh recently when I was in County Meath and she said that she hasn't seen you for quite a while."

"That is correct but, if you see her again, tell her that I'm now a very old lady and that most of my social outings in Dublin are made primarily to the new premises of the United Arts Club in Fitzwilliam Street. It's just across the road from my home. Please tell her that's where she can find me, if I'm not at home. I have two of Caroline's magnificent paintings in the hallway of my home and would love to commission another one from her."

As a smiling Michael assured her that he would pass on the message, he joked that Rosita didn't act like a very old lady!

As he bade her farewell. Rosita took his hand and squeezed it gently, affirming her support for this multifaceted handsome young man and the good job he was doing for his country.

"I'll tell Cormac what you said about him and good luck with your work because it is not easy. Being Chairman of the Provisional Government of the Irish Free State is an onerous job. I just hope that in time the whole country comes to respect your decisions. I believe you were correct with regards the settlement you agreed to and I hope I live long enough to see the day when the whole of Ireland is truly at peace."

"Thank you for that, Rosita, but I must leave you now as there is much done but still much more to do. Farewell, my friend."

Rosita entered the dining room and was greeted by an excited Bridie.

"I saw who you were talking to and I don't know how you could stand there without swooning over such a handsome man!"

Both of them laughed and Rosita replied with a grin, "Perhaps if I was about sixty years younger I might have, but all I can now do is admire his ability to change from a rebellious boy to an excellent statesman. Now let us not even start to speak about the political situation in the country – let's just talk about our family and friends!"

"Yes, let's! My room is beautiful, Rosita," she said as they walked up the elegant staircase to their bedrooms. "Thank you so much for inviting me to stay. It's like being on holidays and I felt like a proper toff when I arrived and they asked me if I was Lady Beconsford's guest. They were all bowing and scraping in front of me!"

A long and enjoyable dinner filled with news and gossip from around Midleton was followed by the hot chocolate drinks that Rosita still loved since childhood.

The following morning, they enjoyed a late breakfast together before leaving the hotel when Jackson arrived at twelve o'clock. As they drove towards the farmhouse in Midleton, Rosita was looking forward to spending a few quiet days in the countryside, eating, sleeping and reading her favourite books, before returning to Dublin.

"I'm getting too old to be travelling so much and I'm looking forward to resting over the next few days," she said, as they set out on the road to East Cork.

"Well, myself and Cormac can't wait for the chance to pamper you. Goodness knows, you've done enough for our family in the past," Bridie said, noticing that Rosita was looking a bit worn out.

Rosita knew that she also needed to carefully pack up the mementos that she had taken from the two houses of the estate, which were now in Bridie's home. The following day she planned to call to say one final farewell to the home of her birth and she just wanted to be alone there without any of her family present. When she had visited there earlier in the week, she felt that it looked shabbier than she remembered it and she knew that it no longer had the feeling of being a home, as the staff had left. But Neill, the estate manager had been there to help her and she spent only two hours before she left, promising herself that she'd also go and sit in the Secret Garden before returning to Dublin.

When Rosita and Bridie got back to the house, Cormac already had a dinner prepared with the help of his stepfather Thomas, who since he was a young man had always been able to cook meals. He had learned how to make appetising dishes when he minded his young brothers, back when he was only a lad himself. The meal was delicious and Rosita again began to feel more relaxed. Having eaten, she happily retired to the small cosy guest bedroom in the farmhouse. I'm glad I came, she thought, because I needed to see the place of my birth just one more time. She truly believed that for a British lord or lady to expect to live as they did in the past in this new Irish Free State was not likely to be an option and she had no regrets that she would never stay in the Big House again.

Before she allowed sleep to take her, she said a prayer for the Irish people. She knew that behind all the smiles of Michael Collins today he must be saddened that with the effort made by so many people to secure independence, he had to contend with Irishmen now fighting each other. She prayed that this internal bickering that was costing too many lives and the destruction of property would end soon. As she finished her prayer, she fell into a deep sleep.

At the first light of day, she was woken by Bridie, who was already sitting by her bed. But she hadn't brought the usual breakfast tray. Bridie continued to sit there as Rosita lifted herself up. Bridie then put a soft pillow at Rosita's back and gently took her hand.

"I have some really bad news for you, Rosita. Don't worry, it's not to do with any of your family, but I want you to brace yourself. I knew about this in the early hours of the morning, when Cormac came to my bedroom and told me, but I decided not to wake you. I am so sorry to have to tell you this. Michael Collins, that beautiful man that you met only the night before last, was shot yesterday evening while he was in West Cork, being driven through Béal na mBlath, just thirty miles from the place of his birth. It was an ambush. It happened at eight thirty in the evening and I'm so sorry to have to give you this news. Michael died of his injuries. I know how much you admired him and so did I. Cormac is distraught and wants to go out and kill whoever did it."

Rosita was stunned. As she endeavoured to get out of the bed, she realised that her legs would buckle if she did. What followed was one of the few times she ever lost her composure except in the privacy of her own home. Within seconds, her tears started to flow and wouldn't stop. Bridie put her arms around her until her weeping stopped and she again lay back down on the bed and closed her eyes. She was recalling her prayer for peace last evening and thought how naive she had been.

As Bridie continued to comfort her, she began to talk. "I prayed last night for an end to this stupid civil unrest and instead it has now taken the life of a great man. I despise man's inhumanity to man. Who did this to him?"

"Nobody seems to know yet but I'm sure they'll find the killer soon. It was one of the other side, love, the men who want the whole island of Ireland free from Britain."

"What you really mean is it was another Irishman and probably another Corkman who did this to him! I thought when the Easter Rising and later the Great War ended in 1918 that we'd seen the last of senseless killing. I now know that I was wrong and that I was stupid to think so. I truly do not know what the world is coming to and I'm now nearly glad that I'm not going to be around for much longer."

"Don't talk like that, love. Why don't you get dressed and we'll go down the town because I think there will be some sort of public prayers said for the repose of his soul. There's nothing else you can do about it."

Rosita looked at Bridie and suddenly announced: "Can you help me pack the stuff from the estate house and after breakfast could Cormac go to the Haven Inn and fetch Jackson. Tell him that I want him to take me back to Dublin as soon as possible, I don't want to meet anyone in this wretched county today. I want to be alone with my thoughts and I want to return to my home in Dublin to be with Charles, Aidan and Maeve."

Bridie understood and left the room immediately. In fact, she was glad Rosita was leaving, as she had nearly forgotten the fact that for those in the town who knew nothing about her might in some warped way try to blame her for being a daughter of a British Lord. As she helped Rosita to pack, she shook her head, realising that nothing in life was simple. Rosita had always been strong-willed, she thought, and no one is going to change her now. I just hope they find the killer who perpetrated this dreadful act of revenge on someone whose pragmatic decisions had caused a rift in Ireland such as she had never expected to see in her lifetime. Irishmen killing other Irishmen. What a tragedy, she thought. As she arranged for Rosita's departure, she just prayed that such an atrocity would never happen again.

It was afternoon before Rosita finally left the county. She had a telephone call made on her behalf to family friends in Durrow in County Laois. In order to break the journey back to Dublin for her, they were delighted to have her stay the night in their home.

As the car drove through Tipperary, Rosita recalled with a shudder that their friends in the Carden Estate had their home maliciously burnt down just a year before and most of them had by now returned to England.

By early evening on the following day, Rosita was glad to be back at her own comfortable home in Dublin. Maeve was waiting for her with open arms, knowing the hurt felt by her friend and employer. Kitty, who was back to being her old bubbly self, was there also, running around sorting Rosita's suitcase and trunks which the driver had brought in, but nothing would stop her gabbling on about the death of Michael Collins.

"I'm so sorry, Lady Rosita," she said again. "I know he was a friend of yours. My dad didn't like him much because he loves De Valera. But even he's upset and says that Michael Collins didn't deserve to be murdered. Sorry if I'm going on a bit but people are talking about nothing else all day but –" Kitty broke off when Maeve gave her the severe stare that she used in the past to quieten disruptive schoolchildren in America. "Sorry, I'll get on with my work unless there's anything I can do for you at all?"

"Would you carry the rest of Lady Beconsford's bags to her room and then come back and help Mrs. Jordan make dinner?" Maeve told her.

As Kitty went to carry some of the luggage up the stairs, Mrs. Jordan called Maeve aside and spoke quietly to her. "She's not stopped talking about him since it happened. I'll try to keep her away from you and Miss Rosita. As you asked, I rang Mr. Dermody and Charles. They will arrive here shortly and I'll have dinner prepared for eight o'clock. In the meantime, I can prepare sandwiches and coffee for her ladyship, if she's hungry."

Maeve thanked her and, with that settled, she went and asked Rosita if she'd prefer to rest for a while or have something to eat.

"I'll lie down first," Rosita said wearily. "I'm exhausted and just need to rest and then maybe I'll be able to think more clearly."

Maeve saw tears glistening in Rosita's eyes as she put an arm around her and escorted her up to her favourite room on the first floor, overlooking the tree-lined square beyond, where Rosita normally loved to sit and read, while watching the residents walking in the park. Maeve settled her on her favourite chaise longue and put a blanket over her, before leaving her to rest.

In the recent past Rosita usually felt a warm sense of time passing in a certain mundane and comforting way while in this room, but the happenings of the past few days had disturbed her deeply.

Later, feeling more refreshed after sleeping for a short while, she felt hungry. Shortly after she rang the bell that was connected to the kitchen, Maeve arrived with her favourite cheese and tomato inside hot toasted bread plus her favourite scones. The two ladies spent a few quiet moments, each alone with her own thoughts, as they ate.

Then Maeve broached a subject that had been on her mind.

"I need to ask you, Rosita, if you are going to attend any part of the funeral procession of Mr. Collins? I know that Aidan will be in the church for the Mass."

"I absolutely am not. I've had enough grief in my life and I refuse to publicly expose myself shedding tears. Also, I think my presence would offend many Irish people at this time. After all, it will be a Catholic funeral and regardless of my support for Irish freedom, I know that I wouldn't be welcome. I'm too close to the British for them to actually like me."

"Don't say that, Rosita – you've done a lot of good things during your lifetime!"

"That may be so, but I'm not attending any part of the funeral. I will read all about it in the days that follow, in the *Irish Times*."

"I'd been thinking that you might like to see the cortege pass by and we have many friends whose upstairs windows face the area where, I believe, it will be travelling. However, I understand your reluctance, but I have your *Irish Times* today and it has reported all the details of the ambush that cost him his life and the opinions from around the world."

Rosita shook her head, indicating that she didn't want to hear the distressing details at the moment.

Later, when Aidan and Charles arrived, they agreed that it was a killing too far in this miserable civil war. Indeed, men on both sides in the conflict were mourning him, as he had been their much-loved comrade for a long time.

For Rosita, the next seven days passed in a haze. She knew all about the funeral with the extensive coverage in the *Irish Times* but especially from Kitty who dealt with the event as if it was something exciting, especially with half a million people thronging the street of the capital, whether expressing their grief, or just to be part of something unique that seemed in a peculiar way to have united the whole country, at least for a day. Aidan talked her through the emotional experience of the church service and the poignant atmosphere at Glasnevin cemetery as the body of Michael Collins reached its final resting place. As the oak coffin, draped in the green, white and orange of the new Ireland and bearing a single white lily, was lowered into the ground, grown men wept openly. Tears of loss, despair and with many hoping that this act of treachery by another Irishman would stop the civil unrest that was beginning to shatter the lives of too many Irish families.

Rosita then shed her tears in the comforting arms of Aidan. It seemed that everywhere in the world where Irishmen and women had emigrated, they too were consumed by grief at this tragedy.

Chapter Twenty-Six

The paradox of the tragic death of Michael Collins was that the Irish people began to heal and the tragedy and horror of the civil war came very slowly to an end. As autumn turned into winter, word got to Rosita that tensions in and around Cork were high, with many people perceived as being linked to England through birth or religion becoming targets for violence. Reading Bridie's letters, Rosita realised that the anger of some pockets of Irishmen in and around her native Cork seemed to escalate when the civil war ended. It seemed that men with guns were prepared to shift their anger elsewhere. Although it was mainly against ex police constables and the English landlords, sadly ordinary Protestant people were perceived by some as being the enemy in Cork.

Rosita spent Christmas of 1922 in a quiet relaxed way in the company of her beloved Charles, Aidan and Maeve. In the new year she had occasional visits from relatives up from Cork, who called and took tea with her. The most important time she spent was with her Charles, who was by now a fully qualified architect. Ironically, a fact that put a smile on Rosita's face was that he was now part of a design team that drew up plans for the many new Catholic churches being built around the country to house the growing Catholic population.

As spring arrived, Rosita rarely ventured beyond Fitzwilliam Street. Holding the arm of either Maeve or Aidan, she continued to make the short journey to the United Arts Club that thankfully was so close to her home in Fitzwilliam Street. She felt privileged to spend her final years sitting in a welcoming environment with poets, playwrights, artists and musicians and it was frequented by many of her friends and acquaintances. It was such a wonderfully inclusive environment for both men and women, and thankfully had never been aligned to any religious or political views. It was a safe haven for all whose interests were creative. Rosita found it was a place where she could totally relax. She would sit in her favourite chair, and join in or not in discussions about whatever was the topic of the day. She was at her happiest listening to the sound of beautiful singing voices, accompanied by piano. It reminded her of her youth in Midleton listening to her Margarita, accompanied by Grandma Eliza or Master Johnson. Her heart pounded with pure joy as she recalled other nights of song and laughter with the Bohemians, especially the occasion when John McCormack joined them for dinner and sang "Machusla". How blessed she was to hear that man sing!

It was late spring before she returned to sit in the gardens in Fitzwilliam Square to watch the daffodils and spring roses blooming in their well-tended flower beds. She loved also looking up at the trees as they changed with every season. Although she loved their rich greenness in the summer months, she also enjoyed watching the golden autumn leaves flutter to the ground. Even in wintertime, seeing a clear blue sky through the barren tree trunks had, for her, its own beauty. It signalled that there was still light even in the darkness of winter. There she sat on sunny days, always with warm clothes and a blanket over her legs. It was also her chance to sit with eyes closed and imagine herself as a young girl back again in the Secret Garden. She felt in her bones that she would not have many more springs to watch the flowers bloom.

As summer approached, she was sitting in the square alone with her thoughts, when a quiet tap on her shoulder brought her out of her reverie. It was Maeve.

"Rosita, I need you to return home. Bridie's son Cormac is in the house and needs to talk to you."

"Has something happened – is Bridie sick?" she asked, alarmed, raising her creaking bones from the park bench.

"No, no, I don't believe anyone is sick, but he said he needs to see you urgently," Maeve said, already knowing that there was bad news waiting for Rosita.

As they entered the house, Cormac came forward and put his arms around his grand-aunt and held her tight for a moment before looking in her eyes.

"We need to sit down and talk," he said tenderly.

Maeve helped Rosita to take her coat and hat off, then escorted her to the parlour and settled her in her chair. Maeve stayed in the room, having told Kitty to bring a tea tray into the parlour. Maeve had also made telephone calls to Charles' office and Aidan's home, before turning her attention to taking care of Rosita.

"Please tell me what is wrong?" Rosita said impatiently.

There was an eerie uncomfortable silence in the room as Cormac pulled up a chair and sat facing Rosita.

"I have some really bad news, Aunt Rosita. It was late on the evening before last that a big group of men, who were not from around the town, arrived in the back of a large truck to Midleton. They then marched onto the Beconsford Estate grounds by breaking through the side gate. They confronted one of the farm hands and threatened him. He had to tell them that the house was shut up with no staff there as his lordship had fired them all. With that, they made their way to the house. A half a dozen of them stayed on lookout and those were believed to have guns with them. The others broke shutters and made their way inside. They then began to loot anything they were able to carry away. By the time the authorities arrived, and I believe they may have been very slow to react, possibly deliberately not viewing it as a priority but that is just my view, the men had made their getaway. By then all the damage had been done. Before leaving, they set fires inside the house and they were all well out of the townland before the firemen arrived. The looters had makeshift rope ladders to help them mount the estate wall and two trucks were waiting for them there, at the far side of the estate. It was almost like a military manoeuvre and by the time the firemen got their water lorry to the building, they were too late. The fire had taken hold and couldn't be quenched. Aunt Rosita, Beconsford House is gone. It is no more. It was burnt to the ground. Before I left in the early morning, I went to have a look. It's a sad sight to see and I'm not sure if you'll want to see it either."

He stopped talking as he saw the blood draining from his great-aunt's face. Maeve gave her water to drink. Rosita sat sipping the water for a long time as Cormac and Maeve wondered how she was going to react.

"I want to go down to Midleton to see it. We'll get Jackson to drive us tomorrow morning if that's all right with you, Cormac?"

"Oh, I'm not sure that's a good idea, Aunt Rosita!" Cormac protested.

"I'm going to get Mrs. Jordon to make dinner for everyone," Maeve said firmly. "Then, when we've eaten, we can have a further discussion on what's best for your health, Rosita. We'll wait to eat until Charles and Aidan come home. I called them both earlier."

They nodded in agreement and Maeve told Cormac that they would prepare a room for him, before she left to talk to Mrs. Jordan.

Throughout the rest of that day and evening everyone went about in a daze. When Charles and Aidan arrived, they too were shocked, although it didn't surprise Aidan.

It wasn't until dinner had been eaten that Rosita said anything. Then, as she spoke, there with a certain sense of bitterness in her tone towards Louis' family.

"That fool Giles Beconsford! He should never have shut down the house and put all the staff out of work. I believe some were even made to leave their homes on the estate. Now he's got his comeuppance because the people in the town have lost their respect for our family and it's obvious that they didn't even try to save the house. Now priceless family heirlooms and paintings will end up God knows where in the world. I don't wish for any discussion about whether or not I should go down to Cork. I'm going. I want to see my old home and stand on its soil for one last time and I don't want any of you coming with me. I have to do this alone because I won't ever be returning to Midleton again in my lifetime, but I do need to say my final goodbyes."

Charles and Aidan were stunned at her outburst and protested that they must accompany her.

"Nothing you say will change my mind, I want to go alone," Rosita said with an air of confidence in her voice that stopped the others from voicing any more of their opinions.

Cormac sat by and listened but he already knew that his Aunt Rosita would never shy away from confronting difficult situations that needed resolving. His Granny Alice had always said that about her.

Two days later, in the early afternoon, the sun shone brightly in the sky in spite of Rosita's mood as her car arrived at the gates of the Beconsford Estate. For Rosita, it would be the last time she drove through the long tree-lined entrance with its gravel roadway crunching under the wheels of the car. As the car turned to where the house had once stood proudly for almost two hundred years, Rosita asked Jackson to stop and allow her walk alone towards the front door of her old home.

Her eyes misted over as she walked with the aid of her stick, and looked at the charred and blackened front door, still sturdy but with its frame crumbling around it. The ghosts of Christmases past flooded her mind. In her head she could hear the laughter and excitement felt in the hallway when in the past Granny Deborah faithfully each year decorated a large fir tree. She remembered the presents stacked around it and each of the children lighting candles that were placed on the ground close by. Deborah had always said it was a family tradition, even before having Christmas trees became a general practice, and it happened there in good times and even bad. The memory of her own father Victor, who stayed alive long enough to see the faces of his three young children on Christmas Day before he died, came to the forefront of her mind. That Christmas still brought a stabbing pain to her heart more than seventy years later. Today she could not smell the pine of the tree even in her head as the air was filled with the pungent smoke from the charred timber despite its being doused with water.

She left the ruined house that she once called home and walked around the side, towards the Secret Garden. As she reached the entrance, her eyes lit up for a moment. The sign carved by Jack Ryan, back in the early eighteen-hundreds, still stood proudly above the entrance. *Deborah's Secret Garden*, it read. As she entered, she hoped that the garden would live on. Sitting in the sun house, she closed her eyes and could still smell the lilac that bloomed, first planted by Old John before he died during the Big Wind in 1839. Sadly, even this beautiful garden now looked neglected. Now, as she sat in the small sun house, she remembered everyone who loved the garden. She continued to sit alone, allowing tears to flow for the loss of the Big House. As she reflected in that safe place a calmness came over her. Perhaps it was a good thing that the house, built all these centuries ago by an English Lord, had now returned to its rightful place, within the soil of Ireland. She knew how much independence from Britain meant to the Irish. Yet she too was Irish. As she sat there, in her heart, she forgave the perpetrators, whoever they were.

When she finally left the garden, she made the short walk to the cemetery beside the estate church and said her final farewells to all of her family who rested there.

As she slowly began to make her way back to the waiting car, she wondered how the new heir was reacting to the news. Thankfully, he had not yet arrived in Ireland and for that she was grateful, as she had no inclination or heart to meet that young man. At this moment, whatever he thought, she decided that she did not really care. Louis' family chose to live their lives away from Ireland and she could only hope they would be good landlords to the many farmers who would work the land and forest in the future.

She didn't look back at the house again as she made her way across the lush lawn in front of it. She recalled her step-mama Margarita speaking often about looking up at the stars from that green space and thanking the fates for bringing love into all their lives.

An anxious Jackson watched her stop and look up at the sky before turning towards him. He was relieved to see that the indomitable woman he knew had a smile on her face.

Chapter Twenty-Seven

1924

It was early summer and Rosita had, much to Aidan's surprise and delight, returned from Midleton with quite a spring in her step. He had promised himself that when she returned from Cork he was going to spend all his time from then on with her. The now fully retired Aidan was glad he had organised to have Jackson at their disposal to drive them wherever they wanted to go.

Rosita seemed rejuvenated as they began taking these trips. They both loved Kingstown, where they often sat in the People's Park, with its fountains and flowers blooming, while the smell of the sea beyond filled their lungs with clean air. They also made regular trips through the heart of the Wicklow mountains, where every turn on the road brought new delights and panoramic views of the landscape. They would then usually enjoy the delicacies served in McGuirk's tea room, where they often met artists and writers they knew.

Late one evening, Rosita was reading the newspaper when she spotted an article about the stained-glass window specialist Mr. Harry Clarke. It appeared that one of his windows had been erected by Monica Ryan in memory of her murdered policeman husband in Christ Church in Gorey, County Wexford. The notion of that took her fancy, and she decided that she wanted to see it.

She read the article to Aidan, before announcing, "We're taking a trip to Gorey tomorrow. You know how interested I am in the lives of others. I would like to see this window with its inscription and dedication. I had thought that Monica might have been embarrassed by her husband's behaviour during the Easter Rising, but it seems I was wrong. Paradoxically, the window is a depiction of the martyr Saint Stephen. I'm sure there aren't many Irish people right now who would have seen her husband as anything but a devil and certainly not a martyr!"

"I would be interested in seeing it myself," Aidan replied. "I knew Monica well when she was a young woman. She was a fine-looking young Catholic girl when she married the English police officer. At the time it was a very unlikely alliance, but they seemed to have a happy marriage."

The following afternoon, having driven to Gorey, Rosita stood in awe reading the inscription on Monica's window in the church. She smiled to herself when she read the engraving. *Lay not this sin to their charge.* As she reflected on the words, she turned to Aidan.

"I wonder did Monica feel that, rather than being bitter at the life and death of her husband, perhaps forgiveness was necessary. I believe that's a good view to have. In my old age I'm beginning to realise that nobody is all good or all bad and that circumstances often dictate that bad deeds are part of the fabric of every warlike situation. Maybe we should all learn a lesson from her and be prepared to at least question why people do bad things and not just rush to judgment?"

Aidan smiled at her as he took her arm and they left the church. "Well, it is a depiction of Saint Stephen who was the first Christian martyr," he said, "but she also has the Wilson coat of arms, so she must have really loved him. I agree with you. She must also have understood the complexities of life in Ireland during its most troubled time. In yours and my lifetime, we've seen enough bad things happen in Ireland and yet, as time passes and people pass away, we tend to recall their good deeds with fondness and forget their past failures. It's a more compassionate view of human failings that I think we should all embrace. Maybe that was how Monica felt as she reflected after his death."

He smiled fondly at the lady whose views had often in the past been both forthright and uncompromising, She had now perhaps mellowed with age.

Chapter Twenty Eight

July 1926

Later that summer, as the afternoon sun was throwing its light over the trees in Fitzwilliam Square, Rosita was sitting with Maeve watching the world go by from her window above. She was still interested and opinionated about the women who walked below and the fashions they wore.

Aidan still came over every day for lunch and dinner, but their trips in the car had become too much for Rosita. She didn't cross the road to the United Arts club very often either, but each evening she loved to listen to Charles and a still sprightly Aidan who kept her up to date with the comings and goings around Dublin. She looked forward all day to those precious evenings.

Later they would both enjoy afternoon tea with delicate sandwiches and the little cakes still much loved by Rosita. Maeve, as she did each afternoon, read articles from that day's *Irish Times* because Rosita's eyesight did not allow her read small print anymore. She regularly interrupted Maeve whenever she disagreed with the opinion of the writer. It always amused her friend. Yet today, her employer and friend seemed quieter than was usual. When Maeve noticed that she had fallen asleep, she quietly left the room and returned to the kitchen. Later, when she returned to the room to tell Rosita that afternoon tea was on the way, she was still asleep. As Maeve walked towards her, there seemed to be a stillness in the room, apart from the gentle rhythmic ticking of the clock. With her heart now thumping in her chest, Maeve quickly reached out to Rosita. Although she looked peaceful, there was a change in her face and her head was to one side, as if still watching the world outside. But her eyes were closed.

Quickly, Maeve put her hand to Rosita's pulse. "*Rosita, Rosita, please, please, wake up!*" Panic was making her heart thump with shock. She could hear Mrs. Jordon rushing up the staircase, sensing the urgency in Maeve's voice.

But it was too late for either of them to do anything. Rosita Beconsford had passed away peacefully in her sleep, just as Maeve had hoped would happen.

Two days later, as the long cortege left Fitzwilliam Street for the short trip to the church in Mount Street, hundreds of mourners came to pay their respects. They all entered the church and listened to the Rector as he spoke of those who shaped Rosita's long life. He reminded the mourners of her Mama Fleur who had died on the day she was born, her beloved Papa Victor whom she dearly loved, her Step-mama Margarita, her beloved Grandpapa Isaac and Grandmama Deborah and Margarita's mama and papa, Jack and Eliza Ryan. He hoped that those she had left behind would on that day celebrate her long life. He also welcomed her Cork relatives and a myriad of friends from all walks of life, before she made her final journey to the cemetery. She had requested to be laid to rest in the city of Dublin, which she had called home for more than ten years. As the coffin was lowered into the ground, just one single rose, picked by Cormac from the Secret Garden in Midleton, was placed on top of the coffin by Charles, to give her an eternal memory of the place of her birth.

Later that evening, Charles, Aidan and Maeve held a very Irish wake in the United Arts Club, where singing and storytelling flowed until the early hours of the morning. Rosita Beconsford's long life was being truly celebrated with much joy and in a way that she would have loved.

Two days after the funeral, five people attended the offices of solicitors Hyde and Barber, a company of great reputation that had carefully looked after Rosita's interests for many years. Those invited were her dearest friends Aidan and Maeve, her grandson Charles, and Giles and Nigel, the two sons of her brother Louis. Immediately after Charles entered the room, Giles Beconsford rudely asked what the hell this man was doing at the reading of his aunt's will. Mr Hyde assured him that everything would become clear as soon as they had all been properly introduced. Mr. Hyde was accompanied by his assistant, Mr. Noel Minogue, who he announced would take notes at the meeting. He cautioned these listening not to interrupt the reading of the will, before he commenced to read the document.

"I, Rosita Beconsford, am of sound mind as I write this will. It is duly signed by me and witnessed by Mr. Hyde's assistant, Mr. Minogue. I wish to leave to my nephews Giles and Nigel Beconsford the Dower House and any other interests that are still in my name relating to the Beconsford Estate in Midleton. I further bequeath two paintings by Turner and my Steinway piano to my good friend Aidan Dermody. To my sister Violet I leave my collection of jewellery, plus one thousand guineas. To my relative and good friend Bridie Sanders, I bequeath one thousand guineas. To my

stepbrother Theodore in New York I leave a music bursary of two thousand guineas to be distributed by him to help young musicians who cannot afford to pay for tuition. I further bequeath two paintings, one by the Irish artist Mr. Jack Yeats and a portrait of myself by the upcoming lady artist, Caroline Donfield, plus the sum of one thousand guineas to my beloved friend and companion Maeve Maguire.

Finally, I bequeath my home in Fitzwilliam Square in Dublin and its contents, plus the financial balance of my personal estate, after duties have been paid, to Charles Irvine. I further entrust a sealed letter to Charles Irvine which is not to be publicly opened at the reading of the will, but only later in the presence of my solicitor Mr. Hyde –'"

There was suddenly a commotion as Giles Beconsford roared, *"Who the hell is this man and why is he getting our aunt's estate!"*

Mr. Hyde looked furious at the unseemly outburst. "Please be quiet, Lord Beconsford, and allow me finish reading! Mr. Irwin is the grandson of Lady Beconsford's longest and oldest friend Doreen Trent, a fact that you should already know. Her son was reared jointly by Doreen and Lady Beconsford. You should also remember that Mr. Benjamin Trent, Charles' father, was killed in the Boer War in Africa at the turn of the century, so please show some respect. Now kindly allow me to continue." He glared at Giles. "'*Finally, if anyone here present endeavours to contest my will, I cannot do anything about it but Mr. Hyde will fight it in any court in Ireland or England. My personal money, bequeathed to Charles Irvine was built up by astute investments, as a consequence of a large legacy received by me from my mother Fleur Montgomery. It was made secure by her mother to ensure this inheritance could not become part of the Beconsford wealth when she married Isaac Beconsford in 1816. Therefore, that money had nothing whatsoever to do with the Beconsford Estate and has all been bequeathed to my dearest relatives and best friends. I just hope that my nephews have enough dignity and respect for themselves and my memory to desist from any legal actions after my death."*

As Mr. Hyde declared the will as read, there was a stunned silence in the room before Giles knocked his chair over as he leapt to his feet and angrily said, "I'm leaving this farcical reading of my aunt's will." He turned to his brother Nigel. "I'm going back to London today – are you coming with me?"

"Yes, I will, but first I want to thank Maeve and Mr. Dermody for caring for my aunt in her later years." Nigel crossed the room and, looking into the eyes of Charles, he smiled and shook his hand. "I hope, Charles, that you become very successful in the future and that you spread some happiness around, as I know Rosita would have wanted."

Charles could only nod as the two men went out the door which Giles slammed shut as he left.

Only then did Maeve stand up, go over to Charles and put an arm around his shoulder.

"I'll help you to deal with things in the house until you decide what to do with your legacy. Just ask either Aidan or myself or even Mr. Hyde. We will all guide you until you've found your feet with this windfall."

Aidan then clasped him by the hand and smiled at the bemused young man. "You are a credit to Rosita, and I know you will continue to be guided by her principles. Charles, she loved you so much."

Charles nodded. With tears in his eyes, he watched Aidan and Maeve leave the room. At the door, Maeve turned back to speak to Charles again.

"We'll be back in the house where Mrs. Jordan has prepared some food. Aidan and I will be waiting for you when you've finished your business with Mr. Hyde. Just remember we are both there for you, Charles." With that, she left the office.

When she had gone, Mr. Hyde asked his assistant to also leave the room. Then he handed an envelope to Charles, explaining that this was the letter that Rosita had left for him.

"I know its contents, lad, and I'll be sitting with you while you read it," he said, gently patting the bemused young man on the shoulder.

They both sat down. Then Charles opened the letter and began to read.

My dearest Charles

My darling boy. First of all. I want to tell you that when you entered my life more than fifteen years ago, my sad heart began to truly mend. By that time, I had lost many of the people who were dear to me but the hurt that I felt at the loss of your father stayed deep in my soul.

I believe that our meeting was the working of providence or even because your father and Doreen were watching over us both. I was lucky to be in England when your mother was ill. Meeting her and hearing her story changed both my life and yours. I had an opportunity to do something good to ensure that the legacy of your father would continue. Sadly, I had done a grievous wrong to your father Benjamin, even before he was born.

What I am now about to tell you will, I hope, not make you judge me too harshly. The sad and awful truth is that it was I and not Doreen who gave birth to your father in Devon all those years ago. Before you rush to judgement, let me try to explain. I was with child, was about to be shunned by society and in terror of losing my nursing job that I loved so dearly. My beloved best friend Doreen, who had no living relatives that she knew of, took on the responsibility of being named as Benjamin's mother. As you know, she did not work as a nurse again. So, what can I say about Doreen?

She was the best, the kindest and the most loving mother to Benjamin and he adored her. I think we equally adored the wonderful young man who was your father. But I was the mother of that beautiful soul and I was never able to acknowledge that fact. It gave me a lot of pain during my life, plus a lot of regret. But I always felt that whatever pain I went through, what I did helped make a better life for Benjamin. I hope you believe that. But can you forgive me? I hope that someday you can find it in your heart to do so. Maeve and Aidan will continue to give you the love and guidance that I cannot give you anymore, but know that you meant everything to me and I'm so proud of the man you have become.

I'm sure you are now asking yourself what kind of man your grandfather was. When I was with him, he was loving and I believed he was in love with me. It was only after he suffered a serious head wound in India, and was sent home mentally incapacitated, that I discovered he was already married with a family. Hence, he never knew of your existence. I finally forgave him in my heart only when you came into my life and I became your guardian. To me you were heaven sent, dearest grandson.

If you find it in your heart to forgive me, please do not waste your life on regrets of what might have been. Just live in the joyous present and hopefully you will have a contented future with a wife and children. If that happens, you can with my blessing tell them that I was your grandmama. I'm sure they'll not believe you if you say your grandmama was a titled lady!

Charles, I have lived a fulfilled life, because Benjamin and you were part of it, but I also made many mistakes. Yet as I now near my end, I have very few regrets.

I love you so much,

Your grandmother,

Rosita

As the young man's eyes misted over with tears that he tried to brush away, Mr. Hyde put a fatherly arm around him and looked in the same eyes as his late client and friend Rosita Beconsford. He then knew that the decent legacy of Rosita Beconsford would live on through Charles.

"Now, lad, walk on up to your own house where both Maeve and Aidan are waiting for you." He felt such sympathy for the poor young man who didn't seem to know if he was coming or going.

When Charles arrived at the house in Fitzwilliam Street, Maeve was watching for him through the window and she hurried to open the door before he reached the top step. Mrs. Jordan and Kitty were already gone for the evening, having prepared dinner. Earlier, they had each been given a generous sum of money by Maeve as Rosita had asked to be done after her death, if they were still in her employment.

Maeve put both arms around him and hugged him tight, then led him into the front lounge to sit on Rosita's own special chair. As he sat down, she touched his hand briefly before taking a seat nearby. Aidan took a seat beside Charles and reached out to cover Charles' trembling hand.

"You know?" Maeve asked.

"Yes," was all he could manage to say.

"I will serve the dinner now and we will eat before we have any further discussion," she said, pointedly staring at Aidan.

Both men nodded.

The dinner was the quietist meal that had ever been eaten in that house, with Maeve making inane remarks about the good weather and the flowers blooming in the square beyond, while Aidan remained extremely pensive.

Then, after Maeve served coffee and chocolate slices, she turned to Charles.

"I hope that soon, only when you are ready to let me go, I will return to my own birthplace in Ballyeoin in West Cork. I have my roots there and last year your grandmother bought the cottage where I was born for me to use in my retirement. Being there for my final days is what will make me happy. Regarding you, Rosita must have known that her hour was coming when she chose to let me know the truth about your birth. She told me only last week, you know. I was so happy for her and for you. She helped raise your father at a time when admitting to his birth would have had her shunned and you cast out by society. Mind you, it's still the same in Ireland. She told me that finding you, her grandson, was a true miracle. She believed that fate and destiny took a hand in her being able to guide you through the difficult days after the death of your mother. Charles, I want you to always remember that you are the proud grandchild of a wonderful woman. Your life has connections that go as far back as 1816, when Jack Ryan survived the sinking of the *Sea Horse* in Tramore. Jack later met his sweetheart Eliza and their daughter Margarita married into the Beconsford family where at a young age she became Rosita's step-mama. Rosita told me that all she wanted for you was to remember your heritage. But more important for her was that you would live a great life, marry and have children, while designing the most beautiful buildings that Ireland will be proud of as it grows into an independent state. She would tell you also that life is too short, so enjoy it! When you have a family of your own, you can proudly tell them that you have French blood from her mother Fleur's ancestors, plus English and Irish blood in you, and when you have grandchildren always remind them that your grandmother was a real Lady."

Maeve stopped as she felt that she was prattling on too much and she knew that Aidan wanted to speak to Charles urgently. She gestured towards Aidan to speak.

He hesitated for a moment, then put a protective arm around Charles who was still bewildered by his unexpected legacy and the letter's contents. Now Aidan knew that he had to add to all of this and he wasn't looking forward to it one bit. But Rosita had asked him to give his word that he would tell Charles another secret.

"Charles, there is only one person close to us, apart from Mr. Hyde, who knows the full story of my life with Rosita. Only Maeve knew our secret. And Rosita insisted that I let you know today." He hesitated again before he continued. "When I first met Rosita, she captured my heart. She was funny and opinionated plus she had a heart of gold. We eventually fell seriously in love in our twilight days, but that is not to say that the strength of our feelings was any less than if we were younger when we met. It first happened in the Savoy Hotel in London when we both acknowledged that we were in love. It obviously was a secret relationship but we didn't mind any of the rumours about us. We always said that we were just best friends. However, it was just over three years ago that we went to London to stay again in the Savoy Hotel for our last holiday abroad. As we waltzed around the opulent ballroom to the sound of *Voices of Spring,* the music of Johann Strauss, I felt so happy that I asked Rosita to marry me. She smiled, as only she could, and then to my great surprise she said *yes*! The following day I approached a Jesuit priest friend of mine in London and he agreed to bless our union. We stayed on in London and, finally, with two strangers as witnesses, we married. We couldn't have been happier. Rosita kept laughing at the incongruity of the situation, with her, as she said, finally becoming a true Irish Catholic wife! We both agreed to continue to live in separate houses as the union would take a lot of explaining for us both back in Ireland. This relationship would have caused too many tongues around Dublin to start to wag. Probably most of them wouldn't even believe it! Yet the most important thing she told me on the night she agreed to marry me was that it was important to her to know that her grandson Charles would have a real grandfather to guide him on his way, if she passed away before me. I laughed when she said that she couldn't think of anyone nicer to be that grandpa. She had told me many years ago that she was your grandmother. She thought at the time that I'd be horrified at her disclosure but I just told her that it made her a more interesting person. Now I am going to be here for you, to be a part of your life, if that is what you want. As Maeve just said, you must live a good life as that is what Rosita always wanted for you." Aidan fell silent, hoping and praying that this wasn't all too much in one day for the young man.

After a considerable silence, Charles stood up and gestured for them both to come to him. Maeve and Aidan came and he put his arms around them both.

"I love you both so much," was all he said.

As tears flowed, Charles held on to them both, as if his life depended on it. They stayed like that for a long time, each with their own thoughts and mourning the loss of Rosita. Finally, the tears stopped flowing.

By then, night had fallen. As Charles guided them both towards the tall window, they stood watching the moon rise above the buildings beyond and hoped that Rosita Beconsford was watching over them from somewhere beyond the bright stars that shone in the dark night sky above.

No more words were needed. As they stood, arms entwined, each believed that Rosita would now rest in peace.

"She's out there, Auntie Maeve and Grandpa Aidan. I can feel it in my bones. She's up with the stars in the sky, looking down on us all. I think she will guide me along the right path in life and if I ever stray off that path, I will think of how well she dealt with adversity during her long time on this earth. Rosita, my beloved grandmother, may you rest in peace. I will always remember you."

Printed in Great Britain
by Amazon

60848577R00163